KT-430-853

The Little Red Chairs

by the same author

FICTION

The Country Girls
The Lonely Girl
Girls in Their Married Bliss
August Is a Wicked Month
Casualties of Peace
The Love Object and Other Stories
A Pagan Place
Zee and Co.
Night
A Scandalous Woman and Other Stories
A Rose in the Heart
Returning
A Fanatic Heart
The High Road
Lantern Slides
House of Splendid Isolation
Down by the River
Wild Decembers
In the Forest
The Light of the Evening
Saints and Sinners
The Love Object

NON-FICTION

Mother Ireland
James Joyce (biography)
Byron in Love
Country Girl

DRAMA

A Pagan Placc
Virginia (The Life of Virginia Woolf)
Family Butchers
Triptych
Haunted

EDNA O'BRIEN

The Little Red Chairs

FABER & FABER

First published in 2015
by Faber & Faber Limited
74–77 Great Russell Street
London WC1B 3DA

Typeset by Faber & Faber Ltd
Printed in the UK by CPI Group (UK) Ltd, Croydon, CR0 4YY

A CIP record for this book
is available from the British Library

ISBN 978–0–571–31628–1 (hardback)
ISBN 978–0–571–31629–8 (export)

4 6 8 10 9 7 5 3

WITH THANKS

Zrinka Bralo
Ed Vulliamy
Mary Martin (aged six)

An individual is no match for history.

ROBERTO BOLAÑO

The wolf is entitled to the lamb.

The Mountain Wreath (Serbian saga)

On the 6th of April 2012, to commemorate the twentieth anniversary of the start of the siege of Sarajevo by Bosnian Serb forces, 11,541 red chairs were laid out in rows along the eight hundred metres of the Sarajevo high street. One empty chair for every Sarajevan killed during the 1,425 days of siege. Six hundred and forty-three small chairs represented the children killed by snipers and the heavy artillery fired from the surrounding mountains.

PART ONE

Cloonoila

> The dirt of his travels, Gilgamesh washed from his hair,
> all the soiled garments he cast them off, clean new clothes
> he put on, about him now wrapped, clinging to him was a
> cloak with a fringe, his sparkling sash fastened to it.

The town takes its name from the river. The current, swift and dangerous, surges with a manic glee, chunks of wood and logs of ice borne along in its trail. In the small sidings where water is trapped, stones, blue, black and purple, shine up out of the river bed, perfectly smoothed and rounded and it is as though seeing a clutch of good-sized eggs in a bucket of water. The noise is deafening.

From the slenderest twigs of the overhanging trees in the Folk Park, the melting ice drips, with the soft, susurrus sound and the hooped metal sculpture, an eyesore to many locals, is improved by a straggling necklace of icicles, bluish in that frosted night. Had he ventured in further, the stranger would have seen the flags of several countries, an indication of how cosmopolitan the place has become and in a bow to nostalgia there is old farm machinery, a combine harvester, a mill wheel and a replica of an Irish cottage, when the peasants lived in hovels and ate nettles to survive.

He stays by the water's edge, apparently mesmerised by it.

Bearded and in a long dark coat and white gloves, he stands on the narrow bridge, looks down at the roaring current, then looks around, seemingly a little lost, his presence the single curiosity in the monotony of a winter evening in a freezing backwater that passes for a town and is named Cloonoila.

Long afterwards there would be those who reported strange occurrences on that same winter evening; dogs barking crazily, as if there was thunder, and the sound of the nightingale, whose song and warblings were never heard so far west. The child of a gipsy family, who lived in a caravan by the sea, swore she saw the Pooka Man coming through the window at her, pointing a hatchet.

*

Dara, a young man, the hair spiked and plastered with gel, beams when he hears the tentative lift of the door latch and thinks *A customer at last*. With the fecking drink-driving laws, business is dire, married men and bachelors up the country, parched for a couple of pints, but too afraid to risk it, with guards watching their every sip, squeezing the simple joys out of life.

'Evening sir,' he says, as he opens the door, sticks his head out, remarks on the shocking weather and then both men, in some initiation of camaraderie, stand and fill their lungs manfully.

Dara felt that he should genuflect when he looked more carefully at the figure, like a Holy man with a white beard and white hair, in a long black coat. He wore white gloves, which he removed slowly, finger by finger, and looked around uneasily, as if he was being watched. He was invited to sit on the good leather armchair by the fire, and Dara threw a pile of briquettes on and a pinch of sugar, to build up a blaze. It was the least he could do for a stranger. He had come to enquire about lodgings and Dara said he would put the 'thinking cap' on. He proceeds to make a hot whiskey with cloves and honey and for background music the Pogues, at their wildest best. Then he lights a few aul candle stubs for 'atmosphere'. The stranger declines the whiskey and wonders if he might have a brandy instead, which he swirls round and round in the big snifter, drinks and says not a word. A blatherer by nature, Dara unfolds his personal history, just to keep the ball rolling – 'My mother a pure saint, my father big into youth clubs but very against drugs and alcohol . . . my little niece my pride and joy, just started school, has a new friend called Jennifer . . . I work two bars, here at TJ's and the Castle at weekends . . . footballers come to the Castle, absolute gentlemen . . . I got my photo taken with one, read Pele's autobiography, powerful stuff . . . I'll be going to England to Wembley later on for a friendly with England . . . we've booked our flights, six of us, the accommodation in a hostel, bound to be a gas. I go to the gym, do a bit of the cardio and the plank, love my job . . . my motto is "Fail to prepare . . . prepare to fail" . . . Never drink on the job, but I like a good pint of Guinness when I'm out with the lads, love the football, like the fillums too . . . saw a great fillum with Christian Bale, oh he's the Dark Knight an' all, but I wouldn't be into horror, no way.'

The visitor has roused somewhat and is looking around, apparently intrigued by the bric-a-brac in nooks and crannies, stuff that Mona the owner has gathered over the years – porter and beer bottles, cigarette and cigar cartons with ornamental lettering, a ceramic baby barrel with a gold tap and the name of the sherry region in Spain it came from, and in commemoration of a sad day, a carved wooden sign that reads 'Danger: Deep Slurry'. That memento, Dara explained, was because a farmer in Killamuck fell into his slurry pit one dark evening, his two sons went in after to save him and then their dog Che, all drowned.

'Terrible sad, terrible altogether,' he says.

He is at his wits' end, scraping the head with a pencil, and jotting down the names of the various B & Bs, regretting that most of them are shut for the season. He tried Diarmuid, then Grainne, but no answer, and at three other joints he gets a machine, bluntly telling callers that no message must be left. Then he remembered Fifi, who was a bit of a card from her time in Australia, but she was not home, probably, as he said, at some meditation or chanting gig, a New Age junkie into prana and karma and that sort of thing. His last chance is the Country House Hotel, even though he knew they were shut and that husband and wife were due to leave on a trekking holiday in India. He got Iseult, the wife. 'No way. No way.' But with a bit of soft-soaping she relents, one night, one night only. He knew her. He delivered things there, wine and fresh fish including lobster from the quayside. Their avenue was miles long, twisting and turning, shaded with massive old trees, a deer park on one side and their own bit of river, sister to the town river, a humped bridge and then more avenue, right up to the front lawn, where peacocks strutted and did their business. Once, when he stepped out of the van, he happened to catch this great sight, a peacock opening his tail out, like a concertina, the green and the blue with the richness of stained glass, an absolute pageant. Some visitors, it seems, complained about the cries of the peacocks at night, said it had the weirdness of an infant in distress, but then, as he added, people will get funny notions into the head.

A youngster came in, to gawk at the strange figure in the dark glasses and went out roaring with laughter. Then one of the

Muggivan sisters came and tried to engage him in conversation but he was lost in his own world, thinking his own thoughts and muttering to himself, in another tongue. After she left he became more relaxed, let his coat slide off his shoulders and said he had been travelling for many days, but did not say where he had travelled from. Dara poured a second drink, more liberal with the measure this time and said they could put his name on the slate, as hopefully he would be coming in and out.

''Tis an honour to have you Sir,' and he left the tired man to his meditations as into the little passbook he wrote the date and itemised the two brandies. The visitor said that in his part of the world, the brandy was made from plums and damsons, known as *rajika*, and at least forty per cent proof. It was mandatory at baptisms, weddings and the graveside of warriors.

'Mandatory.' Dara liked the fullness of that word in the mouth. And where would your part of the world be, he ventured to ask.

'Montenegro.'

At the word Montenegro, he recalled another stranger from there, bit of a hermit, lived in a big house overlooking the sea and walked his cross dogs very early in the morning. His untimely death in his early sixties, that bit fishy. Only three mourners at the grave down in Limerick, three people all hunched under the one umbrella. Never knew him, but heard various stories from the sergeant to the effect that he was wanted elsewhere. Didn't think it was an appropriate anecdote for the visitor.

He had come outside the counter, gobsmacked, as he would later put it, by the sagacity of this man, the knowledge, a walking university to himself. He heard of the beautiful scenery of Montenegro, mountains that rivalled the Alps, deep gorges, glacial lakes that were called the eyes of the mountains and valleys abundant with herbs. Hewn into the rocks were little churches and monasteries, without windows, where people came to pray in the same way that Irish people were known to pray. Celts, he was told, had lived in the gorges of the Dolomite Mountains and along the river Drina in the centuries before Christ and the link between Ireland and the Balkans was indisputable. Scholars who had studied hieroglyphics in scrolls and artefacts in the several museums had traced the resemblance in the type of weaponry and armour that was worn.

'So your people have suffered injustices just as my people have,' he said.

'Oh 'deed we did . . . My mother who comes from Kerry, used to tell us of the Ballyseedy massacre, nine men tied together and a grenade put down between them. Only one survivor and that was my grandfather and he appeared to her every year on the anniversary, March the 24th, God's truth . . . stood at the end of her bed.'

The stranger hearing it, pondered it and then bowed his head in sympathy.

'You are familiar with Siddhartha?' he says after a long silence.

'Well, not exactly,' Dara replied.

Siddhartha, he was told, lived thousands of years ago and one day, at a ploughing match, he had a vision in which the sufferings of all mankind were revealed to him and he was told that he must do all he could to alleviate that suffering. While not being Siddhartha, as the stranger was quick to say, he too changed paths midlife. He withdrew to various monasteries to meditate and to pray. The question that perplexed him was how to get back the something he had lost. That something lost to modern man, call it soul, call it harmony, call it God. By withdrawing from the world and giving himself up to the magic carpet of learning, he entered, as he said, the rose garden of knowledge, esoterica, dream divination and trance. With careful study he arrived at a simple observation, which is the analogy of opposites and from that he hit upon the idea of combining ancient medicine with modern science, a synthesis of old and new, the one enriched by the other.

'I bring it to you,' he said, and offered his hand as an assurance.

'Cripes' was the only word Dara could find.

'A woman brought me here,' he said then with a touch of mischief, describing how one night in a monastery, there appeared to him, pale-faced and with tears streaming down her cheeks, a woman, saying *I am of Ireland*, entreating him to come there. Dara, with his smattering of history, said that crying woman was well known and in every child's copybook and she was called Aisling, which meant dream. Then he was handed the visitor's card, with the name *Dr Vladimir Dragan*, in black lettering, plus a host of degrees after it. Further down he read *Healer and Sex Therapist*.

'But I am known as Vuk,' the man said with a tentative smile. Vuk was a popular name for sons in his homeland, because of the legend attached to it concerning a woman who had lost several infants in succession, deciding to name her newborn Vuk, meaning wolf, because the witches who *ate* the babies would be too terrified to confront the wolf-child. They were getting on great, when to Dara's utter annoyance the bloody telephone rang. It was Iseult from the country house, wanting to know when the guest was arriving and if crab claws would do for his supper.

He stood in the doorway and under a sliver of moon, watched the man go down the slip road, the ice cracking under his feet, footsteps getting fainter and fainter as he crossed the bridge, away from the roar of the river, to a sister river that was not nearly so rapid. He took gulps of the air, priming himself, knowing that presently the bar would fill up and he would have to provide a blow-by-blow summary of the encounter.

Desiree was first, a strapping girl in her pink mini-dress, her stout arms bare and a coat over her head, bursting for news.

'God I could do with a fella, haven't had a fella for half a year,' she said, curious to know if the guy was presentable and married or single. Did he wear a ring? The Muggivan sisters were next, slinking in, in their grey coats and their knitted caps and ordering peppermint cordial. Fifi came with a few of her friends and Mona, alerted by the hilarity, came down from her living quarters, and like any customer sat on one of the high stools and ordered her usual tipple, which was a large port wine with a slice of orange. A widow for over twenty years she always dressed nicely in dark crepe dresses with a corsage of cloth violets on her ample bosom and she spoke in a soft, breathy voice. Mona had two staples in life: one was Padre Pio, in whom she had unswerving faith and the other was the romance novels of which she could not get enough. She devoured them, the way she devoured fudge in bed at night and looking around she welcomed the fact that the bar was filling up as things had been woeful since Christmas. There was also Plodder policeman, Diarmuid the ex-Schoolmaster and Dante the town punk, with his dreadlocks and his black gear, flanked by his cohorts: Ned, who'd done time for growing marijuana in window boxes and Ambrose, for stealing lead piping from the contractor he worked for. Business had bucked up. Seized with enthusiasm, Dara was proud to announce that the stranger was a gentleman, an out-and-out gentleman down to his pointy shoes. Soon he had them in the palm of his hand, as he pieced events together, adding a few flourishes, such as the man's transfixing eyes, his long fingers, expressive as a pianist's, and the signet ring with the crest of an eagle, the colour of red sealing wax. Although a toff, as he had to remind them, there was also this aura of one of those holy men, pilgrims that used to travel around, barefoot, doing good. He mentioned the plum brandy, *rajika*, that was mandatory at baptisms, weddings and the graves of warriors and how the Balkans and Ireland had shared ancestors in times gone by.

Was the newcomer one of those sharks, speculating for gas or oil, to bleed their green and verdant land?

'No way . . . he's a doctor, a philosopher, a poet and a healer.'

'Jaysus, that's a mouthful,' Plodder policeman said, coming to his own conclusions. Close to retiring and a bit of a joke in the barracks, he was only sent out on small jobs, missing taillights or straying sheep, but he felt in his waters that this visitor was dodgy, a con artist of some kind, or maybe a bigamist.

'Where is he from?' Mona asked.

'Montenegro,' Dara said and then relayed the story about Irish and Balkan Celts being blood brothers and how the artefacts found in fields et cetera were similar to ones dug up around the Boyne.

'Bollocks,' Desiree said.

'He's staying . . .' Dara said, pleased at his timing and then dropped the bombshell about the man intending to set up a clinic as an alternative healer and sex therapist.

'Sweet Jesus,' the Misses Muggivans said blessing themselves.

'Oh, oh, oh . . . Sex therapist.' Things got heated. There were those who smelt vice and corruption, while a few lone voices were insisting that he might be an *artery* for good. They were shouting each other down. It was too much for ex-Schoolmaster

Diarmuid, who had listened to this twaddle and was now asking them to please give him a chance to voice a sensible, mediating opinion:

'There was a man called Rasputin,' he began and walked around, scolding and pugnacious, still the Schoolmaster except no one was in awe of him anymore, 'who hailed from the wilds of Siberia and infiltrated himself into the very nucleus of the Russian court, presenting himself as a visionary and a healer. He was going to lift Russia from its lethargy and darkness, he was going to cure the sick child of the Czarina, the future heir, of his haemophilia and he was going to perform miracles ad infinitum. Did he cure the heir? No. Did he save the Russian family from the firing squad? No. He was a fornicator and an imposter who got drunk every night and had carnal knowledge of most of the women in the court.'

He could hear titters and shuffling, but determined to have his say, as he made for the door, he warned them that Rasputin's last supper was a plate of biscuits laced with cyanide.

'That's a grand story Diarmuid,' Mona called, entreating him to stay, because she never liked a customer to leave in a huff.

Dante had been listening and presently, with a nod from Mona, he began to play on the bohrain, his soft brown hair falling over his face, his team waiting for their cue. Demands for Irish coffee were legion. Dara was being complimented on the fact that he could keep talking and still have a nifty way of getting the cream down the back of the spoon, before it trembled into the coffee. The music got wilder, thumpier, the cohorts doing their scherzos and trills with the spoons, while Desiree improvised her mock striptease. Dante was on his feet, tiptoeing around, hovering above each one, the Shaman, whispering the prophecy:

Santa didn't come
His brother took his place
Santa's dead
Santa's dead
That's what he said
Annihilated on his sled
That's what he said.
So this is it, Son
This is it
Dark dark shit.

Mona, a little tiddly on her perch and nostalgic now, pressed the violets on her bosom and said, 'Maybe he'll bring a bit of Romance into our lives.'

Outside, the thermometer on the Folk Park gate read minus three, and inside they basked in the warmth of a fire that had been going since morning. Spirals of smoke drifted through the room, the faces curious, jovial, dreamy, wreathed in smoke, like beings captured in some strange nocturnal bacchanalia.

Fifi

Fifi wakened hearing voices. It could only be John, John dead almost three years and still paying his regular visits, 'channelling' as he would call it. He might as well be alive, she could picture him so clearly, with his tousled black hair, wild black eyes and the old green jersey with strings hanging off the sleeves, spouting the mysteries of the Divine, of which he was an initiate.

She never feared his ghost, it could only be an influence for good. They were soulmates, both having travelled the wide world, returning from their wanderings, to the sea mists and the ground mists, the Fomorian darkness as he termed it. There was nothing romantic of course, as she ruefully admitted to being 'a dried-up old bird' from all that sunshine in Australia, whereas John with his shock of hair and his wild eyes was still Orpheus, singing to some lonely Eurydice, whoever she may be.

Ah, the high-flow glorious nonsense of those times.

For two years he lived under her roof, in the back bedroom, which he named Manaan Mac Lir, Son of the Sea and God of the Sea. He did rough work, digging and hoeing, quite content to do it since it kept him close to nature, and pursued his mystical studies at night. The original agreement was for bed and breakfast, but with time things changed and moreover, he would bring back a hare or some trout and she would cook for him and they would sit and talk at the kitchen table, John expounding on God, paganism, Gaia, and St John of the Cross. Often he would contradict himself, saying that the way to religion was to have no religion at all and they would almost come to blows at the kitchen table, shouting one another down, regarding the authenticity of the Virgin Birth and the Resurrection of Christ. She was a believer but for John, poetry was the true faith.

He disapproved of her summer visitors, camped out in the bog or by the seashore and gave the odd seminar at summer schools, which she was too busy to attend. Her guests came back year after year, some for the fishing, some for the shooting or festivals that went on all year round, along with nature walks and God knows what else.

Her breakfasts were legendary, with all the troupe, minus John, at the long oak table, her best bone china, cotton napkins warm because she would have just ironed them, then folded them to look like a large envelope with the letter flap turned over, exactly fitting into the space between the arrangements of silver cutlery. They came down to the smell of warm potato bread and scones, honey from her own hives and marmalades and jams of different flavours. She dragooned them to eat those breakfasts whether they wanted it or not and then sent them out on their various pursuits.

Leaving her little 'ashram' as John called it was the great mistake of his life, because he died not long after and she always maintained that he had died of homesickness. It so happened that a nearby pub, shut down for many years, was auctioned, done up and reopened, so that the noise of cars and revellers late at night drove him insane. She could hear him in his own bedroom cursing, shouting at being hauled out of his paradisal dreams. He went south to where he thought he would find peace only to learn that a disused quarry was reopened and after that it was the noise of men and machinery all day long.

'So what have you to say to me John?' she asked sitting up in bed and pulling on a cardigan as the room was freezing. With her big toe she pressed on the button of the floor lamp and then got into her snug pink slippers. Going down for the first cup of tea, she envisaged Bibi, her little dachshund, with her wiles, waiting for the first saucer of milk with half a spout of tea in it. Like a human Bibi sensed things, knew that her mistress was soon going away and kept bolting at the slightest opportunity. January was the month to close the shutters and go for a week over to Leenane, to Mickey the basket weaver, to learn again how to make cribs and baskets from willow.

The doorbell took her by surprise – *Closed for the season* was printed on a cardboard sign and left on the inner ledge of the conservatory window. She went out holding the brown egg, that she might or might not boil for breakfast and seeing the bearded figure in the doorway, like a picture of Moses, she remembered the craic in the pub the night before and rued the fact that she had mixed gin with Irish coffees.

'Good morning . . . Dara sent me,' he said, in a quiet courteous voice.

'Good morning . . . Dara should not have sent you,' she replied tartly. There was silence for a moment as he admired the view, the river as it sprawled out into a broad sweep, eel nets, creels for the crab and the lobsters, and two swans so sedate, as if they were made of china. The hazed horizon seemed to be resting itself on the mountain tops.

'January is the month I do all the painting and redecorating,' she said by way of apologising for refusing him.

'Your house is most unusual,' he said.

'Ach it's tumbling,' she said but she was proud to hear it. Her house was two-storey in one part, single-storey elsewhere, with a crescent-shaped conservatory and ruins of cottages to one side. There was a front garden with ornamental shrubs and a back garden that rose in a steep incline to the woods. It was fifteen years since she acquired it, the cottage that her ancestors had left, the walls sprouting mushrooms and toadstools, cockroaches wherever she stepped and yet she knew that somewhere distantly, a man or woman born there, into hardship, was responsible for the peppery glints in her hazel eyes and her scalding temper.

It was a crisp bright morning, sun glinting on the bushes and on a few straggling dog roses that had survived the winter, the green snouts of the crocuses poking through the clay. She brought him around to show the lime walk, the apple orchard and the beautiful sun dial with its verdigreed peacock, that had come from a grand house in County Wicklow. Pointing to the ruins of three cottages, she said that one day she would make them into artists' studio apartments. Suddenly she looked around and there was no sign of Bibi. Bibi had run away and little snob that she was, probably to the Castle grounds to mix with the noblesse. First she rang the Castle, only to be told there was no sign of Bibi, and she ran hither and thither, calling and coaxing, then blew a whistle that made a shrill, peremptory sound. Bibi, she feared, could be stolen or poisoned, because many people coveted her.

He helped in her search and soon it was up into the woods, where they moved stealthily, listening for any little stir. By the base of a birch tree, he noticed that leaves had been disturbed and a small seam of earth opened up. He stooped to listen and said he could hear some movement.

'She's in there,' he said.

'Why isn't she coming out?'

'Mother nature,' and he explained how most likely, she had gone down the burrow on the scent of a rat or a stoat, with all her senses quickened, so that she could get through the eye of a needle, because she wanted to. But coming back up was a different matter altogether. The adrenalin was gone. It was lucky, as he said, that they had come so soon, because if she were there for days until she got thinner, so as to squeeze her way through, she would probably die of thirst.

He worked the spade gently, until the frozen clay began to shift and then with a trowel he kept digging, carefully, so as not to break any bones and when the seam had opened sufficiently, he put his hands in and eased her out. She looked like a rag, muddied, one ear torn, and quivering all over.

'She's been in the wars,' he said.

'My little rambler,' Fifi said and cradled her in her arms and they walked back in silence. They stood her in a tub of warm water, Fifi washing and sponging, while he cut all the toenails broken from scraping. She was still quivering, as if she did not know where she was and she flinched at having the clay taken out of her nostrils with tweezers.

He was soon made welcome, admiring the things in the kitchen, the old-fashioned dresser painted green, the different cups and shaving mugs, plates wedged in at the back and jam dishes of a milky Vaseline glass, partaking of a hearty breakfast.

She sat across the table from him, cutting the willow rods into near-identical pieces, while sizing him up. He was a handsome man, and no doubt about it, a swell, the scarlet silk handkerchief in his top pocket complementing the more muted red of his silk tie. Somehow she got talking of John and what an inspiration he had been and on impulse, she fetched the shoe box with pictures of him, smiling the minstrel smile, sayings that he had copied from the Upanishads and things he himself had written. The visitor read them, clearly impressed, and then read them aloud:

If I repair a little of myself, I repair a little of you, for we are all joined in the Cosmic law of the Divine.

Oh my mother Asia of the Heart Sutras, guide me.

Let us return to the Bird Reign of Conaire Mor in which all things live Ecumenically with each other, man and beast uniting with nature in the Divine scheme of things.

'He lived here?' he said.

'He did . . .' she said proudly but before things got too spiritual altogether she said John could be a demon with drink and described him in his cups on Friday nights, with Fergal, another Orpheus, both on the one bicycle, stopping at the hill by the eels' bed and Fergal saying, 'You're nearly home John,' and John answering, 'I am, but am I on the otter's way?'

In the Manaan Mac Lir room, he looked out, as John had so often looked, at the apple trees, the ruins of the cottages and the wood where the little birches had withstood the ravages of many winters.

'We are now in the Silence,' he said and the sight of him standing there, so solemn, so episcopal and yet masculine touched her in some forgotten way.

He said then, how enjoyable, how enriching the morning had been and that he would not forget it. It was all it took to sway her.

They settled on a price of one hundred euros per week and as fortune had it, he could now look after Bibi and her six hens, while she kept her promise to go over to Mickey in Leenane.

She watched him go down the path, lithe, straight-backed and thought that the ladies of Cloonoila, married and unmarried, would be doffing their bonnets at him.

'It's for you John,' she said, in a rare admission of loneliness.

Men of Faith

'Shocking . . . shocking morning altogether.'

Waves pounding in over the rocks in a vaulting vengeance onto the promenade, drenching all before them.

Yet two gallants are out there braving it, a youthful Father Damien in brown sandals and cassock and Dr Vladimir in long great-coat, red scarf, white gloves and dark glasses rimmed in bright steel. The wind lifts the young priest's cassock, so that it billows up around his face, muffling his few awkward words.

He is new to the parish, having been recalled home suddenly, as one priest died of an aneurysm and the second, being too fond of the greyhounds, was more often at the race track than fulfilling his pastoral duties and eventually moved away. How he misses his work in the slums of Leeds and Manchester, that was his real calling, helping the poor, giving them hope and not this sparring match.

They pass the poop scoop with the big black sullen waves rolling in to lash the two benches that are already drenched and head for the dunes. Earlier they agreed it was wiser to be outdoors, because in TJ's or the Castle there were bound to be eavesdroppers, or, as Father Damien nicely said, 'Walls have ears.'

'Malfeasance,' the doctor pronounces it again, the voice mellifluous but his manner curt. He had smarted at the word when he first heard it, as the young priest paid him an unexpected and flurried visit, blurting it out, in the consulting room. There and then he consulted his dictionary, read the meaning and knew that it did not bode pleasantries. *Malfeasance – Misconduct or wrongdoing, especially by a public official; the wilful and intentional action that injures a party.* He had copied it into his notebook, which he now reads and rain falls on the open page.

'The Bishop has concerns,' Father Damien says, that bit beholden.

'I am sorry to hear that,' the doctor says calmly.

'The thing is – word has circulated that you intend to practise as a Sex Therapist and this is a Catholic country and chastity is our number one commandment.'

'But of course . . .' He assures his friend that in his country, his beloved Balkans, for thousands of years wars raged, to defend the faith against the infidel.

'As the Bishop sees it,' Father Damien continues, 'we have to be ever vigilant and Sex Therapist sends the wrong signals . . . experimentation . . . thrills . . . deviances . . .' and here his voice falters in shame. He is torn between deference and duty and what with his stammer and the doctor's aloofness, hidden behind those dark glasses, their eyes never meet, so that he cannot tell if he is getting anywhere.

'You must remember I have taken the Hippocratic Oath,' he said and recounted the swearing to Apollo, to healing gods and goddesses, always mindful of upholding ethical standards. As for intimacy, he went on to say, it was unthinkable, always keeping far from seduction or the pleasures of love with one's patients, be they men or women.

'But you are alternative and that entails a lot of new-fangled ideas . . . and a whiff of Darwinism maybe,' Father Damien says, woefully self-conscious.

Mainstream and alternative (he is told) go hand in hand, a prodigious leap due to the discoveries in neuroscience and cognitive physics, an acoustic resonance, a dance within the body's particles, by which illness can be stopped in its tracks, good cells, like good soldiers, fighting bad cells. He is Messianic in his enthusiasm, citing the secrets in plants, in fern, in the husk of a sunflower, in the innards of a nectarine stone, predicting that a time will come when medicine can enable patients to listen to the sound of the soul itself.

'That's awesome,' the priest says. He is completely flummoxed now. *Defixi.* The Bishop's word is ringing in his ears, the Latin for fix, pin down, taken from the nails used in Roman times, to pin curse-tablets on opponents. *Defixi*. He is half-blind from rain and the ground is full of holes, so that he is staggering when he should be upright.

'I don't like to press the point,' he says, 'but if we are to picture a man or a woman, lying on your couch, and the words Sex Therapist keep running through the mind, might they not be expecting something' (and here he gasps at the word) 'kinky?'

'I thank you for having put it so succinctly, but let me say, I am not here to snatch away souls or bodies from your faith. I am here to do good.'

'You see, many feel a vacuum in their lives . . . marriages losing their mojo . . . internet dating . . . nudity . . . hedonism . . . the things I have heard in confession . . .'

'Well, that is for the confessional, between them and you and not between them and me.'

'Does the Orthodox have confession?' the priest asks, mustering some courage.

'Yes and no . . . in our Antiochian jurisdiction every priest is invested with the faculty of hearing confessions, but not all priests choose to do so.'

'My Bishop won't buy that . . . repentance and sorrow for sin is woven into our DNA.'

'I should remind you we also recognise the seven sacraments, including penitence, which you call confession and anointing with the Holy Chrisms.'

'But you are sending an incendiary message . . . it's the red rag to the Gallic bull,' the priest says bluntly.

'Ah,' the doctor exclaims. Now he understands, he has grasped the nettle, he no longer sees through a glass darkly – *Sex Therapist* is the bogey.

'Why not erase it!' he says to his distraught interrogator.

Nothing could be simpler. He will have new cards printed, that will set down the rigorous disciplines and methods of his practice.

'Hallelujah . . . the Bishop will sleep sound tonight,' says Father Damien, much too cravenly.

'We will all sleep sound tonight,' the doctor replies as he wipes the spray from his lenses with a clean, dry handkerchief.

They are almost in agreement, except for one final hurdle. Father Damien envisages himself in the Bishop's palace, in the drawing room, the Bishop with his icicle eyes and his pointed nose, the parish priest perspiring, and all the other priests on edge, grilling him. The important thing now is to get clarity on the difference between Catholic and Orthodox churches.

The doctor welcomes the question, admitting to differences and quasi-differences down the centuries that led to schisms and dualism, adding that many of them were a mere matter of interpretation, but scholars on both sides were reluctant to concede. As an example, he said that to one, God was essence and to the other, God was experience, but to both Plato was the thief of truth and Christ its messenger. He then glories in the insoluble marriage between the churches, when in 1964, at Vatican II, Pope Paul VI met with Patriarch Athenagoras, to finally settle their differences, and proclaimed to the whole world, 'Now we are breathing with both lungs.' Rome, as he went on to say, was more empirical, orthodox more mystical, Hell was a spatial place to one and to the other it was the soul's despair at the exclusion from the sight of God. For the mystical supper of communion, Rome have leavened bread or *zyme*, and for the orthodox, unleavened or *azyme*. Yet both churches could trace their roots back to Holy Scripture, when in AD 310, the Emperor Constantine saw the Chi-Ro sign in the sky, the XP signifying the first two letters of the Greek word for Christ. Henceforth he was directed to fight under the Christian standard, which he did, securing a victory over Maxentius and subsequently asking to be baptised. Proof of his conversion was that his remains were laid to rest, alongside the Twelve Apostles, in a sarcophagus, at Patmos, deeming him the Thirteenth Apostle.

At the mention of Patmos, Father Damien thinks of sunshine, turquoise-blue waters, cedar woods and the remains of the saints, snug under glass and gold, white satin tucked around their chins to disguise the shrivelled yellow of their skins, emanating Holiness. But he is shocked to hear that all those remains are gone, not a bone, not even a rib left, from centuries of war, looting, pillage and plunder.

'What about relics?' he says aghast.

'What about relics!' is the answer and they both sigh.

Father Damien is already wording his report for the Bishop and the Fathers. They will buy the matter of breathing with both lungs, bridling a bit at Hell being a spatial place to Rome and to the orthodox despair at the exclusion from the sight of God, but Vatican II will be his trump card. He will keep Plato out of it. They will be intrigued to hear about Constantine's remains alongside the Twelve Apostles. Constantine, who also had a vision of the Transfiguration at Mount Tabor, the same vision as revealed to the Apostles who followed Christ.

'I am wondering . . .' he says aloud and the doctor wonders for him and with him. It's like this. He, Damien, would like an olive branch extended to the community. Suppose they hold a public meeting, not from the altar but say in the back room of TJ's, where the faithful could fire questions and be given answers, clear up any grey areas that might persist.

'You mean a Q & A,' the doctor says enthusiastically. He is anxious to get acquainted with the local people because he intends to make Cloonoila his home, sensing in it that primal innocence, lost to most places in the world.

That clinches it for Father Damien. He has a sudden impulse to embrace the man, represses it, kneels down on the wet grass, reciting from the Creed – *God from God, Light from Light, True God from True God, Consubstantial with the Father.* The doctor repeats the prayer in his own tongue, much to the edification of the little ratty dog who has momentarily quit his yapping.

Then they stand, wipe their knees, and with the camaraderie of men who have at last understood one another, begin to breathe, to the mantra of Pope Paul and Patriarch Athenagoras – *Now we are breathing with both lungs.*

The heavens opened, the rain came slanting and vengeful as they walked back in silence, puddles slopping about their feet. Near the promenade they come on Fidelma, the draper's wife, all muffled up in grey raincoat with a squirrel collar, a wet sheen on her face.

'What are you doing out on a rotten morning like this?' Father Damien asks.

'I love it . . . I love the rain,' she says as she passes and the doctor acknowledges her with a regal bow.

'Lovely woman . . . lovely Christian family,' the priest says when she is out of hearing and they continue, buffeted this way and that by the raging storm.

At the car park, they find that both sets of windscreen wipers have been ripped off their cars and thrown on the ground and the priest's new radio has been stolen.

'Youths . . . nothing better to do,' Father Damien says, as if he is responsible for the morals of the entire community. With pride, he hauls out a tiny cell phone and rings a garage in Sligo, where he has a contact. He listens, smiles, ends his call and recites in lofty incantation, '*He will send his angels and they will gather.*'

Sister Bonaventure

No fanfare, not even a reporter from the local newspaper and certainly no photographs, as the doctor believed that a person's soul was stolen by the influence of a camera. So it was just a tasteful sign in black lettering, on white parchment, announcing that Dr Vladimir's clinic would open on Tuesday 22 February. In smaller print it said *Holistic Healing in Eastern and Western Disciplines*.

He was there almost a month, but still something of a stranger, a curiosity, glimpsed in the very early morning, his trouser legs rolled up, gathering stones from the river and on other mornings, he went with the shearers to gather seaweed for his massages and body wraps. Herbs and tinctures from China, India, Burma and Wales were despatched day by day and the postmistress, the town Sphinx, said that some of the stuff had a smell of cow dung.

He walked a lot and sometimes, after a long stretch, he sat on the bench over at Strand Hill, in his big overcoat, beside the letterbox that read *Poop Scoop*, sat there spouting verses in Latin as big waves came faithfully in. No one approached him in his reverie, until one day, Taig, an eager pupil, dared ask him whose poetry it was. He was told it was Ovid, a poet of the third century who had been exiled from Rome to the Black Sea. In his poems, he cursed and pleaded with those who had banished him, yet was always asking to be allowed home. So like Ovid, he too was a poet and an exile.

Fifi his landlady got to be familiar with his tastes, lamb or pork with red cabbage, which she bought in a jar from a supermarket, and crepes with different fillings, including a curd cheese with sugar. His wine was ordered from a vintner's in Galway. At night, he pored over his medical journals and encyclopaedias and sometimes, very late, he went up into the woods with the big flash lamp to make phone calls. He had two cell phones, one for work and one that was private and in these late calls she often heard him shouting, up there in the woods, yet at other times laughing when talking to a comrade. He played a stringed instrument called the gusle and recited some of his poems on Sunday evenings in the front room, she being his only audience. Some he translated for her and she found them very macho, rigmarole stuff about bullets being slender and majestic and strapping wolves coming down from the hills. It was not like Yeats, no, not like Yeats's wandering waters in the pools above Glencar.

Smoke rose from the chimney in his clinic and stacks of logs had been neatly piled in the front hall, yet no one had the courage to cross that door. In the end it was Sister Bonaventure who decided she would be the guinea pig. A nun, she had no fear of him and his Latin charm, prided herself on her free thinking, liberated as she was by the humane teaching of Pope John. John was her man. Yes, nuns, like everyone else, had to move with the times.

She and three other nuns now lived in one wing of the old convent, the major part having been sold off for a school, and as she put it, quoting from scripture, *The sparrow hath her house* and so they settled in. Faithfully each day, unless she happened to be gallivanting, she was able to get her school lunch for three euros, the same price as the children paid; meat or fish with a vegetable, potatoes, boiled or mashed and what more did anybody want. She never drank. She had seen the harm and the woes that drink wreaked, families torn apart and farms auctioned off for half of nothing. So as to set a good example, she wore her total abstinence pioneer badge on her lapel. She no longer dressed in a nun's habit, except for the veil, which she called her 'bonnet'. She wore a navy skirt, navy jumper, black stockings and good strong black shoes for the journeys she made to isolated places, up by roads and bog roads, where she wouldn't dare risk her little Mini, her chariot of freedom. The four nuns had their different duties, she doing charity work, visiting the sick, bringing Holy Communion in her wooden pix to those who were crippled and housebound. Sister Austin did the grounds and the gardens and Rosario took classes in Science and Geography, which meant that she was the most earnest. Poor Pius, who was the eldest, did the altars and the sacristy, helped the parish priest and the curate, laid out their vestments and lit the candles for Mass and benediction. Bonaventure loved her charity work, tireless at raising money for causes. She collected stamps. Always badgering people for stamps, especially from faraway places, which she then sold to a bureau in Dublin, using the money for a water scheme in East Africa, from where she received letters of profuse thanks and photographs of children with infectious smiles. She also made jams, which she sold at a car boot sale on Sundays. At first she was a bit of an oddity, with her nun's veiling, standing behind a fit-up counter, but once people tasted the jams, which she put for them to sample, on tiny squares of water biscuit, business flourished. The 'apogee', as it was described in the local paper, was her marrow jam with chunks of crystallised ginger.

Her appointment was for eleven o'clock and all that morning she prayed that she was doing the right thing and not sullying her body. She took extra care when she showered and with the big powder puff, dusted herself with lily of the valley talc, a gift from Mona at Christmas.

He answered the door himself and bowed as he welcomed her in. He was wearing a loose-fitting blue overall, which gave him the likeness of a monk. A fire blazed in the small upstairs grate of the waiting room and they paused to have a brief conversation, she saying there was nothing that seemed quite so vacant as an empty grate and he regretting that the chimney smoked, but that the builder assured him with a good coat of soot on the back breast, the smoke would travel upwards.

She halted before a glass cabinet, staring at all the medicines – drops in glass-stoppered bottles, blue jars, their insides silvered from the powders they were filled with, see-through bags with herbs and grasses, bits of bark and forked roots that reminded her of a picture in Rosario's science book of the mandrake that shrieks when dug up. All of a sudden she felt uneasy. This was more incriminating than she had imagined.

The treatment room itself was a temple, lights so very dim and intriguing, and sacred music issued from the four corners. Out of the open mouths and empty eye sockets of wooden figures, gods and goddesses, plumes of light poured, gold one minute, then blue, then rose pink, at the touch of a tiny switch, which he held in his hand, the Magus, as the ex-Schoolmaster had called him.

He left her alone to undress, saying she could leave her panties on, if she wished, or he could give her a paper pair. She opted to leave her woollen on and then cautiously undressed, having to sit on a stool to roll down and remove her tights. She nearly fell off that stool twice, because of the way it swivelled. On a side bench were two big saucepans, one fitted with an electric element to heat water and one with stones, a great mass of stones, smoothed to various sizes and shapes, smooth as pumice and tiny chinks of white marble.

She lay on her back, peeping through the slits of her almost closed eyes, for fear of any hanky panky. He looked like a devil, or maybe a Red Indian, because of a bandana that kept the hair out of his eyes. Yet warmth flowed from his hands when he touched her and sought out the various knots and nodules and cricks. When he leant on her chest and caused it to ease under his weight, she feared she might dissolve altogether. His hands were so capable and so far-reaching and it was as if he had more than two hands, so that gradually she felt herself giving in to it, with him persuading her to let go. He placed stones on the flab of her stomach, which he had not touched, and ran the sides of other stones along her veins, the heat just this side of burning, her insides warm and gooey and as a precaution, she uttered a quick ejaculation to her Corpus Christi and the Holy Innocents.

Sing, my tongue, the Saviour's glory,
Of his flesh the mystery sing,
Of the blood all price exceeding
Shed by our immortal King.

When the time came to turn her over she felt happier, it was more private, away from the lights that pulsed from the orifices of the wooden gods and goddesses. Away from his eyes also, that were so penetrating. She jumped at the feel of something warm in the palm of her hand and then realised it was a stone and she met its grasp as she would that of a trusted friend. Then he placed different ones down the length of her body, as he massaged her legs, held her ankles and gave them a quick, smart swivel in both directions.

She did not want it to end. But end it soon would, as she could tell by the diminuendo of the pressure and the stones falling away off her body, onto the bed and onto the floor. Lastly, he placed the chinks of freezing marble over her lids and the thrill of the cold penetrated to behind the eyes and to her mind itself and she felt a flash of blinding light and was transported to the ethereal. Then, from a censer, he sprinkled water over her, like raindrops, but smelling of musk, which was meant to waken her up, except she longed to linger.

He left her alone to dress. The holy chant still filtered from the four corners and all the stones that he had applied to her lay in a rugged heap.

When she paid him, she was impressed by the fact that he refused a tip and moreover, escorted her down the steep stairs to the door. There with folded hands he wished her good health: repeating the word *Namaste, Namaste*, until she was out of sight.

Five women were waiting for her in the coffee shop that was known as the Parlour. A rustic room with basket chairs and a slab of slate for a table, it was where locals could exhibit their drawings, or their etchings, or leave stories they had written, to be read by others. A Book Club organised by Fidelma, the draper's wife, held their meetings there once a month.

She would tell them about the coloured lights slicing the air in the room, and the effigies of gods and goddesses and she would tell them about the sacred music, the offer of the paper panties and the marvellous splay of his hands. But she would not tell them that when she got up from that treatment bed and he had left the room, her energy was prodigal, a wildness such as she had not known since her youth, out in the fields when she pissed against trees, the way men did, pissed unashamedly. She would not tell them that.

Upcock

Upcock Upcock Upcock.

The beaters were flushing out the birds in the wood opposite, their cries high-pitched and faintly hysterical, coming near and far and intermittently, the sound of gunshot muffled by distance along with the joyous yelping of the hounds.

It was Fidelma's favourite walk, a winding path by the river in the Castle grounds. The Castle with its turrets and ivied walls was a five-star hotel which attracted celebrities and regulars who came for the fishing and shooting. She could do that walk in her sleep, over the bridge, down three steps, by a sign that read *Please Close the Gate* and all of a sudden the sound of the river, squeezing its way under the bridge and then bursting out as it opened into a wide sweep, making its way upstream, girdling the small islands that it passed. The sound was like water bursting in childbirth, or so a woman who had had many children once told her, and she remembered it.

She loved those woods, especially in winter, trees without leaf, trunks sombre and grey, fallen boughs caught on one another and a hush, despite the roar of the river and the far-off sound and yodel of the hunters and their gillies.

It was where she could be most herself, more than in her own garden with its verbena and its roses, or in the rooms which she had so lovingly furnished, envisaging a different and more scintillating life. Rarely did she meet anyone, except for visitors from the Castle who would politely salute and walk on. The path itself was muddy, embedded with bits of rocks and the raised roots of the trees forked crookedly. The walk took her to the far end, where path and river met, and there was a thick palisade of reeds to bar the way. Always on her return journey she sat on a bench, where a particular robin, or one identical to it, flew about, then hovered so close she could touch the little plump terracotta chest and the suede-brown wings, except at the very last instant it eluded her and flew back into the rhododendrons that grew densely under the thick cover of trees.

That bench and that robin were witness to her many secrets. It was there she shed tears at losing the shop, the boutique, as it was known. She never did believe she would lose it, it was her empire, her salon. The wives of rich builders and developers came from far and wide to try on the latest fashions and they would walk up and down past the long mirrors, pretending to hesitate, but already buying and concocting the lies they would have to tell their husbands. She was renowned for her modish collections, hats for all occasions, funerals, weddings, race meetings, garden parties (though there were none), knitwear in indigo and violet and silk shawls that cried out for the click of the castanets. Once, to the titillation of many, there was a pink corset in the window, made of broderie anglaise and studded with diamanté. She had bought it at Pigalle in Paris.

There were as well the less affluent customers, who paid on the instalment, knowing she would relent and let them have their finery long before the full amount was paid. There was Deirdre, who worked in the Castle, having to try on a dress for an American called Mary Lou, that her forester sweetheart was sending to her in Connecticut. Yet Deirdre believed that he was keen on her, since he made her keep the dress for weeks, where she modelled it for him each evening in her apartment across the hotel yard. Then one Saturday morning she came to the shop in tears, saying, 'I hate men, I hate men,' as the dress had been posted to Connecticut.

But the boutique lost its cachet. She and Jack sensed it the day they read that there was a motorway to be built six miles away. It meant that ladies could then drive to the city for their couture and moreover, summer visitors would not stop to admire the novelties in her window. She knew for quite a while that their days were numbered and she hid the bills that came from wholesalers and stockists in London and Paris, deluding herself that with the coming season business would perk up.

'God Almighty we're paupers,' Jack said the day he found the bank statements and he scolded her for her extravagant nature and sulked for days, eventually conceding that they would have to close down and sell the good stock to wholesalers in Galway and give the remainder to charity shops. After that, she began to notice a change in him. He pottered less in the garden that he had for years so lovingly planted and tended. He did the crosswords and then sat staring out, the pink of his scalp so scaly under the thinning white hair and his eyes had a kind of rebuke in them.

The difference in their age had begun to matter, she had just turned forty and Jack was in his sixties, no longer the 'Brooding Heathcliff' that used to sign birthday cards to her. He wanted less and less to meet people, keeping her to himself, shutting the world out, drawing the heavy velvet curtains too early on a bright evening. If she announced that they might invite a few friends, he worried, began to wonder what time these friends might arrive and more importantly, what time they would leave. Only on Christmas morning did he become his old self, in his maroon smoking jacket, fires in both grates, himself and old Dr Carmody sitting on the chaise longue, recalling their fishing feats, mostly at night, on camp stools, waiting for the fish to bite and the lure, oh yes, the lure of the fly in the dark, like love itself a conundrum. That moment was then the cue for Jack to open the drawers of a little bureau, with its tray of flies, boyishly calling out their names: Cascade, Green Highlander, Collie, Munro Killer, sparkling away in their louvred confinement. Later, he and Dr Carmody did their party piece, singing the love duet of Molly Bawn and Brian Og, in which Jack impersonated the wronged Molly –

Oh Brian you have been drinking, Brian Og,
I can tell it by your winking, Brian Og.
Since you 'listed in the army
No more those eyes can charm me,
Oh I hate you, oh I love you, Brian Og.

Then they vowed that come the spring, they would go over to Lough Corrib, that vast archipelago of blue, with its three hundred and sixty-five islands, one for every day of the year, and troll for the brown trout and the occasional salmon, come there after running the many rivers.

Opposite to where she sat the water was a boggy brown, but not too far along it was a dark violet colour, always changing, the way the sweep of the current changed, but as she saw it, her own life did not change at all – the same routine, the same longing and the same loneliness.

Father Eamonn was the only one she could confide in. He was from the south and had been defrocked, a disgrace he had brought upon himself by loving a woman. She knew how isolated he must be in that bungalow, looking out at the mist, nursing his sin, unable to walk because of his arthritis, along with suffering from gout.

It came about that they met in the library and had a brief conversation and subsequently, they began to discuss different literature and loan each other their favourite books. He had all the Catholic writers that were new to her – Bernanos, Gide, Mauriac – and she gave him the story of Abelard and Heloise, the twelfth-century lovers, nun and priest, who, for their illicit and rhapsodic passion, were forced to withdraw to a contemplative order, never to meet again.

Once a month they drove to Strand Hill and sat on the bench facing the rocks that looked as if they would growl, the waves pounding in and the surfers in black, with the stealth of seals, far out, seen and not seen in the troughs of the waves. They discussed the Russian writers, she sometimes having copied out a paragraph to read to him and one day he put it to her that the reason they loved books was because the crimes in people's hearts were rendered more fatefully and more forgivingly in literature. It was that day or perhaps a different day she told him how much she yearned for a child and how this yearning intensified with time, so much so that she imagined holding it in her arms, hearing its first disconsolate cries.

Twice in her married life she was pregnant and Jack bought her pieces of jewellery, but she lost it both times, and believing the failure to be hers, she grieved alone. One summer Jack booked a holiday in Italy and everywhere they went, she kept seeing paintings of the Nativity, mother and child depicted in such sumptuous colours, their expressions so serene, adhering to one another, and she found, when they came out into the hot street, with awnings over shops shut for lunch, that there were tears in her eyes and down her cheeks.

She once considered going to China to adopt a child. Why China she could not say, except in a dream, she was already in labour and the midwife at her bedside was Chinese, holding a rod of bamboo with three green shoots. According to her reckoning, she had a few years at most, which was why she went to a psychic for guidance. The woman listened attentively and told her she must pray more, pray to her Earth-Angels, out of doors, close to nature and her prayer would be answered. It couldn't not be. Without even thinking, she looked both ways, then waded through the rushes, over the clumps of seeping fern and at the water's slobbery edge, she knelt, feeling the shock of its coldness, as she cupped it in her hands, then brought it to her face again and again. But for the prayer to be efficacious, the psychic told her she had to plunge her face right into the water, and so she did, staring down through those teeming whorls of dark, praying as she had never prayed before. Afterwards she got up, flattened the dents on her knees, dried her hands on the wet grass to no avail and walked on, her hair still wet and water streaming from her eyes.

It was where a young tree had fallen onto the path that she stepped to one side and almost collided with a figure who had come on her unawares, her sudden scream breaching the quiet of the oncoming dusk. He apologised. It was Dr Vladimir. She recognised that voice, so low and distinctive, not like any of the voices she was accustomed to. She recalled the morning weeks before, when Dara brought him to the shop to ask for rooms to rent for his practice. She had gone there to do a bit of dusting, pick up the circulars and flyers that had accumulated, crestfallen at the emptiness of the place. The drawers still had labels in her own neat handwriting – plimsolls, children's socks, ladies' hosiery and lingerie. The two men had come on her unawares, Dara blowing between his mittened hands and the stranger with such a steadiness in his gaze that it unnerved her. Dara had put the question to her at once, while the doctor walked around, admiring a few antiques that they were intending to send to auction – the tall silver and glass floor lamps, mirrors, the pale Flemish tapestry with its fauns and its cupids, and the gentleman's travelling trunk that seemed to intrigue him so. At first she demurred, then said they intended to sell, not rent and Dara countered with the fact that the place would be kept warm and aired and free of rats, until purchasers materialised from the great blue yonder.

'I'll have to talk to my husband,' she said, which she did and that was that. Jack agreed, made all the practical arrangements congratulating himself on his good judgement, because the new doctor's praises were increasingly hailed.

It was in the car park at the front of the Castle that he caught up with her again that evening as she stood looking up at the sky, a cold sky with a few stars up there, faint and distant from one another. Huntsmen were also returning, bluff and garrulous, some with their breeched guns under their arms and their gillies also with guns, went towards the side entrance down the three steps, over which a sign read *Bar*. The dogs were straining on their leashes, knowing that they were about to be cooped up in an outhouse, while their masters slaked their thirsts.

Edmond, the manager, stood at the front door welcoming the troupe and seeing her, he came out calling her by her name, saying she and Jack had become loners since they sold the boutique and scolding her for not having come to the most recent poetry evening. He welcomed the newcomer effusively, said it was an honour to have him and as he led them in, he relayed the Castle's three hundred years of variegated history, the clans that owned her and the clans that lost her, her woodlands, her flora and fauna, red squirrels, pine martens, the peregrine falcons, spoilt for riches as he said. In the hall there was much commotion, men dismantling and cleaning their guns before they were taken to the safe overnight. He led them through to the bar and sat them on his own special window seat, where they had a fine view of the room, the hunters and the locals all so convivial, enumerating the day's thrills and adventures. Through a side window they could just see the stretch of river, dark as it crept between the wooded shores and then gone from sight, as it broadened out into that final journey before reaching the sea. Pointing to a spot way beneath Edmond said, 'That's the maternity ward,' and recounted the salmon, back from the lonely oceans and the winds and the trade winds of Greenland, who had made the hazardous journey to hatch her eggs in the very spot where she was born. Himself and the gardener had been watching her closely and what a production it was, to see how carefully she prepared her bed, like a belly dancer, moving back and forth to get it smooth, emptying it of clay and silt, then making it porous for the fresh water to flow through and that done, she sat back and evaluated her suitors. Several swam around her, swam ceaselessly until the strongest fella, the one with the most spunk, got it over her and as he said then in mock lament, the honeymoon was cut short. The funny thing was that the poor males, limp and exhausted, were still dancing around her, still hoping, like those eejits that hung around the court of Penelope in Ithaca.

'Some of us caught those eejits and ate them,' a voice was heard to say among the boisterous crowd.

'So we did,' another voice joined.

'It was called the Christmas Pot . . . it's what poor people had to make do with,' the first man said and his comrades agreed and there ensued a friendly altercation as to whether poor people had broken the law in those times, poaching fish from a river that belonged to the gentry.

Like them, Fidelma was in her element, basking in the warmth and the banter. There they all were, locals she knew well, perched on their regular stools, next to the glass cases with the prize trout and photographs of the men who had caught them. Written in silver on the top of the two cases was the weight of each trout and the length of time it had taken a fisherman to hook it in. Now and then they called across to her, as Edmond and the doctor were exchanging hunting expeditions, in Europe, in Africa and all over. Suddenly she heard Edmond ask the doctor did he not think that this woman, the lovely Fidelma, born and bred in the west of Ireland, was some throwback to a noble woman in Spain or Italy. He remarked on her black hair, her porcelain skin, the long neck and the Gioconda smile.

'Ah now,' she said, blushing fiercely, the colour running up and down her neck in ripples, as if cochineal was trickling through her. An evening like no other, what with her plunging her face in the freezing water earlier on, then meeting him, the banshee scream that she had let out and now here, he fixing her, with his dark, untelling eyes. She looked up at him in that first sweet exchange of a glance and felt a sudden gladness, for the sake of which all other things were forgotten.

When they came out, he bowed and went on foot along the

back avenue, to the outer gate that led to where he lodged with Fifi. She had scarcely exchanged a word with him in the bar and yet she had a sense of him, how attentive he was, his hands so expressive, as if they too talked, absorbing everything around him, infinitely courteous, yet mysterious and inscrutable.

There were more stars than when they had gone in, a cold silvery night that now seemed full of sudden and sourceless promise.

On the Veranda

It is after midnight and all is still at the Castle. The guests have gone up to bed, windows dark with heavy curtains drawn and the entire place, its ivied walls, its turrets, its broad walks, its steep steps, all engulfed in night.

The kitchen staff have gathered on the veranda, as they do most nights, for the smokes, the odd beer, to unwind. They sink into the bockled armchairs, in their coats, huddled around the tall gas heater, chatting and joking. They are a mixed group, Irish, Burmese, Italian, Spanish, Czech, Slovakian, Polish. In their small bedrooms, which lead off the courtyard, are the emblems of their own land, maybe a flag, or a map, electric and acoustic guitars, family photographs and in Ivan's room, cookery encyclopaedias. In Mujo the mute's room, there are no emblems, as he has no past and no family that they know of. They knew so little about him, except that he had been sent from Holland to Ireland, and spent time in a hostel in Dublin. The supervisor there got him the job in the hotel as she was a first cousin of the manager's. He was called Mujo, short for Muhammad, and with his big sad eyes, kept his silence, always listening with wonder to what others said. His was the lowliest job of all, kitchen porter. His principal duties were to keep floors and surfaces spotlessly clean, to fill the dishwashers and clean all pots and pans separately. Sometimes he did not talk for days, but he could speak in an emergency. He spoke when he was interviewed for the job and Ivan, who shared a bedroom with him, said that he talked in his sleep and sometimes got very agitated, shouting and thrashing about.

His doves were his friends that he kept in the barn, going to them at all hours and all his wages went on them. They lived like royalty, their nests were terracotta pots, lined with straw, corn and maize for their grub. How quickly they had bred. Five pairs within half a year. He gave them names, names of people from his own country. In the very early mornings when they were let out, the yard was a cascade of white, wings fanning out, as they readied themselves to rise, then up and up towards the woods, where he followed, his tumblers, unerringly roaming and circumnavigating the upper air, long before the songbirds wakened, or the seagulls with their cold caws came swooping in from the seashore.

In a tin box was his most secret possession. It was to be opened in case he was ever taken to prison.

Earlier in the evening, the kitchen was bedlam, shouts and commands and arguments, Olive the assistant chef calling everyone 'Shithead'. Shithead this and shithead that, staff going up and down the narrow stairs to the dining room, where all was elegance and candlelight, calling 'Coming through, coming through' to avoid a collision. Yet inevitably, the unwieldy metal trays kept grazing one another.

Hedda, the tall beautiful waitress from Lithuania, has turned twenty-five and has been crying on and off, at the misery of growing old. Now on the veranda, she has cheered up, demanding that everyone tell her a story. That is her birthday present, along with the Sachertorte, which Ivan the pastry chef has made for her and has arranged on a beautiful cake plate with an elaborate pink frilled ruff. Nobody is willing to start, they keep teasing each other and even Dara, normally a spinner of tales, can only remember as a kid three boys and one girl trying to make sleds out of cardboard boxes, to skate on the disused railway line.

'Is that all . . . is that all?' they tease him.

'Ah, buying the first condoms and texting girls over in Galway,' he says and suddenly baulks.

Tommy takes to the floor. Normally, he would be driving home by now, but has stayed to have a slice of the famous cake. They know all about Tommy, his one hundred and eighty acres of arable land, all along the coast, his expertise with dosing cattle, his Rouge French ram bought at a cost of eight hundred euros, the lambs he has delivered and later castrated so as to get more fat on them. Tommy's motto is 'Keep the money turning'. They also know he has a beautiful girlfriend, Camilla, half English, and they have seen pictures of her on his phone, dark-haired, teeth like pearls, always in very high heels and an off-the-shoulder black dress. They know that he's a volatile man and that he once killed a sheep that was acting crazy because she wouldn't go in the door of the outhouse and how he struck her with a blackthorn stick, several fierce blows and she fell down dead. Then the dogs and the foxes got her and soon after as he told it, the seagulls came for the guts and the contents of the stomach and how Camilla didn't talk to him for three days.

'It's like this,' he begins and waits till the sniggers died down, 'I'm stressed out, I'm going crazy, I drive the whole fecking way to Mayo to get new aluminium wheels for the Volkswagen. I drive in Camilla's car. I have the measurements and yer man the dealer gets his ruler and measures and assures me that his wheels will fit my VW exactly. Deal done. Three hundred euros cash. I come home, jack up the car, and the effing wheels are out by half a millimetre. I'm fucking psycho. Camilla says relax, relax, we'll put them on Dundee. We'll never fucking sell them on Dundee I tell her and she tells me to relax and she takes a picture and the measurements and she puts it on the site and in five minutes the wheels are sold for exactly the same price.'

Andre, the Polak, is next. He coughs a few times, apologises for his English and begins very seriously, 'In my small town, they say Ireland good place, good wages. Homeless for one month when I arrive to Dublin. I go to one shelter and another and another, ask *Can I please spend night here*. Mattresses on floor, many men in one room. I keep one eye half open, for I fear I lose my flash lamp, my one possession. In morning, janitor hand out small dishes with cornflakes and we all go out search for work. Anything, anything. After two weeks I get job down in Limerick working with cows. Place very lonely. Only cows and shed where I sleep. I ring my mother and she say *You won't make it Andre . . . come back*, but because she say that, I am determine to make it. Late one night I am called from agency that say *Come tomorrow morning eight a.m. for interview to start in restaurant in Finglas*. No trains so early. No bus. I set out in night and I start flagging when I get to main road. Walk. Walk. Walk. At petrol station woman in wellington boots ask me where I going. I tell her I have to be in Finglas before eight o'clock for interview for job. She tell man filling his car *Bring this boy to Finglas* and I get in and he give me coffee in cafeteria in O'Connell Street and afterward money to take taxi. One year there I save and now my friends I am here.'

Hedda is reluctant to tell a story, even though it is her turn. She tells them that her idol is Baudelaire, but he is dead and she cannot write poetry now, as she has no love in her life. She tells them that she cries a lot and that her only relaxing is cleaning her small apartment. Not lucky in love. It is why she has left the previous job and come here, to get away from Milos, to think. 'It is like this,' she says and then begins, a bit shyly, holding back the tears. 'Milos and me, we work in the same dining room in County Waterford and get to know one another and find us falling in love. He go home on holiday for one month and I think when he coming back and I pray he don't find another woman. I hug him when he appear. I make marzipan. Light candles. Marzipan cut up in slices and along with it, cheese and wine. He say, "Let's go for a walk Hedda." He very insistent. We go along by a river and he stop me and he say, "Don't move." Then he say, "Don't jump in the river." I am shaking like a little little girl. I say, "What is it." He say, "Don't ask," then he go on his knees and take a small box from his pocket and snap it open and he say, "Marry me." I am bewildered. One of me feeling "Stay" and one of me saying, "Run to the motorway Hedda." So many different feelings. He put the ring on. In that moment almost husband and wife. For two months enjoying our feelings. Then we decide to have a holiday in the Caribbean and we start to fight. It is all about arrangements. I pick hotel and he say not enough palm trees. Next hotel he say, mould on the picture frame in the lobby. I throw my computer on the table and tell him do it. What he do then, he call his mother. She find hotel with many palm trees and we go. When we are there he say mans is looking at me, he say I smile at them behind his back. Temperature thirty degrees. Everything go wrong. I book a table for dinner and he doesn't come. Holiday separated us. We come back and work together and his jealousy is getting worse and worse. He say I talk to girls more than I talk to him. From the minute I wake up in the morning he criticising me, every bit of me. Everything I do is wrong. If I say I am coming in one hour and am five minutes late he is shouting. He complain to his mother. She say if she was not his mother she would marry him. I say, "Why are you and I quarrelling since we got engaged, is it the piece of metal?" and he say yes and I throw the ring back at him and I leave the hotel and find myself a job here. I did know myself, but not any longer.'

When she has finished she buries her head in the armchair and Ivan, who has been consulting a little notebook, sits back in his chair, willing them all to listen to him. 'My country Czechoslovakia. My family nine hundred years in same place. We aristocrats. It say so in chronicles in museum. I am a little Russian from my mother's side. My mother she say my grandmother every night have small shot of plum brandy for sleep. Then war happen. My family they lose everything, their estates, their money, they move to one small place, then another and finally we are in a little dingy house in a city. My mother a widow. I am very close to her all the time, I wash her hair and she wash mine. She have three jobs. I learn to cook alone. I make my first cake age seven. It has three flavours, chocolate, sponge with cheese and vanilla. A grand uncle he pay for me to go to food college in Austria. I graduate after two years and get work in Graz, not far from Vienna. I work later in Italy, then France. In each country I learn something new, in France baguette. I have no personal life, but then in hotel in Switzerland, where I have moved, a girl come and she from another part of Czechoslovakia, also aristocrat, pictures of castles in her photo album. We like one another, we talk in our language, we go skiing two weekends in wintertime. After one year we decide to go home and tell our relatives that we intend to marry, to settle down. Her people eleven kilometres from mine. After two days she come to me. She find me in orchard pruning trees and I am so happy to be in my own country. She say to me, "Ivan, my family think you too old for me." I say, "Be honest Wanda," and she look at me all sad and she say no, it is not her, it is her family. I do not believe her. I do not know why she change her mind. I say thank you, goodbye and good luck. I go back to Switzerland and am alone. In time I recover. I think in basement of cousin's house I have plum brandy from 1967, fifty per cent proof. I tell myself that when I have son I will go there and open that bottle and be drunk. When I have son. I decide to come to Ireland because I like Tolkien and Tolkien he like Scotland, New Zealand and Ireland. I speak no English. I bring recipes from Czechoslovakia, Austria and France, I learn a few things here, for example scones. I move from city to this place because I have forest, I love forest, forest and river. I cannot say how long I will stay. My friends I tell you this, we are a jolly group but put us in uniform and all that change. In war I don't know who my brother. In war I don't know who my friend. War make everybody savage. Who can say what lies inside the heart of each one of us when everything is taken away.'

Then it was Mujo's turn. *Ne. Ne. Ne.* He rolls himself into a ball and Hedda kneels to console him, but he fends her off. He could not tell his story the way others did because the words had stopped inside him. He was dumb, dumbstruck.

Into the Woods

The new Doc brought our class to the woods, to walk in the footsteps of the druids and learn the healing properties in nature.

We were fifteen in all, boys and girls, and we walked in pairs through the town, over the bridge and about one mile more to Killooney Wood. We sang as we walked and when we could remember no more songs, the Doc sang folk songs from his own country, in his own tongue. Everyone wanted to be the person walking next to him. We were such a merry group that people waved to us from their passing cars. It was a sunny day and it was nice to reach the woods, where there was shade. Leaves were just beginning to sprout and were, as he said, at their most tasty. The boys were running and scampering around, climbing trees and one boy peed from a height, but the Doc just ignored it. He looked a bit funny in a long black smock, with his white beard and his white hair tied up in a topknot. Lena Lally asked him if he was married and he just smiled and said that perhaps she had a wife in mind for him. He had brought illustrated books with pictures of trees in them and another with pictures of mushrooms and in his chip basket there were two knives, a secateurs and a trowel.

Then it was time to pick some leaves. We were allowed to eat them or put them in the basket for a salad. One girl, Cliodhna, said hers was buttery and so everyone said buttery and we were all laughing and vying with each other to describe the tastes – lemony and apricoty and peachy and orangey and nutty. The little wild violets under the trees were minute, and we did for them, gobbled them up and they had no taste at all. In our copybooks we wrote down the properties of each tree, the leaf, the flower, if it were a flowering tree, and the root. The oak leaf was fibrous, so everyone wrote fibrous. He told us then the medicinal value attached to each tree. Hawthorn for the heart, something else for the liver, willow for the gall bladder. The needles of the big cedars were oily, good as a breath freshener, but too intense for the mouth. Eating the catkins was like eating maggots. Lime flower, which was moist and mucilaginous, was a cooling yin tonic and especially, as he said, suitable for women during menopause. There were a few giggles at that.

Then it was time to pick mushrooms. Before we did, he warned us *Never touch a mushroom that you are not sure of*, as many were deadly poisonous. From his book, we looked at pictures of mushrooms, including the poisonous ones and they looked identical to the harmless ones. They were on very thin little wobbly stalks and had a vivid red cap with thick white spots. The mushrooms we were allowed to pick were called chanterelle. He knelt down and got one knife to sever the stems and then the second knife to lift it away from the root, so that more mushrooms would grow next year. They grew in clusters, clinging to one another. While he was cutting, his topknot fell down over his face and he looked like one of those hags in a fairy tale who steal children and boil them in a big black pot. There were several kinds of chanterelle and they crumbled easily in our hands, like soft biscuits and we devoured them.

*

Later we were on a summit, with a view of the wood all around, the trees so nice and breezy and the sky above as blue as in the holy pictures of Our Lady, ascending into Heaven. We sat in a circle, our frocks spread out neatly at our sides and the boys stood, or else sat on their haunches, just to show how cool they were. Two bigger girls that were in charge of the picnic laid out a big plastic cloth and then plastic tumblers for the lemonade. The Doc said that in times of old, kings and queens always built their castles and their keeps on high places, so as to spot the encroaching enemy and then from the slit holes in the masonry aimed their bows and arrows, which were already dipped in poisons made from plants. He said how people barely realised the potency in plant and vegetable life and then he talked of poisoning, state poisoning and individual poisoning, saying that in the larger scheme of things, all wrongs were avenged and there was a cosmic payback for every bad deed.

In ancient China for instance unwanted people were disposed of at ceremonial dances. Feathers already soaked in several poisons were thrown onto very hot coals and the fumes asphyxiated the unlucky ones, who minutes before had been dancing merrily. In Roman times, it was also at banquets that unwanted family members were done for. Sometimes it was a knife already dipped in poison and normally used to cut meats, while more often it was in the wine, laced with arsenic, which was tasteless and without smell. Naturally, suspicion began to spread, which is why the unfortunate eunuchs and servants were made to taste the wine first. Craftily, goblets had been set in a particular place for the doomed. Suspicion was such that kings and queens were ever cautious. King Henry IV of France was so afraid of being poisoned that he cooked his own eggs on his own little portable stove and drew his own water from the Seine. Napoleon believed there was arsenic in the wallpaper in his prison cell in St Helena, and believing he would die from the gaseous fumes, he insisted on being moved to another cell.

In an old Norse saga, a certain tribe ate a mushroom that was so lethal, it caused disorder in the mind and deprived them of their true feelings. They went wild and even the princes, to whom they were bonded, were terrified of them. They stopped at nothing. They bit their own shields, they uprooted trees and slaughtered all before them. The Berserks they were called.

'Crikey, a Berserk,' Cliodhna said and we all turned round and there was a strange guard in uniform, coming up the hill, bawling his head off. The Doc got up and told us to get on with our picnic and then he hurried down the slope and they met halfway.

*

'What are you doing out here in this wood with these children?' the guard asks in a broad country accent. He is red and breathless from the climb and is a cocky young pup, a bit overweight and trussed into his uniform. He repeats the question, only more threateningly and soon Dr Vlad realises that this accidental encounter could land him in treacherous waters.

'We were having a nature class . . . we studied the various attributes of different trees and I told the children the particular medicinal value.'

'You need a Garda clearance to take children out.'

'Well, I was not aware of that . . .'

'Only parents, grandparents and teachers are allowed to bring children out . . . it's the law here in this country and we take it seriously,' his interrogator said, bristling now with the importance of his own authority. The questions are not so much asked as pelted at him. Who is he? Is he a schoolteacher? Under whose authorisation has he embarked on this?

'I am Dr Vladimir Dragan. I have lived here for several months and practised as a healer in the town.'

'Oh, one of the New Age quacks,' the oaf says with a sneer and then asks if he has the qualification to be a healer and certificates to prove it.

The doctor is telling himself to maintain composure at all costs. He looks down and at that moment a juicy pink worm is wriggling its way over a bit of fallen bark to get to its prey and he has a terrible instinct to tread on it, to squash it just as he would like to squash this upstart. He pictures his grandfather's sabre sinking nicely into the folds of that thick neck. He has begun to perspire and blames the humidity. What humidity, he is asked.

'Let me see your identity,' and carefully from his wallet he retrieves the documents that he has always carried, including an ID card and driving licence. He watches every muscle in the oaf's face as he reads, peering into it as if to find something incriminating. Then he is asked to turn around, for the guard to study him sideways, look behind his ears, compare the man standing in front of him to the man in the passport photograph. Pernickety to the last. He knows the type, he knows all the types. A few years further back and he could have had him executed.

'You know you have broken the law,' he is told.

'Mea culpa.' He is at his most beholden now, wipes his face with his handkerchief and comments once again on the hot day.

'There's a nice westerly breeze,' the oaf says and then asks if the schoolteacher, who allowed him to take this nature walk, had Garda clearance.

'I couldn't tell you the answer to that.'

He explodes, asks loudly what the country is coming to: civil servants and government officials sitting on their arses not doing their jobs properly, shirking their civic responsibilities. Did the teacher not know the law?

'She's a woman.'

'Woman or no woman, the law is the law.'

The doctor is seized with rage. The same murderous and subversive rage that landed his father and that father before him in prison. Yet he manages to keep a grip on himself and in a guise of holiness, he takes the crystal pendulum that is hanging from his neck and waves it back and forth at his opponent, as though in a blessing. The guard ignores it, takes out his phone and moves a distance away, obviously to ring his superiors, to put the country on high alert.

In those moments, as Dr Vlad watches and waits, he remembers his wife's last letter, saying they must never ever correspond again, since it was becoming too dangerous. He recalls her description of searches in the various houses he had lived in since his disappearance and at the end her begging him to give himself up. *No, no my dearest. If I am to give myself up it will not be to some imbecile in a wood in Ireland.* He remembers then his mistress of the dark tresses, whom he met through their occult interests, her tendresse, white poodles that she walked in back streets and maybe was walking at that moment and thinking of him. Those last two years together – while he was still a free man – were happy ones, feted in bars, greeted openly, pictures of him all along the walls, in combat attire and everyone knowing who he was.

The oaf has returned, even more het up, as obviously there is no signal in that wood and he has not been able to reach head office.

'Let me see your identity again,' he says, and this time, having stared at them, he takes out a small notebook and biro, for the defendant to make a statement.

'Why do I have to make a statement?'

'Because I'm telling you to.'

With utter confidence, the doctor gives his name, his age, his occupation, Alexandria where he was born, the various countries where he was educated, the Balkan countries he has lived in, the academies where he has studied, the cities in which he received honours, and the date when he arrived in Cloonoila. Then in Latin and French and English, from memory he lists the various medicines he has imported and for which he secured the correct permits. Mother Nature of course has also supplied him with cures, gathered in those very woods and local environs. He lists them: willow, dandelion, valerian, moss, not to mention the seaweed which he, along with others, harvests in the early morning and which he uses for his seaweed baths. Several times he has to repeat what he has said, because the scribe is not familiar with the words, and then, to compound the comedy, his biro has run out of ink, he licks it to set down a few more syllables and finally, has to resort to borrowing his captive's fountain pen. This would be a farce, if discovery was not only seconds away and his true identity about to become known.

'I'm arresting you,' the voice says and it is like a thunderclap. *I'm arresting you.* He balances himself against one of the tree trunks and at his most persuasive, like a gentle father talking to an errant child, he remonstrates, saying if he were the type of person intent on harm he would hardly take fifteen children out in broad daylight. He would take one in his motor car and that under cover of darkness.

'Dragan,' the guard repeats, asking if that was an unusual name and is told that there are plenty of Dragans, scattered all over the Balkans, Transylvania and Ukraine.

'Is it related to Dracula?' he is asked.

'No . . . but that's an interesting variation,' and then, with a brazen recklessness, he says, 'I took the name in honour of a lame shepherd of wolves.' *I took the name, rather than I am that name*, but the blustering idiot didn't get it. Inside a warning voice is saying *Beware arrogance*, and he is thinking of a recent encoded warning, that his enemies might be closing in on him.

'Could we not do this in a more mature way?' he says.

'What mature way were you thinking of?'

'I was thinking of the children . . . the shock it will be, the trauma, seeing me carted away in such circumstances. Why not let me walk them home and drop them off at their houses and then I can meet with the teacher and you and subsequently, we go to the local guard.'

With each passing moment, the noose is tightening.

Very soon he will not be nice Dr Vladimir Dragan, he will be the most wanted man in Europe, with a price on his head. He can see it all with an eerie clarity, both of them going into the local station, Plodder Pat looking up in disbelief, the young pup explaining the gravity of the matter, as his fake identity papers are handed over. One guard will study them, a second will log the information into his computer, then a whoosh as the data goes through cyberspace and reaches a head office in Dublin or Brussels. Within minutes, when the information is downloaded, checked and found to be false, he will be handcuffed, brought in the back of a car and driven through the green complacent land, where he believed he was safe, to meet his downfall.

Shamelessly now he wrings his hands, berates himself for his carelessness, utters craven apology, saying that there are those in the town who will vouch for him as a healer.

'What kind of healer?'

'Quantum energy . . . radiothesia . . . human sensitivity to the various energy fields . . .'

'Is that so?' the guard says, totally perplexed.

'But on Sundays I coach young people in football,' the doctor answers quickly.

'So you like the football.' The fellow is taken aback, and asks what kind of coaching he does.

'Well, we run, then I sit them down and talk about motivation . . . their dream of playing for their country one day.'

'Do you watch the football?'

'I do. I like it on the flat screen in TJ's . . . for all the games . . . unless of course you are determined to lock me up.'

The thaw has not happened, but something has shifted. He takes out his crystal and waves it repeatedly, lost in prayer.

'You strike me as a military man,' he is told and he laughs and says what could be less militant than a man with white hair, a straggling beard and a smock. He plays a last, audacious card, even while recognising the risk. He decides that by openly admitting to having been a cheat once, he will be seen as a man of truth.

'I avoided military service,' he says with a colluding smile.

'How come?'

'I was eighteen and due to be called up, but they forgot me . . .

so with money from an uncle who had no children, I took myself off to Japan, where I was lucky to meet a Zen master. It was he who started me on the holy path. I learnt alternative medicine and also studied the language, both written and oral, but I've forgotten most of it. A year later I came home and unfortunately, some punctilious clerk noticed the error and I was called up. By now I was determined to devote my life to medicine, not to serve in an army or go to war. I knew from a friend that one way to avoid conscription was to plead deafness.'

'Go on,' his interrogator said, his mouth half open in wonder.

'It was a lengthy examination, lasted all day, they spoke to me, questioned me and then with a vibrating tuning fork tested the middle ear, the inner ear, at which I professed to hear nothing. Then they tapped on the bone of the skull and I knew from my studies that sound travels directly to the bone, independent of the ear and is transmitted to the listener. Had I said I couldn't hear anything, they would have known I was lying, but they believed me and I was let off.'

'The way you think I am letting you off,' the guard says, but not so aggressively.

'As the elder of the two, may I propose the following – we will both go to the local guard, in his house, and explain everything.'

'Is that Plodder Pat? He's more interested in the bungalow he's building than in the law . . . You think I'm a sucker.'

'On the contrary, I congratulate you. You saw a potentially dangerous situation, you stopped your car and you gave me a grilling.'

'To tell you the truth, I was going to a funeral . . . I almost didn't stop.'

'Is it a relative?'

'It's a second cousin. It was sudden . . . he was serving petrol from his own petrol pump, talking to the guy, and he keeled over . . . Dead.' At the word he blesses himself.

They then talk of family ties, blood knots, the necessity of mourning and the folly of taking life for granted. The danger has passed. The guard says he had to do what he did, for the sake of the children, as children are sacrosanct to him.

'The things I've seen, 'twould break hearts,' he says.

Deliberating for a moment, he decides to go, but not before saying that maybe his mother could do with some of that quantum energy stuff for her arthritis. He is told that she would be given special treatment.

*

Dr Vlad takes the swim in his secret cove that night, a swim he had promised himself to wash away the day's provocations. Afterwards, he lies on the bank and drifts into a sleep: *Sleep that knits up the ravelled sleeve of* . . . then falls fast asleep. Soon he is dreaming of the long ago, his mother's polenta cake, the ice-green rivers that roared down from the gorges, the children in the wood, their voices calling to one another, the chanterelles that they broke and wolfed down, along with the young pup of a guard, licking his biro to squeeze another word out. Suddenly, into the dream there walks his old friend K, not in his usual tweed jacket with the leather elbow patches, but all in black, altered through death.

'Brother,' he says, wagging a finger. 'That was a near thing today, you must have been shitting your pants,' and uninvited, he sits, and begins to talk.

Townspeople soon followed to eavesdrop – Young Dara, Fidelma, the draper's wife, the nun with the big thighs and the crabbed sisters. He is paralysed, helpless to send them away, in what he knows to be a dream, yet he cannot haul himself out of it, his limbs are inert. There is K jabbering away and he who was once master is now on the rack. *I am undone* he says, but his words are also clogged up within the dream.

'That siege', K began, 'broke many hearts but not ours, in our fortress in the hills. We could hear the constant rat-tat-tat of the mortars and sniper fire, eliminating *the scum down in the city*. One thousand, three hundred and fifty-nine days and nights of it. The human spirit is indomitable. Such were the sentiments of outsiders who nevertheless could not imagine the carnage, rotting bodies, rotting garbage, dogs roaming wild and a few stalwarts creeping along the alleys to scavenge for bread. Since then they had a celebration, a way of remembering, red chairs erected in our beloved city, your jewel as you called it. Yes, eleven thousand, five hundred and forty-one red chairs in commemoration of the fallen. It is said that tourists only began to cry when they came upon the six hundred and forty-three little red chairs of dead children. Yes, the living, the mangled, the scarified, with the crazed responsibility of remembering everything, everything. The evening we were told of the market massacre we drank a toast, we drank many toasts. No song without suffering, as you said. What a gruesome sight it must have been down below, quite surreal, limbs, arms, heads, torsos, all mixed in with potatoes, cabbages, onions and kohlrabi. A conglomerate. You insisted to the outside world that those dead bodies were mannequins and corpses from wars long past, planted there by our enemies. The waitresses were invited to drink with us. They had the hots for you, with your thick, black, glossy hair and your voice so deep and so resonating. They wrote billets-doux on your napkin and you pulled the plaits of your favourite one, Helga. Another incident that caught the attention of the world was a little girl of twelve on her bicycle, oblivious, when a shell hit her and soon the blood rippled out, a leitmotif of red rose petals on discoloured yellowish snow. Yes, that caught the attention of the outside world and some foreign intellectuals ganged together and put on a production of *Waiting for Godot*, to bolster the morale of the people. That annoyed you. It stole your thunder. After all, you were the Commander, the supreme leader, the mastermind whom diplomats and big shots came to appeal to, to implore you to call the siege off. How you bamboozled them with your charm and your procrastinations and sometimes your fierce temper. You insisted you were ready to negotiate, while also demanding human rights, placing yourself and your people in the role of victim – *We are mice in the jaws of cats at play*. At the outset, these dignitaries were always given a history lesson, our wronged race, starting with the Battle of Kosovo in 1389. When questioned about the atrocities you always had an answer. Either they never took place, or were fabricated by the enemy, and questioned about corpses down in the square, you insisted they were mannequins, which the enemy had planted there, to delude the world. You even said, "I have an abhorrence of war," and maybe there was a grain of truth in it. You promised the earth, without meaning it. You promised the siege would be lifted, the shelling would stop and food and aid convoys would be allowed in, except none of that happened. It was all a lie, but lies can be just as persuasive and as palatable as truth in desperate times. So these diplomats and big shots went away moderately reassured and in any case, they were always in a hurry to get to the airport, lest you might already have ordered it to be shelled. Around that time you stopped writing. It stands to reason, with so much going on you had no time to reflect and maybe no wish to. As I say, I read more while the siege went on. I re-read *Hamlet* and thought for all his protestation of loving Ophelia more than forty thousand brothers, he too was a specialist in the macabre. Things began to get less robust down in the city, which is to say there were fewer corpses. You raved, you ranted, your Utopia, that diamond city enfolded in hills was beginning to slip from your grasp. Everyone was betraying you, the whole world was against you and you resolved on even greater conquest. There were more territories to be taken. Ethnic purification must happen, even if in the end you ruled over a land of ghosts. Shakespeare must have come to your mind – that *tide in the affairs of man*, yet you mastered any doubts you might have had. So came the next bonanza. Srebrenica. A killing spree. Eight thousand Bosniak men boarded onto buses, assured of their safety, driven off and herded into a concrete emporium, where, it is said, the shooting began after dark. We heard that the gunners were so tired from killing, they asked for chairs and chairs were provided. Then replacements took up the grisly task. Four days, four nights of it. Those cries, those screams, those expirations, the apotheosis of all bloodiness, with carrion men groaning for burial. As for the bodies, that was a matter for the engineers, hence the zillions of secret graves that litter our land. A hot night and the blood of so many in such a short space of time. I did not picture it and I did not want to. But as time went on it got to me, befouled by death, the stench of blood, in the mouth and especially on the palate. There was no escaping it. The spree seemed to have paid off, but as happens down the ages, our fortunes began to wane. We lost whole swathes of land to the east and before long, our enemy got to be as bloodthirsty as us. They learnt, it was said, from our butchery. Soon the diplomats and the bigwigs were not so credulous and there were even whispers here at home of your having gone too far, of maybe your surpassing yourself, because for you, enough was never enough. There was sullenness up in our fortress. You in your shirt sleeves, pacing, shouting, sensing treachery on every side and mouthing your rationale, like all the cast of crazed monsters that have come before you in history. Then other times you sat like a wronged child, silent, biting your nails, biting, biting, down to the quick. I was the one entrusted with talking to you. Why wouldn't I? After all, between us there was that oath, we were brothers, best friends in our youth and university days, a little competitive in our reverence for William Shakespeare. We loved Goethe and Musil, but Shakespeare was God. You had been christened Young Törless because of the two terribly contrasting aspects of your character, the sane, the reasonable and the other so dark, so vengeful. In summertime we took vacations together, lay on riverbanks, meadows full of flowers, and veins of snow beautifully ridged the mountain caps, while down below we breathed the scent of newborn flowers. In winter, we plunged into ice-green rivers that had flowed from the gorges and lay on our backs braving it, then other times, cycling through snug little towns and to the amazement of people, spouting Shakespeare. We loved our country and vowed to leave it a better place than when we had been born into it. But poetry came first. In the mountain, where we had gone to cram for our examinations, it happened. One night you called me outside, in the snow, and with your little pearl-handled penknife, you slit both our fingers and we swapped our blood. It almost froze as we tasted it, because the temperature was twenty-eight degrees below zero, up there. Blood brothers from that moment on, the keepers of each other's soul and each other's conscience. That was what you said. You said something else that I will never forget. You said we were like mountain climbers with a rope and that if one let go of the rope, the other fell into the abyss. You said that. So I began, as things unravelled up there in our lair, to talk to you, as in the old days, to talk of literature and why not, since we both loved it so. I said, "Do you remember Mr Kurtz?" and you said of course, because that time in the mountain, along with Goethe and Musil and Shakespeare, we read every word of *Heart of Darkness*. Who wouldn't. We followed the pallet on which the dying Kurtz was carried and pictured the crazy woman, who came abreast of the steamer, with her wild incantations, her necklaces of glass and I said to you, "Do you remember Kurtz's last words?" and you went silent and I spoke them to you, *The horror! The horror!* and I put it to you if Kurtz was not trying to expiate his own horror and ask for remission of some kind. You looked at me and I trembled because I knew that for you, at that moment, my death was as necessary and as meaningless as all the other deaths that had gone before. You had let go of the rope. As time went on my nausea worsened. That warehouse, with its seven thousand men of reproductive age, kept coming into my mind, along with the leitmotif of the spattered roses on the square. I began to believe that I could breathe better dead than alive. You see, we all became unhinged in our bastion. I would like to dwell for a moment on the manner of my death. It was not for fear of you. It is also said that I was drunk when I blew my brains out, but were we not often drunk in deference to the Kremlin mountaineer? You never wrote the book you had hoped to write. What a book it would be. For only you knew the full story. A Book of the Night. Those unfortunates, 'the scum down in the city', in their apartments, no light, no heat, no water, no hope, no nothing. What a book that would have been, your beloved, Sarajevo, with its eleven thousand, five hundred and forty-one empty red chairs, including the little ones for the children. In our quasi-mysticism, that surely has not completely abandoned you, the book you will never write will be full of cries. The lamentations of the dead, seeking their others in the underworld, not knowing if those others are already dead, or still in the zone of the living. Yes, a Book of the Night. As you exit the world stage, with the Angel of Death waiting to settle your account, or as you put it to the children in the forest, earlier today, for the cosmic payback for evil that has been done, even you will tremble. Goodnight my friend and brother, and Viva Sarajevo.'

He wakens, ready to deny, to refute, to attack, but they have all gone, instead there is a big black dog rolling its tongue along his forehead, big larruping licks, and as he goes to strike at it, it too disappears, vanishes into the shadows.

Then he opens his eyes to a night of such infinite calm, stars numerous and bathed in gold.

The White Mist

His name is on everybody's lips, Dr Vlad this and Dr Vlad that. He has done wonders for people, women claiming to be rejuvenated, just after two treatments. It is tantamount to a miracle, what he has done for Hamish's wife. She suffered from seizures and they had tried several doctors, including a specialist in Dublin but with no luck. They were told that her illness was psychosomatic and in part, caused by their winding each other up.

There, in his clinic, having been stone silent for the first twenty minutes, the wife was taken with one of the very seizures they had come to discuss with him. She fell to the floor and her husband rushed to hold her. Dr Vlad took control. He said, *Don't hold her . . . it ties her down*. What they had to do was allow her to lie on that floor, watch over her to contain her and just be present. In that way, the fit would subside of its own accord, which it did. She was then given a thorough examination, with Hamish waiting outside and the conclusion was that her condition was neurological because of her being allergic to many things. It was quite an unusual case. He proposed various remedies – lymphatic drainage twice monthly, sulphur and magnesium baths regularly and a very specific diet. She was to avoid foods with preservatives, cleaning fluids and soap powders with any chemical and public places where rooms or curtains had been sprayed. She began a hermetic regime, no longer going to her weekly hairdresser's or to any cafe, but according to Hamish, she had begun to smile again and they believe she will be one hundred per cent cured in a time. Like Jesus, Dr Vlad will soon be walking on water.

Since the evening in the Castle I had only glimpsed him, passing up or down the street or in the river, in the very early morning, gathering stones for his healing massages. It happened without my knowing. A fixation. I began to dream of him.

In the very first dream he walked brazenly into our kitchen and took Jack's favourite coffee mug off the dresser where it always hung. A white china mug, a shaving mug, with side handles and a fading gold crest at the rim. We searched everywhere, indoor and outdoor, in the shed and even in the holes in the hedges, where it might have slipped down. In the dream, Jack said that this was serious and the culprit would have to be found. I had a sense of him knowing that I was party to the theft.

In another dream, he was delivering me of a child, in my own bedroom. It was slippery and he eased it carefully out, every little twist so slight, until it was freed, and then he slapped it smartly for the circulation and I heard its cry. A piercing cry and one that I could not forget. Our bairn, our traitor-treasure. He held it up for me to see, Jack in the bed beside me.

*

It was the mist that did it. A white mist, like a winding muslin, enfolds our part of the world from time to time. Sometimes it occurs in the night, other times in the very early morning. It breaks boundaries, so that adjoining counties are as one. I was invisible in it and so was my little pale green Citroën, buoyed along unseen. The side door of our shop was on the latch and I went up that stairs, transported. I tapped, knowing, or rather guessing, he would be in there meditating. In the tittle-tattle of our universe, all is known, including the verbena aftershave that he uses.

'You are very welcome,' he said, masking any surprise at my impromptu visit at such an early hour.

'I have come for the cure,' I blurted it out.

The cure. He repeated the words.

'The cure for what?'

'*Nerves.*'

He sat me down, without pressing me to elaborate on my condition. He said there were things that could and would be prescribed, but that of course Nature herself was the primary healer. He said I ought to go to the mountains, now that the snow had begun to melt and spring flowers were showing their little modest faces. He made our mountains seem like the Alps.

He had a small bottle with drops and repeated the various plants and other ingredients that were in it. I was to let the drops dissolve under my tongue and wait. The silence was so immense, you could almost touch it, almost reach into it.

Later on, he enquired if the nerves dated back to a particular cause, a bereavement perhaps, or a childhood trauma. I told him I lost a child, that it happened twice and that curiously, I believed both children were one and the same and that afterwards we took a holiday abroad. He asked my age and also my husband's age and said that nothing was impossible nowadays, as science, drawing on nature, had advanced with the advent of in vitro fertilisation. I could see his hands, as in my dream, delivering the child: *Mary took all these things into her heart and pondered over them.* He recognised the words and smiled, a friendly smile.

I watched while he made up a batch of powders and put each amount into a sheaf of paper, which he then folded, his hands so adroit. Then he dated them, one for each day, twenty-one days in all, when he would like me to come back. He said he was grateful that I had come, that I felt I could come. I said were it not for the mist I would not have ventured, but the mist had made me daring.

Before I left he proposed an idea that had just occurred to him. Once winter had passed, why should he not organise some walking tours. Myself and many other ladies could walk with him in the very early morning in the mountains and it would be a wonderful stimulus to the libido.

'That is a promise I will keep,' he said.

I could not believe my eyes. Jack was outside, half standing, half sloping on the bonnet of the car and with a chastising look. He was also quite perplexed, said he had wakened, found me not to be there and had come in search.

'I thought you had gone to the river,' he said.

'Why would I go to the river?' I said, not wishing to be robbed of my wanton happiness.

On the way home, the mist was lifting, bits of it flying around in shreds, and the rest vanishing, as if one of those big forks, that they lift earth with, was gobbling it up. Not a word was spoken.

Dido

The Book Club was in its second year and Fidelma had recently been appointed chairperson. It was in a downstairs room, halfway up the street, that had once been a coffee shop, but that had folded. Flossie had loaned it as she had moved closer out to the sea. The furniture was rickety, two old sofas, kitchen chairs with no backs, and a long stool near the entrance, for latecomers.

The loyal few were there, and some new faces, along with the rowdy family who, for some reason, had been christened 'the Naublers'. There was the father, who was blind, with his Alsatian, his stroppy wife, several young daughters and hobo sons. They hated books. They detested books and came only to make a disturbance. They always brought refreshments, chips, miniatures of gin or vodka, with cans of tonic water and a generous bag of ice. The Alsatian was thrown cubes of ice, which he gnawed at, until it melted into Flossie's carpet.

Fidelma was surprised to see Dr Vlad come in, and stand by the back wall, and suddenly the room was full of him.

As was usual, the evening opened with a short reading, in order to refresh people's minds. Fidelma wondered if Bridget might like to read and from her wheelchair, in her old torn clothes and her green suede boots, she read the chapter called Dido from the *Aeneid*, Book IV, with all the poise and ceremony that it deserved:

Every field, all the farm animals and the colourful birds were silent, all that lived across miles of glassy mere and in the wild country's ragged brakes, lying still under the quiet night in a sleep that smoothed each care from hearts which had forgotten life's toil. But not so the Phoenician queen, her accursed spirit, her torment redoubled, her love came back again and again to haunt her.

'Feck' was the first word, followed by a slew of fecks and it set the tone for the invective that was to follow.

'Pissed me off it did.'

'Nothing to do with our lives . . .'

'Exactly, Moira . . . there's homeless people . . . there's single mothers . . .'

'Yeah yeah.'

'. . . People signing on . . . bastards up in government screwing us and we're asked to feel sorry for Dido . . .'

'She should take an ad in the *Leitrim Echo* – "Lost in Leitrim" – and the lads will put a bun in her.'

Then the most brazen of the Naubler sisters, in her short skirt and fishnets, stood on the stool to mimic Dido, rising from her saffron bed, sprinkling herself with river water, pouring wine between the horns of a white heifer and speaking into the open vitals of slaughtered sheep, to find an answer for her tormented love.

'She's pathetic' was her verdict.

'Are you sure?' Mona asked, seething.

'Bloody right I'm sure,' and her sentiments were echoed by some of the younger in the audience, who found the story too antiquated, and not relevant to the modern world. Dido was no role model and anyhow, love was past its sell-by date.

'Not for me mate,' Fifi shouted.

'I'm the oldest person in the room,' Bridget said, then, rising from her chair, like a tattered empress, looked around and said resolutely, 'Love is everything . . . love is sacred . . . love is your last chance.'

'Oh, Granny's on a trip . . . she's a wanker' was heard amidst the numerous jibes, but undaunted, Bridget looked at her assailants and said, 'Because you have never felt it . . . you have no right to mock it.'

Phoebe, who had been knitting, as she always did at the meetings, threw her needles down for her moment – 'I'm a small child, I'm walking home from school in the rain, I'm soaking wet . . . my father is driving cattle in the field and he sees me and comes in and says *Take them clothes off and get your mother's coat* and he starts a fire and makes me a sandwich of bread and sugar, before going back out to the cattle. If that's not love, what is?'

It was too much for the Naublers, who rose en masse and trooped out, the dog straining as if there was something in the room he still needed to sniff. The bickering girl was yelling into her phone – 'We're out of this 1900 BC shithole . . . See ya.'

As things became vituperative, Fidelma, feeling she should bring some order to the evening, asked what they felt about the character of Aeneas.

'Aeneas the True' was shouted in scorn.

'Aeneas the Rat' and so the ridicule heaped on him far exceeded that which had befallen poor Dido. Here was a man, a semi-god, who had skulked off in the night, and so sneaky was it, that the rough oars of the sailors still had the leaves of the trees on them.

Amidst a tide of restlessness and invective, foolish and irrelevant things got said, in the name of love. Desiree had a friend who had seen Placido Domingo on an aeroplane and they had locked eyes, Mona was not ashamed to tell them that she and her dead husband communicated morning and night, and a blustery-ish girl announced that she was going bisexual, as she had never found true happiness with a fella.

A young student, who had been taking notes, turned to Fidelma and though very shy, he asked if she could give him a definition of love. She hesitated, yet knew it was incumbent on her to give an answer of some sort – 'It is a feeling . . . it is beyond words . . . it is for another person and also for something larger . . . in love, you know that you are living . . . every nerve in you comes alive . . .'

Schoolmaster Diarmuid rose, his lean face suffused with scorn, eyes glinting, saying that without putting too fine a point on it, their book club was no longer the acme of culture. But what could they expect from someone of the Emma Bovary mentality, who had graduated from the milking stool to the literary salon.

It was too much. There were audible gasps, the student, now with a pronounced stutter, asked for the remark to be withdrawn and Bridget wagging her finger repeatedly, told him he was a pup and an ill-bred pup at that. He chuckled, said, for Fidelma's benefit, that he was only *codding*.

Mary Kay, a retired nurse, said she would not stoop to his level, since she wished to point out the connection between love and loneliness.

'I was in my thirties at the time and my job took me to all sorts of outaway places. The things I saw were weird, sometimes sad, other times hilarious, husbands and wives hiding wills from one another, but a particular incident has stayed with me. There were two brothers, Michael and Finbar, twins, and Michael suffered from epilepsy. I'd go every so often to make sure he was on his medication and try to encourage them to clean up the kitchen a bit. It was a mess. One evening, just before dark, brother Michael saw me to the car. When I sat in, he put his hand through the open window and felt my breasts inside my blouse. I did nothing. I said nothing. It was the wisest thing to do. Brother Finbar watched from about twenty yards away, but you couldn't tell what either of them was thinking. When Michael had finished the fondling he took his hand out and I drove down that mountain helter skelter.'

It was followed by an awkward silence. Rain was pelting on the flat tarmac roof and plopping into the bucket left in the passage, as Sister Bonaventure, looking heavenwards, said, 'I thought it was supposed to be scattered showers and now it's the Flood again.'

Phyllida, wishing for things to end on a high note, held up her phone and walked around, for everyone to see the picture of a new foal, biscuit-coloured, standing on its wobbly legs – 'I was feeding the horses a few weeks back and I thought, that mare Tessie is awful fat . . . little did I know she was on the increase, so we've called our little arrival Brio, because brio she is and full of life and I want to tell you, I couldn't do it without Samantha, we're not well to do, but we're full of love, we love our animals, our geese and our hens and our chickens and our dogs and we love each other and I'd like to close the proceedings, to give the yea vote to love and to hell with the begrudgers.'

To everyone's surprise, Dr Vlad took the floor and walked forward to the centre. With deference, he then asked Fidelma's permission to say a few words. He began by saying he understood why some readers were disappointed in Dido, her self- immolation, her negativity, but suggested they might give the story some further thought and place it in its historical context. Dido, as he reminded them, was widowed young, her husband poisoned by an avaricious brother and subsequently she was driven from the lands of Tyre, and had to make her way to Carthage. There, as he said, using torn pieces from the hide of a bull, she mapped out and procured her territory. She trained armies, she built walls and defences, she created governments and she gave orders to men. It was the woman in her that gave shelter to Aeneas and the Trojans and could she be blamed if the flame of love had consumed her, and which, in all seriousness, she regarded as a kind of marriage. This was her downfall and became an excuse for all the African chieftains, who had been jealous anyhow, to seize back territories and usurp her powers. Her added crime had been that she had fallen in love with a foreigner. When Aeneas abandoned her to continue his quest for a homeland, she had not only lost him, she had lost the admiration of the citizens of Carthage.

'Pity my sinking house' were among her last fateful words, he said.

By damning her, he suggested that they had perhaps been too hasty and that love was of far greater consequence than they had deemed it to be. He reminded them then that when Achilles, the Trojan hero, lived among women, he had taken another name, because of the softening influence of woman's love.

You could hear a pin drop.

Those who had disdained Dido now found merit in her and some of the women detected in his address an oblique compliment to Fidelma.

To her surprise, he stayed on while she cleared up, and he helped her to gather the Xeroxed pages of Virgil, which had been relegated to the floor.

'Why such antagonism?' he asked.

'Oh . . . it's like that around here . . . lies . . . hypocrisy . . . bitterness . . . we don't trust one another . . . we get depressed . . . blame the weather . . . we book a package tour to somewhere sunny . . . we come home . . . it's not the weather . . . it's us.'

'So literature is not enough,' he says.

'I wish it was . . . but it isn't . . . sometimes I think I'm choking . . . choking,' and she put her hand to her throat to contain her gasps.

He looked at her for a long moment, then stood before her, her hands wringing, as a colour rose in ripples from the V of her neckline, to the neck itself, and to her face, so many hues of red, in a wandering, dappled enchantedness.

'At the risk of being too blunt . . . it seems to me Mrs McBride . . . that what you want is a lover.'

'It is,' she said, surprised at her boldness and putting it down to the chaotic evening.

They went out together and she put the key under a pot, on the windowsill, where Florrie would find it.

Just by the schoolhouse at the top of the town, a sprig of forsythia, the first of the season, had branched over the wall and he broke off a spray.

'What was the name Achilles had, when he lived among women?' she asked.

'We don't know . . . we will have to think of one,' he said, and put the forsythia into a side comb, that held up her hair.

Surfing

Fidelma had the bench to herself. It was at Strandhill, where he often came, as she knew from Father Damien. On the horizon, the water was a baby blue, same colour as the sky, but as it travelled in, it was grey, and nearer still, where the waves whooshed and gathered, it was indigo, like the dye in the lovely shawls that were so popular in her boutique.

The surfers were watching for their moment, to disappear, to be lost from sight and then to reappear, like marionettes, arms, legs, torsos, flying and flailing, as they reached for their surfboards. In the brief lull, white foam carried on into the rocky shore, where it spent itself and went back out, leaving behind lazy pools and patterns, so that the foreshore seemed as if tubs of suds had been emptied into it.

A surfer, slippery as a seal and dripping wet, stood near where she was sitting, just to observe the ocean, his last view of it before he left.

'You're not local,' she said.

'No ma'am. I am from the United States of America.'

'And you've come all this way . . .'

'This beach brings folks from all over. It's the topography . . . the land under the sea here is perfect for the surf waves.'

'Can I ask you something? What do you feel when you go under?'

'Scary . . . scared.'

'So why do you do it?'

'It's kinda mystical . . . it's the nearest I know to God.'

Dr Vlad appeared at that moment, with the swiftness of an apparition and gave her a single, knowing glance. He did not stop to talk, but it did not matter.

It was not long after that when she broached the matter of a child, though very obliquely. She went, as usual, for her supply of powders and tinctures that he had prescribed for her and in answer to his question, if she felt better, she said yes, but she was not complete. He knew what she meant and in a voice both quiet and regretful, he said, 'In the past I would have said yes . . . But I am a monk now.'

And yet she did not give up. If anything, her perseverance made her more determined.

It was Ash Wednesday and she was the last to run up the chapel to the rails, in order for the penitential ash to be put on her forehead. Dr Vlad was kneeling nearby, which came as a surprise, since he never attended Sunday Mass. The parish priest was in a hurry, probably dying for his breakfast, so much so that he put a load of ashes on her and it flaked down her face. In the porch, as she began to wipe it off, Vlad came out, looked quickly around and then grasped her arm, to stay her the bother of doing it. He touched her cheeks all over, his fingers deciphering the untamed passions within and as his palm moved downwards, she heard *Ssh, ssh*, and silencing her lips with his forefinger, to her utter amazement, he said 'Yes.' Yes.

Clouds

Clouds chased each other across the heavens that bright afternoon, when she drove into the hotel car park. It was much further south and the air was balmy. Yes, clouds on a great maraud, up there staging a tournament.

The elderly porter came forward and greeted her effusively. He wore grey coat tails and a grey top hat and on his lapel were numerous badges of distinction and a turquoise fishing fly.

'A hundred thousand welcomes madam,' he said, translating directly from the Irish, then with a practised deference, he touched her arm and led her in. The front hall was of pale stone slabs, bordered with diamonds of terracotta and as it was just after four o'clock, the lobby had a tea-time flurry, with waiters carrying trays, wheeling trolleys of cakes and gateaux, as the porter extolled the 'haute cuisine'. In tall glass cabinets were knickknacks, pearls and pendants set among the several framed photographs of Grace Kelly, who was also wearing pearls.

Fidelma had come alone. It was how they had planned it.

The suite was opulent, French windows opened onto a lush garden, tall cedars at each of the four corners, flowering trees and shrubs in different clusters and the stone wall that led to a kitchen garden had thick copings of ivy.

Through the open window and as in a distant memory, she heard the lilts and hollers of children. Little girls in white Holy Communion dresses, with coloured sashes around the waist and matching ribbons in their hair, ran in and out under the shade of the trees, hiding from the boys, also in their best Holy Communion attire. At first, the girls hid and the boys pretended not to see them and then suddenly, at a certain enlightened moment, they did see them, caught them and squeezed them amidst hallelujahs of triumph and mock terror. Then the game was reversed, the boys hid and the girls sought them, pretending not to see them, then saw them and amidst hoops of resistance and name-calling made them prisoners. When it began to spatter with rain, their elders called them from inside, pleaded with them, but they ran recklessly, as the rain plopped onto their best clothes and into the numerous flowerbeds planted with white and purple flowers. It fell also onto an ivory plaster lady, safe on her pedestal, her robes gathered up and kilted around her, a figure which the porter pronounced earlier as 'Greek and Roman to the core'.

She ran around to familiarise herself with things, the light switches, the window latches, the wardrobe, with its nest of side drawers and various side tables. Someone had put yellow roses in a white enamel jug with the name of a bakery on it, the very thing she would have wished for. The bathroom was almost as big as the bedroom, mirrors everywhere, mirrors watching her every move. Various essences, soaps and talcum powders were placed beside each of the two washbasins and quaintly, little sewing kits in embroidered pouches. At the side of the bath were three long loofahs and she wondered if he would bathe there or in the separate room that she had booked for him. All the arrangements were done by her.

Then she sat on one of the high chairs, far too restless to read the book she had opened – *The Kreutzer Sonata*. She could hardly believe that it was happening, that they were actually going to meet here, incognito, that he had yielded after so many refusals. She remembered the impassioned letter she had improvised asking for a child, and the recurring dream she had had of his delivering that same child. Then the cheese straws and pies and trifles that she had left on the stairs of his consulting rooms, hoping that he would guess they had come from her. What had made him change his mind. Her pleading, her openness, or maybe he was lonely for a bit of tenderness. He said it would be a question of three or four assignations, as they were not going to embark on a seedy, clandestine affair and he hinted at commitments of his own. He made her swear to secrecy, which she did, crossing her heart, yet full of illogical hope and happiness. Had she not heard Jack say more than once that a house without a child was an empty nest. Yes, carried away in the rapids. She was already dressed for dinner, a russet dress of shot silk, with a pleated skirt that opened and closed concertina-wise. The cameo brooch at the cleavage had belonged to Jack's Aunt Violet.

The room was almost in darkness when she heard the knock, jumped up and it was in near-darkness that they met, then the voice of which she was enraptured – 'I am here Fidelma, I have come.' From the slant of the hall light she saw a spray of rain on his hair and thought how much younger he looked, almost jauntier, no longer the healer in the loose smock and the bandana, a huntsman, in his high black polished riding boots. He wore no shirt, instead a green, knitted sleeveless sweater and she reckoned that when he took off the jacket, she would see his armpits and for the first time she was overcome with a terrible shyness. His lateness was due to the fact that the signposts were awry, pointing left when they should be right and moreover, all the names were written in Gaelic. He talked of the changing landscape, the poorish soil from where he set out, the dry stone walls dividing the small fields and further south, lush land, the black-and-white cows, their udders pink and pendulous, barely able to walk to the milking station.

Opening his arms very wide, he gauges how many metres is the width of the four-poster bed, so inviting, with its canopy of soft pink silks and a snow-white counterpane. Then he spies a miniature golf club and golf ball, which he hits, the ball arriving on a little tray that serves as a putting hole and she watches as he does it. The golf club, small though it is, unsettlingly reminds her of Jack's, propped in the corner of the sitting room at home. He says that for dinner he must put on a good shirt and taking one from his bag, he sets her the task of lifting off the knitted sweater and putting on the clean, starched white shirt. She ties the cuff buttons, the two tiny buttons to fasten the collar, then he tells her to tuck the tail of the shirt inside his trousers to his '*boule d'amour*', which she does. She blushes, burying her face in the crook of her elbow, and seeing this, he remarks how especially beautiful she is looking, like a contessa, with all the intrigue of a mistress.

The bottle of wine was already open and pouring two glasses, he raises his to hers and says, 'Let us hope for good results Fidelma.' Then he sat back on the reclining armchair and raised his legs onto a stool, for her to take off his boots. She imagined that if someone were to look in that window, it would be like some painting in a grand house, the huntsman home from the chase, the wife with her sleeves rolled up, doing the bidding of her master, an intimacy that was a prelude to love.

'We must', he begins sitting back, 'if we are to make a baby, know something of one another, our roots, our race and the loins from which we have sprung.'

'You know a bit of mine,' she says suddenly tongue-tied.

'So I start,' he says proudly. 'The women in my life have been the stronger force, totemic figures who never raised their voices, yet I knew that I must not disobey them. My grandmother was Cath-ollic and every day she made her prayers and listened on her radio to the Vatican Mass at six in the evening. No matter what happened, she never must be interrupted while listening to the Mass. One day, visitors, cousins, have driven a long way from Ukraine and arrive at our house. I knock on her door and say Grandma and she say, "Go away Vuk, I am listening to my Mass." The house revolved around her. She make a cheese, a soft cheese not unlike mozzarella. One room was where it was made. I see her there in her big striped apron, heating the milk on the little stove to the exact temperature, then pouring it into enamel pots that were blue with white lids. After some time she take the settled milk and put it into squares of muslin to mature. No one allowed in that room. The door was never locked because our word was our oath. One night, I do mischief, I steal down and through the muslin I feel the crust growing around the squares of cheese and I take one and eat it. I am caught. I am punished. At breakfast I must stay in the upstairs room, while downstairs they are eating the soft cheese and the warm bread that my grandmother has baked, along with the bacon from our own pigs. I smell the hot coffee and I know what is happening, mugs of coffee for the grown-ups and a little coffee in the milk for the other children, except that I am banished. My mother exactly similar to my grandmother, all daughters the same. My mother make the same cheese that her mother made, though she didn't listen to the Orthodox Mass. My father he steer me from boy to man. A wolf come around our neighbourhood. We have not seen it, but we have been warned. We know it is from the opposite side of the mountain, where our enemy lives. Two nights it circles our house. We hear its cry, a cry like nothing else, that baying so fierce. One night our dogs are howling in the barn and my father he lift the gun off the wall and he beckon me to follow him. I am ten years of age. The snow is higher than I am. We walk along a path where snow is shovelled away and we see the wolf on a height above us, very still, watching with its yellow eyes. My father he look down the muzzle and even now I think I hear the skid of the bullet that goes into the shoulder next to the wolf's heart. My father he an expert shot. Then another and another and the wolf begin to stagger and fall down the slope, the blood richer than the red of red wine. My father make me walk to where the wolf lies dead. Look in the eyes. Look at the flank. Now touch it. Then he made me lick the blood from my finger and he do the same. He make warrior sign on my forehead and initiate me into the mystery of the kill. You see, there is deep inside man the instinct to kill, just as there is deep inside woman the instinct to nurture.

'And now you,' he says and she hesitates, because the story she wants to tell is of the evening when chance first brought them together on the path, after she had plunged her face in the river and that somehow, surreptitiously, was where it all began. But that was too dangerous a story to tell and too binding altogether.

'In the town,' she begins light-heartedly, 'women argue about the colour of your eyes.'

'My eyes?' he asks, unable to conceal the sudden flare of vanity.

'I said they were a dark green, what we call bottle green.'

'And now that we are alone?'

'I say the same thing – bottle green.'

'And what does that signify Fidelma?'

'It means that they change colour . . .'

'You think I am a Don Juan.'

'No.'

'Then why are you shivering?'

'I am a little afraid just now.'

'Do you want to call the whole thing off?'

'No, I want it too much, to not want it.'

'Then we have crossed the Rubicon,' he says holding his hand out and she shook it and not long after they went down to dinner.

*

As they were late, the dining room had half emptied and so they were offered a choice of tables. Curtains of glass crystals hung on poles, luminous screens dividing different areas of the room and as they walked, hailstones of pink and violet light danced on whatever they could find. A world of shimmer, tall flowers and grasses in huge metal urns, paintings, drawings, a room into which such taste had been poured. He spoke to the maître d', who led them to a corner table next to a wine rack that was filled with the empty bottles of vintage wines that had been drunk on festive occasions. Vlad reeled off the various names, the chateaux – Meursault 1962, Chassagne-Montrachet 1972, Lynch-Bages, Margaux, while the eager young waiter, who stood in awe, complimented him on his excellent French. The door to the garden was ajar and she felt, or believed she felt, trees and grass and earth drinking in the moisture.

Everything was being done with ceremony.

Vlad looked at the basket of bread, naming the different varieties and then took a slice of rye bread, telling her that a nice combination was to rub warm rye bread with garlic and lemon rind. He had made bread himself, having grown up in that house of women, when various ancestors had died on the battlefield and later his father, who was a partisan, imprisoned as a traitor. All of it so exotic to her. She did not question it. She did not question the fact that he had been born in Alexandria, but that the family had to leave there in the exodus of 1956. She did not question the fact that he had been in a seminary for four years, wishing to be a priest, to walk the *terra sacrata*. All she wanted was his arms around her.

'So we start with the bread and the wine Fidelma,' and he looked into her eyes as if he was seeing her longings and seeing her soul.

To start with they ordered scallops on a bed of chive foam, which the waiter assured them was delicious, ''twas like eating gossamer'.

'Of course, cooking is all science now because of the gadgets we have,' he added proudly.

'But the libido is in the taste buds,' Vlad said and the young boy rushed off, scarlet.

He ate heartily, said he was a behemoth, whereas his companion ate like a bird. The elderly porter was determined not to leave them alone, coming with this and that, first it was a leaflet which he had printed out, with a picture of the stairs that they had been admiring, pointing to the mahogany newel posts, the ash treading and the side panels with forkfuls of dipping hay. The next time it was to tell them about a series of sculptures called 'Love

Letters' in a pasture nearby and how he would run them over there in the morning for a quick decko, if they felt inclined. The strange thing was, as he said, that despite the title, there was no lettering at all, just hoops of variously twisted bronze. Fidelma guessed that he sensed they were not man and wife and this gave a piquance to his evening.

'You have not told your story,' Vlad said and she looked at him and then all of a sudden began to blurt it out.

'I always wanted a father . . . a father I could talk to and go cycling with, like other girls who cycled with their fathers on Sundays and weren't afraid. It's what drew me to my husband Jack . . . such a kind man . . . he always brought an umbrella when we went for a walk, because he knew I was fussy about my hair. I was about fifteen when we met in a kitchen garden in West Meath. The raspberries were ripe on their canes and Moira, the daughter of the house, had invited me over to pick some. He came in with another man and spoke to us and he asked me what I wanted to be. I said a poet maybe, because I had written little verses. He said he would set me up as a lady of letters later on. He waited three years before he asked my family if he could take me out. They were very surprised. He worked in a bank, whereas we were very poor, we scraped all our lives. He and I would go for walks by the river and in time he proposed. The way he did it was that he asked me to meet him, along with a friend of his that also worked in the bank, at lunchtime and it was there, on the steps, that he said to his companion, "This is my intended Donal," then looked at me for an answer. The engagement was announced in the Social and Personal column of the papers. My parents were too shy to come to the wedding in Dublin that was in a beautiful church, I had a white dress and a tiara of orange blossom. You see, I was heartless then, I had gone up in the world, I didn't think too much about my poor parents, nor visit enough when they were sick and when they were dying. I had cut myself off. I remember the skeleton of a rotting horse that died on us, its bones bleaching in the field and somehow my parents are mixed in with it and shut out. But I changed with time. At first I did not want a child, but as time went on the longing grew in me. One day I was on an aeroplane going to London and beside me was a mother with an infant on her lap. She was from the north of Ireland, but her husband was from Fiji, he was one of the small platoon of foreigners serving in the British army there. The child had this gaze that I shall never forget. It looked so beautiful and so knowing, it was a half-caste, the skin brown and creamy and the mother said to me, "You've hypnotised it," and I said, "No, it's hypnotised me." I wanted to stroke it, I almost wanted to eat it and then I put my index finger out and its fingers gripped mine and began to suck, all the time gazing with this beautiful understanding smile and for the rest of the journey it was like that, staring at me and I staring back and I thought if I could have this child, my life would be different, my life would be full. It would break my husband's heart if he knew I was here telling you this.'

*

She came out of the bathroom, her hair unpinned, wearing her own lilac-coloured dressing gown and not one of the towelling robes that were in a pile on a stool. The bedroom was almost dark. Small candles flickered on a tall bureau and in the grate under logs pencils of light pulsed and gave to the brass fire dogs a brazen reddish tint.

'First Science, then Eros,' he said as he stood above her and with an instrument, began to trace what he called her neuron path, the chakras from the crown of her head to her frontal cortex, her earlobes, her throat, her chest and her belly. Afterwards, he poured freezing drops of oil over each point, allowing the heat of her body to melt it. Then turning her over onto her face, he ran a hot mocha stick over her vertebrae, hot to the point of burning. It was not how she had imagined it and it was not how she wanted it. She was his patient, his puppet. Once again, he turned her over and as she lay on her back, he blindfolded her with a black scarf that smelt of verbena. With a pendulum, he searched for the different energies she emanated. Not once did he touch her. She put her hand out to be held and when it wasn't, she pulled the scarf off and asked what was he so afraid of.

'Afraid of?' It nettled him.

'It isn't right,' she said.

'What do you mean it isn't right, Mrs McBride?'

'It's an experiment . . . you feel nothing . . . all you have is your power and your pendulum.'

'It's a procedure,' he said coldly.

'It's a very bizarre procedure . . . are you afraid of love, is that it?'

'Why should I be afraid of love?' he said and drew back as if she was one of the untouchables. Soon he began to put everything back into his doctor's bag.

She sat up, clutching the scarf, unable to look at him, unable even to remonstrate. They were enemies now and would be back in Cloonoila. Just as when she was a young girl, she broke into song, it was a kind of appeasement, when things got ugly –

I am a king's daughter from the town of Cappaquin
In search of Lord Gregory, oh Gregory let me in.

He was gone by the time she had finished the verse:

The rain beats on my head, the dew it wets my skin,
The babe is cold in my arms love, oh Gregory let me in.

She sang it to the garden, to the night, to anything that might listen.

In her nightgown, she went down the spiral stairs into the garden, too ashamed to stay in that room. The garden was empty, no echoes of the giddy Holy Communicants or the group who sat out after dinner, guffawing. The grass was damp and cool under her bare feet and there were several smells, from the grass itself, from the clay of the flowerbeds and above all, from the night-scented stock that flourished everywhere. Bats flew in random erratic swoops and the air was filled with tiny insects and gnats.

His white shirt seemed like a banner under the half moon, unless it was another man in an identical white shirt coming towards her. How long had he been there? He had heard her sing in the bedroom and came down to say how beautiful her voice was, how haunting. Uninvited, he sat on the bench and like the plastered kilted lady, they remained in silence.

'I thought I could be the scientist and not the man,' he said eventually. She didn't answer. He said other things too, but throughout she didn't answer. Had she imagined him to be a man without desire, particularly with an enchanting woman like her? He told her the moment when he was first attracted to her and how, many nights when he swam alone in Killooney Cove, he thought she might just be there and they would meet under water, sea creatures. He put his arms around her then and said, 'You are mine now, I can drown my eyes in your hair,' and he carried her across the garden, up the spiral steps and onto the tossed bed. The candles still burnt and she asked him to light the taller ones that were in a sconce on the bureau. Then they sat side by side and she helped him to undress. She had broken through to the real him, the poet, the man of feeling, that she always knew to be there. She held his beard and wagged it, as she had so often done in her imagination, fingering it like it was flake tobacco. He asked what poem or piece of literature in her country best expressed the wooing of a lady. She said it was a Playboy, who said he had killed his da and wandered into County Mayo to boast of his feats, where the women of Connaught fell for him. He chose one girl, envisaging for her moments out on the side of Neffin, where he would kiss her, 'unto her necklace'.

'Unto your necklace,' he said and kissed her and they lay down, his body next to hers, seeking her with his hands, with his mouth, with his whole being, as if in the name of love, or what she believed to be love, he could not get enough of her. Her breath came in little gasps, their limbs entwined, the healer and she, the stranger and she, like lovers now, as in a story or in a myth. At the moment of immolation he shouted, 'Take it, take all . . . I am yours,' and she teased him with her knuckles, which he bit into, with a primal hunger.

Afterwards, he spread the strands of her black hair along the pillow, and he smelt it and kissed it and tasted it. She would remember this forever, the room with the candles burning down, the smell of warm wax, yellow roses opening in the heat, as outside the sky was a deep blue, that soft satiny blue when night has her to herself.

'I will let you sleep now,' he said and gathered his belongings, with his boots and his laptop under his other arm.

It was early when he knocked on her door, already dressed to leave. He would not be staying for breakfast. She guessed it was caution, but she did not say anything. She was happy, still half inside a dream as she got out of bed and stood on his insteps, so that he could kiss her and smell the different perfumes of the night that clung to her body and the crumpled nightgown.

'The coming weeks will answer all our questions,' he said.

'But we will meet,' she said.

'We must not get your story mixed up with my story Fidelma,' he said.

'And what is your story Vlad?' She could barely hide her dismay.

'My sacred duty to God and my own people,' he said in the words of a preacher.

Later, she went with the porter, as she had promised, to see the sculptures. There they were by a wall, hoops of bronze, black and ambered, affixed to a wire mesh, but with no revelation, no trace of the passions that had informed them, tall grasses growing up around them, guarding their weathered silence.

*

Jack was waiting for her in the doorway, a reproachful look in his eyes because she was one hour later than she had promised.

He believed she had gone to a Carmelite convent for two days of silence, fast and meditation, because that was what she had told him. He wore an old brown leather glove that was usually kept on a shelf in the potting shed and thrusting it at her, he said, 'Look, look.' Then he opened it to reveal the ooze of a bat that he had squeezed to death. Two, as he said, had come in, in the night and when he got up and later went to wash his hands, he found them in the washbasin, clung together like vampires. The moment he touched them they began to fly, big circuits, out of the bathroom, into the hall, up to the ceiling, passing back and forth before his eyes, in winding, evil loops. He had to go outside and get the stepladder and then stand on the top rung, hitting out with the sole of his slipper to lure them down where he could do for them. Eventually, he belted one that fell into the tallboy with the maidenhair fern and seizing the china flower-pot, he squashed it to death, blood and pus spewing out like slime, black and bloodied, while the second one, the she-devil, escaped through the open window.

'I would have pulped her too,' he said. Such seething words from a man who had never harmed anyone in his life.

'Oh poor Jack,' she said.

'Oh poor Jack,' he said sourly, adding that he had not had a wink of sleep. She heard herself say that they would go out for dinner, go over to Renvyle, where they went each June on their wedding anniversary. He said they could not afford it. She parried. She had buyers for their pair of antique mirrors and the silver lampstands in the shop. She had discussed it with the porter, who promised to try and find a purchaser for her. Eventually Jack agreed and she brought him upstairs, drew the blinds in their bedroom, put a wool rug over him and went out.

It was downstairs that she confronted herself. The daylight of crime. Images kept crowding in, Vlad's high boots, the rim of one toppling over the other, the miniature golf club, the scarf that smelt of verbena, crusts of wax like spent roses on the wooden bureau and his two selves, the passionate one and the ruthless fugitive. She remembered the dream she was having when he knocked, first on the outer door, then on the inner door and how she jumped up. In the dream, she was in some mountain place, a terrain so real that the scrub pricked and bled her skin. Then three dogs came to unseat her in her lair, circling it, yelping, but instead of trying to chase them away, she began to think up ploys and strategies to deceive them. It seemed to her that her night of passion had made her both deceitful and animal-like. She disliked the alacrity with which he had taken his leave of her – *We must not get your story mixed up with my story Fidelma.*

Long before they were ready to set out, Jack was in the hall with his coat on, pacing back and forth, rattling the small change in his pocket, as he always did, and urging her to hurry up. How the sound of those footsteps, the rattle of loose change, his punctuality, his bursts of affection, repelled her.

The dining room where they sat, so contrasting with the previous evening, everything shabbier, frayed embroideries, dust in the folds of the taffeta curtains, faded photos of ancestors and little knickknacks, all falling into neglect and melancholy, the world she was retreating from. From the two sherries, Jack's eyes had clouded as he leant over her with a terrible and weeping ardour, saying too loudly that no man had a wife so beautiful and so constant. He began to reminisce, the dancing lessons they had taken in Nassau Street in Dublin, the evening in Formentor when she lost her ring in the sands and how he dug and dug until he'd found it, the yew trees they put down and that would outlive them.

Mujo

'I am not going up there,' Mujo tells them, 'I am staying down here . . . All boys he round up. Many thousand in one day. He go on TV and say it not happen. My mother and sisters say our brothers are gone. So are our cousins. They are down in the ground but not dead. My mother and sisters they taken in a cart. I am not going up there.'

For one known as the mute, it is the longest speech he has ever made and could not have come at a worse moment.

'This is fecking crazy,' Carmel says and the pan she threw into the air in temper, drops with a zing on the stone floor. Two major functions. Sister Bonaventure's sixtieth, an English shooting party and Mujo will not carry trays, because the man at table seventeen is a bad man. Mujo had been sent up earlier with boxes of candles and saw the bad man. But, as she reminded him, last week the man at table seventeen was a bad man and he turned out to be a missionary, home from Africa.

'It's the fecking table,' she says, but he is adamant.

'He done evil.'

'What evil?'

'He take everything.'

'You have no memory . . .'

'I don't need memory . . . it happen . . .'

'Oh . . . feckin' clairvoyance.'

Mujo has begun to cry.

'Why are you crying Muj?' Tommy has brought him to the pantry to talk sense into him.

'I am not crying.'

'Look, son, all you're asked is to carry up heavy trays, not to serve tables and if you don't do it, you have no feckin' family here either . . . it's back to some piss hostel, in the middle of nowhere . . .'

A truce is reached. He will carry up the trays, but he will not go near the table, where the bad man's wine is already breathing, in a special decanter, red circles, manifest on the white tablecloth.

'Thank Jesus,' Carmel says, as she plunges lobsters into vats of boiling water and prays for the repose of their soul.

'Coming through . . . coming through,' the voices on the stairs are now heard, as they pass one another, going up and down, up and down, careful to avoid a crash.

Upstairs all are in thrall. Bottles of wine and water placed along the length of the table and the colours within the wedges of cut glass, dancing like billy-o. Sister Bonaventure is lost for words and also worried about the palpitations. She can hardly believe it. A surprise party and she thinking she was going to the chapel to say the rosary. Mona had various people in the town contribute and had chosen the menu. Celeriac and apple soup or pâté to start, with pheasant or lobster Thermidor for the main course.

The second large party is a group of English people who have come for the shoot and the mother, or perhaps it is the grandmother, holds court as she describes to several young men her fall in her own house in Devon. It was like this: she had just put the pot pourri in the guest room, came out onto her landing and somehow must have been distracted or else exhausted, because she missed a step. Yes, tumbled on her own stairs, never letting go of her little dog, her little Winston, even though it transpired that because of that, she had sprained her neck and dislocated her right shoulder. Her voice carries through the room, but she is oblivious of that and the fact that people are laughing at her.

Mujo stands holding the tray, and the group at Sister B's table are marvelling at the sight of the piping hot lobsters, their pink tentacles branching out, holding onto one another. They stand up in twos and threes, in order to be photographed. Desiree is taking the photographs on her smartphone. Then when all have been photographed, he helps to pass the plates around, while Hedda crosses to the sideboard for dishes of potato dauphinoise and mixed vegetables, from the burners.

Mujo is now asked to capture their faces, their elation, as they behold the feast set down before them. First he refuses, says he does not want to, but they insist and for it he is told to stand back, and get a wide shot. The doctor's table is just to one side, which means he might be in the picture. Suddenly he is shouting, '*Stani, stani – ne, ne, ne,*' as he tries to seize the phone, except it is too late, the picture has already been taken. Mujo will not hand the phone over, as it belongs to Desiree and not this man.

'*Glupa budala.*' Stupid idiot.

'*Ja znam ko si ti,*' Mujo says. He does know him. The voice is unmistakable. This is the voice from before, the voice he heard on television when he was three, or maybe four, the voice that put terror into people and filled him with fear before he fully knew what fear was. But he is fearless now. He will fight. It is for everyone, it is for the dead people. They stand, as on the battle-front – man and boy. It seems to Mujo that something he did not know, or rather something he half knew, is happening. The wanted man, the mass murderer.

'Beast,' he says in an instantaneous righteousness.

The doctor rushes suddenly, his fury unleashed, and strikes the boy several hard slaps on the cheek. He catches him by the hair and whirls him round and round, like a circus exhibit, Mujo hitting any way he can. They stumble and in that brief hiatus he breaks loose, leaving a tuft of hair in the man's fist, then hooking himself to the man's breeches, like a goat, he begins to kick, the kicks tremendous, athletic, almost phantom-like. They fight, the one with his hands, the other with his feet, in an entwinement that could be farcical if it were not so fierce and then, together, they fall over the table, where the red wine from the overturned decanter begins to spill harmlessly. Amidst screams and cries that are both desperate and despairing, Salvatore, one of the waiters, and Plodder Pat pull them apart and a cluster of waiters surrounds the healer, craven with apologies, while Mujo is thrown to Carmel in the other room. She lugs him by the ear down the back stairs, as he is still kicking and on the last two steps, flings him down.

He lies where he has fallen, with staff having to vault over him, carrying their trays.

The kitchen is aswirl with gossip, how the healer stormed out, refusing any offer of apology or hospitality, Desiree's phone was confiscated and the manager had driven over from his own house and ordered complimentary Irish coffees, for everyone, sending the staff ballistic.

A sort of calm has descended, cutlery and cruets are put away, the linen is bundled up, the drinks fridge locked and the various dishwashers rumbling away. The brouhaha will soon be forgotten, but Ivan thinks differently, that poor boy's head is full of demons. Once, on a Sunday, he had looked in a scrapbook and seen the same words over and over again – *Blood. Bleed. Brother.*

Bleed like pig. Brother. Krv. Svinja. Brat. Blood. Pig. Brother.

For over an hour Mujo lies there, bunched up, and every so often his body arches into sudden aghast spasm.

'Get up for God's sake.' It is Tommy who moves him and sits him on a chair. Then they wash the wounds and the crown of his head from where the hair has been pulled and put disinfectant on them. It is as if they are not there. He is all alone, his eyes terrified and hopeless and with the frozen lostness of the abandoned.

Next day he is called to the office in the yard, where the manager and his young assistant Conor are waiting. They sit him down. It is a leather chair that swivels and he feels lost inside it. They speak reasonably, saying this unfortunate incident has to be cleared up. They ask him to give an account of himself and why he had behaved like a whelp. He is unable. He is almost a mute again. The manager's retriever keeps chewing the tongue of his boot that he hasn't laced. Was he out of his mind when he insulted the gentleman? They have looked up photographs of wanted war criminals on the internet, which they now show him and none remotely resembles their healer in his black outfits and his white hair. No way. Only a madman would see a resemblance. No. *Ne. Ne*. So why did he do it? Why did he name him? Had he mistaken him for someone else? He doesn't know. He isn't sure. He isn't sure of anything. Could he please explain himself and his violent actions. He looks up at them, his face blank and tragic. Always bad things, bad things long ago and bad things last night and bad things just minutes away. The moment they say that they will take the matter up with the police, he begins to shake, uncontrollably. *Ne, ne, ne*. He asks to be let back to the kitchen, as the peeling for the dinner is now. They tell themselves it was all an unfortunate misunderstanding, a fantasy, from a boy given to fantasies.

It ends with his scrawling his name on a letter of apology that had already been typed, even with knowing that he probably couldn't read it. It was to be sent to the doctor, along with a first edition of Yeats's *Stories of Red Hanrahan*. The edges of the pages are gold-flecked like a prayer book and the manager lets it be known that he is loath to part with it.

In the first dusk he walks back. Flowers and fallen confetti, from a wedding two days earlier, lie trodden on the wet grass and he knows in his heart that he is sure who the man was, but that nobody in the whole world, not even Tommy, not even Ivan, would believe him.

Jack

It was a brown envelope, of the kind circulars come in. My name, Jack Colbert McBride, was typed in full, which I found odd, as Colbert, my mother's maiden name, was not known to many. Inside a smaller envelope, again with my full name, but written in ink.

Someone, it said, had an important secret to impart to me and confidentiality was essential. All I had to do was reply to a post box above, granting authority for a poste restante letter to be sent to my local post office, where I could pick it up. The secret, it said, was gobsmacking. I had better know before it was too late. I guessed it was something to do with Fidelma, the soft spot she had for the new doctor, that all the women had, but I ignored it, knowing it was a passing fantasy. I hated this threat, so slyly conveyed. I was filled with anger at whoever had sent it and my deepest instinct was to protect her from slander. Yet it shook me. I remembered shortly before I married, when Malachi, my best man, and I went night fishing in a lake in Longford and his saying out of the blue, 'If you buy a canary, you have got to let it sing.' Later on, we wound the lines in, put the rods aside, and spread our coats on the grass for the man-to-man conversation, that happens on the brink of marriage. The funny thing is, we said nothing at all about it. I knew he wanted to say things, but hesitated out of loyalty and that it probably concerned the big gap in our ages.

I first saw Fidelma in an orchard, a young girl just ripening, with a crop of black hair and the whitest skin. The face and features that they used to say were descended from the knights who came with the Spanish Armada. She was with her friend Moira, picking raspberries off their canes. It was in the big house where I played tennis with Aubrey the son, and the two girls at first ignored us. I asked Fidelma what she did and she said she worked in a beautician's, but that it was temporary. It was Moira who spilt the beans, said Fidelma wrote poems and hoped to be a poet one day. Her shyness was touching. She did not act shy, she just was, turning aside from us as if we weren't there. I wrote to her and surprisingly she replied and so our friendship was epistolary until I plucked up the courage to ask her parents if I could take her out. We met mostly on Sunday afternoons, walked for miles, climbed mountains, searched for the periwinkles in the rocks and later, had tea in a cafe in some town where no one knew us. Getting her to open up was difficult. She talked in bursts, the way shy people do, and she was such a trusting girl and with an innate reserve. If she had written a poem and I had enquired about it, she would tuck it into my pocket as we parted, saying it was never to be mentioned again.

Our honeymoon was in Rome, where it was still warm in November and a flowering creeper bloomed above the entrance door to the hotel. It was an old hotel down a side street, with a plash of fountains not far away, where we had earlier tossed pennies for our marital bliss. The staff were so courteous, that while waiting to be checked in, instead of queuing at the counter, we were seated and given coffee with petits fours, while my passport, with my wife's name on it, was being studied.

Fidelma was transported, gazing at the paintings and an icon in darkly hued wood, in a niche just above us, with an image of a mother and child. The whole place exuded grandeur, armchairs covered in red velvet, with gold-threaded braid and small tables for visitors to be entertained at.

Later that night, on the third floor, I sat outside our room on one of those velvet chairs, as Fidelma had gone in to prepare. That landing lives on in my mind. There was an open cabinet lined with embroidered silk, platters on the shelves with designs of cupids and fauns. One platter in vivid colours bore Picasso's name. I was burning with desire.

When I let myself into the room, Fidelma was not there. Where had she gone to? How had she escaped? I looked in the bathroom, then on the small balcony, where a sensor light had come on the moment I stepped there. The leaves of a little tree, possibly a lemon tree, had plaited themselves into the railing that I leant over, to see if she had climbed down, or worse. Back in the room I searched again and eventually found my frightened wife crouched in a corner, behind a chaise longue, over which a long panel of velvet dipped. She was cowering like a child and like a child she was weeping. She asked me to tie the drawstring of her nightgown, thereby asking me not to violate her, which I did, and then I carried her onto the big four-poster bed.

She insisted on washing the sheet in the early morning. We had breakfast out on that balcony and the faint atlas of discolour, on the otherwise white sheet, that she had hung up, was both a triumph and a rebuke to me.

We came home. I took a lease on a carpet shop that had been empty for years and we refurbished it in order for Fidelma to open her boutique. Soon she was singled out for her flair with fashion and complimentary articles appeared in local and national newspapers. We gave brunches, I joined a golf club and Fidelma disarmed all those she met.

But alone she withdrew. I felt I never really got to know her. She was elusive, like thistledown.

I folded the anonymous letter and put it in the drawer, between my summer shirts, wishing neither to explore it nor to destroy it, the ditherer's way, while ringing in my ears were Malachi's words – *If you buy a canary, you have got to let it sing.*

Where Wolves Fuck

Fidelma stood staring at it, hot and cold by turns, the paint still wet and with a glisten to it – *Where Wolves Fuck*. It was scrawled on the pavement in front of their shop, which was now Vlad's clinic. The lettering was lopsided. In cardinal red: *Where Wolves Fuck*. Her first instinct was to stamp on it, except the sludges of wet paint stuck to her Sunday shoes. She had been on her way to first Mass, to the chapel five miles away, and had only come into the town, as she did each Sunday, to pick up two papers from the pile that was left in the passage, corded and covered with plastic. She had a prior arrangement with Nora the newsagent, to collect them and pay monthly.

She knew that Vlad coached youngsters in football up at the playing fields, early on Sundays, and she ran towards there. Passing TJ's she saw that his blue Opel car had its tyres burst and its windows smashed in, the strewn glass on the street, like crushed ice. She kept running and at that moment, just as she neared the bridge, she saw him coming along the road in his togs, with a raincoat over his arms.

The last time they were together was on Muck Island, when he had told her that they could not meet again, as it was becoming too dangerous. That time, he brought a boat on the roof of his car so that they could go to the islands. She sat on the bridge and watched as he undid the ropes and hauled the boat down into the water and she remembered the slip-slop of the water as she got in and his helping her to her seat. They were the only ones out on the lake. Damselflies, like slivers of blue, darted above the water, and just underneath, as in a mirage, a luxurious green weed, languorous, drifting. Pointing to the ruins of cottages, he said whole communities had lived on those islands and whole communities were buried there, their bones sunken deep down. He had been researching in the library, intending one day to compile a history of the place, the place he had grown so fond of.

They moored at an island further along, where hares, droves of them, were chasing each other in a wild, wanton sport. Yet, at their arrival, the sport stopped, the hares on their hind legs, their dark ears cocked, watched everything that went on, circling around their two half-naked bodies, recumbent in a hollow.

Later, he rowed along the lake, passing the several islands, and when they came to an extremely low bridge, they had to lie flat on the boat and she searched for his hand as the boat idled in, to what would be their last lagoon. He was at his most reachable. The roots of the willows had half collapsed into the water and water lilies lay on the surface that was scummed with willow seed from many years and shrivelled with age. There was such stillness there, everything totally sequestered, nature at her most prodigal, away from the prying world.

As with Dido, birds were singing in her head when they rode back to the shore, but suddenly her mood darkened. Sitting on the bridge was a figure, whose presence somehow struck her as ominous. A stranger in a dark suit, with sunglasses, smoking a cigarette. The way he stared at them unnerved her, following their every move. He watched as Vlad hauled the boat onto the dry land and with the ropes, eased it up on the bonnet, while she held the other end of the ropes, for him to tie the various knots. For a moment, she thought of approaching this mystery man, but Vlad told her to get in the car. As they drove off, she looked back and saw the silhouette, a harmless tourist on a bridge at eventide, and yet, and yet she flinched.

Ten weeks passed and she knew. In the mornings she went down to the bottom of her garden, so that Jack did not see her vomiting. She was inventing stories to tell him, all of them lacking credence, like a child making sandcastles that the incoming tide will sweep away.

She blurted it out to Vlad, the broken windows of his car, the punctured tyres and worst of all, the graffiti. As he was hearing it, he was already running.

Where Wolves Fuck. He loomed over it, stared at it, then knelt and smelt it, as if he might guess the perpetrators.

'It's someone who knows us,' she said.

'You must deny everything, Fidelma.'

'I can't . . . I live here.'

'I thought I could trust you to be discreet,' he said with a cold contemptuousness.

'I am discreet,' she said far too loudly, hating the hysteria in her voice, in her being, in her headscarf, in all of her.

'We must go to the guards,' she said.

'Don't be so stupid,' he said. His plan was already in place. She was to waken one of the local bums and get him to bring black fence paint and erase it completely. He himself would go to Plodder Policeman's house, report the damage done to his car, but insist that he would not be pressing charges, as it was obviously the work of some passing hooligans in the night.

'What do I say?' she asked.

'Nothing happened . . . no broken window . . . no graffiti . . . no rendezvous . . . nothing . . . *ne . . . ne . . . ništa*.'

'But we're . . .'

'Start forgetting . . . Fidelma.'

'Forgetting what?'

'Everything . . .' He was wiping his hands in a gesture of wiping her out. No more letters. No communication. No tears. She is a grown-up lady, she can look after herself.

Then he was gone. Gone to where she would not find him. So this child, this wolf-child, was hers and hers alone to give birth to. Oh Jesus and Mary, she said, as she headed for the squat where Dante and the boys lived. *Start forgetting Fidelma. No rendezvous. No letters. No communication. Ništa.*

Dante brought all the clobber in a wheelbarrow; tools, brushes, rollers and several pots of paint. She stood at the edge of the kerb to deflect pedestrians, but luckily there was not a soul about, only a pair of rasping tomcats on the wall of the crèche. She watched, as first he poured pools of black paint onto the offending red and then with quick, sure strokes he rolled it again and again, black upon black, and then with a thin paintbrush he jabbed and jabbed, so that every speck of red was gone. Who might have done it, Dante wondered. Obviously, it was in the very early hours of the morning, as they were all in the pub until after three, Diarmuid, Plodder Pat, the sisters, Fifi and a big crowd back from a funeral in Manor Hamilton. The buggers must have come after that.

'Have you an enemy missus . . . someone with a grudge?' he asked.

'I didn't think I had . . .' she said and began to cry, looking down at the black slabs, as at a funeral bier, and pretending not to notice, Dante began to paint the next and the next set of adjoining pavement, so that it would seem the whole street had been defiled by hooligans in the night.

Not once did he mention Vlad, but she knew then that he knew, just as she knew that day when she came home from her first tryst and Jack held out the glove, smeared with the bloodied pus of the bat, that he had guessed her crime.

Capture

When to everyone's astonishment Dr Vlad returned and he emerged from the back of the hire car, people were shocked to see the change in him. He looked like a cave man, his hair scruffy and unwashed and he wore thick dark glasses.

The poetry reading had been planned months before, the idea being that he would read his own poetry at the foot of Ben Bulben, in homage to Yeats, and accompany himself on the gusle. Afterwards, there would be a picnic, with others invited to sing or recite as they wished. But since his sudden disappearance, the outing had lost momentum. Were it not for Fidelma, Fifi and an actress from Dublin, the event would have been quashed altogether.

The bus was hired for the occasion and the name McDonagh was splashed in gold lettering on both sides. The driver, who was Polish, was very affable.

'I show you the beauty of Ben Bulben,' he said to each one as they got in, mostly women in their Sunday best, flowered dresses and matching jackets, the younger ones in T-shirts and jeans, while the actress who had come specially from Dublin to recite was in a cream trouser suit and wore a green chunky necklace. She had been booked as a substitute to recite his poems, which she deemed 'Mystical and Quasi-Philosophical'.

They sat in pairs. Vlad had taken the single seat behind the driver, bent over his sheaf of papers and making corrections. Fidelma kept hoping that he might turn around just once and give her even the semblance of a smile. Since the morning of the graffiti she had heard nothing.

They were an animated group. Fifi and her help Maggs were reeling off the delights of the picnic in the green rush basket – sausage rolls, cheese canapés and egg-and-cress sandwiches, all wrapped in moist linen to keep fresh. Cora, the supervisor in the seaweed spa, had brought her mother along, the poor woman scattered and *distrait* as she looked around at the unfamiliar faces, and seeing Vlad, she pointed and said, 'Is he the devil?' The wide brim of her straw hat, held down with two metal curlers, gave her a somewhat childish, stroppy look. There were whispers at how awful sad it was that she a schoolteacher for almost forty years, was now asking people their names and then forgetting them and saying her husband, her dead husband that is, spent far too much time on the computer. Phyllida showed the more recent pictures of her foal Brio, who unfortunately was losing her nice biscuit colour and was more khaki now.

Minerals and sweets were passed around and the excitement was palpable. Those from different neighbourhoods sat in huddles, but as the day went on it was hoped that everyone would mingle. Two silent men sat together as they did on fine days on the town bench, rarely exchanging a word.

'A sign say *No Climb* but I climb,' the driver told them, boasting of his pride at having stood on the summit of Ben Bulben and searched for shells and coral, as souvenirs for his daughter. Yes, stood there and between the wide bays of the sea, had a view of another mountain, with the tomb of an ancient queen and from where it was forbidden to trespass or take stones.

They left the town and after a few miles came on the woods, beech trees, that met and mashed overhead, an oasis of green.

Further on ash trees grew in little clumps, and the sun slanted through the window creating different moments of light and shadow, the same sunlight that sent dimples of gold into the pools of rainwater that had lodged in the fields from a downpour the previous evening.

'Aren't we blessed with the day that's in it,' two elderly women kept repeating, tears in their eyes, grateful at being included in such select company.

They had a fine view as the road was high, having been built on mounds of earth to prevent flooding, but the ride was bumpy and Cora said what a pity that they did not have an important politician up in Dublin, that would ensure good roads for them. Her mother kept thinking she saw the sea, which she couldn't have, as they were still passing fields, sheep cropping the young grass and clover, lambs suckling and running away and running back almost instantly, as if they feared abandonment.

'Look, there's the sea,' her mother said and Cora kept apologising for her, and her mother's harmless smile disappeared, just as if someone had wiped it off with a face flannel. Her expression was hostile, as if to say *I see what I see, I understand what I understand. You'll all be old one day*. One of the silent men swapped places with Cora and began to show the mother pictures in his illustrated bird book and she imagined they saw these different birds in the air, soaring and circling.

As they came out onto a dual carriageway, cars were whizzing by at a reckless speed. It was a dangerous road, where the many small white crosses, wreathed in meadowsweet and set at a distance to one another, were reminders of those who had lost their lives. They had not yet reached the sea, but the air smelt salty and with a tang to it. Vlad had not engaged with them at all, never once looking up from his papers and Fidelma wondered if, after his poetry reading, she would manage a word with him alone. She craved it. She knew that there was to be no further communication and she accepted it, but she hoped, if only for the child's sake, he would be there, at the rim of her existence. She had not yet told Jack. How to tell him. What to tell him. When to tell him. These were the questions that assailed her hour after hour, as she faked good cheer at home and cooked the things he liked, flans, steamed pudding and crème brûlée, things he didn't have to chew too much. But soon the gourd of her belly would show and there would be no hiding from him or from anyone.

'Holy Jesus!' Fifi was the first to cry out as the driver braked suddenly, the bus came to a stop and people were thrown onto one another, the open tin of sweets rolling along the aisle, toffees and chocolates spilling out.

A guard in uniform had put his hand up, signalling the bus to stop, then had a few words with the driver through the open window. Traffic was building up behind and the driver was asked to move the bus into a lay-by, which he did. Everyone assumed it was about his licence, or if he had been insured to drive a bus at all. Then two guards, who were not local, boarded the bus, both with revolvers attached to their holsters, and made a quick survey of the passengers on either side. They approached Vlad and asked for proof of his identity. He looked in his briefcase and after what seemed an interminable time, he took out his passport. Both guards studied it and nodded to one another in silence. Then one, who spoke with a country accent, said, 'I'm afraid we have to ask you to come to the station with us.'

'I'm afraid it's impossible because we are heading for a poetry recital,' he answered, quite nonchalant.

'That will not be possible sir . . . we are arresting you,' the second, more senior guard said.

'My dear fellow, you must be mad . . . arresting me . . . you are chasing shadows,' Vlad said, still in total command of himself.

'You have been living under a false name,' one said, and his colleague, who was not quite so bristling, said that they were just doing what they had been instructed to do, as he held up the arrest warrant for him to see.

'But this is preposterous,' Vlad said and turning to the others, he shrugged as if to say 'I have fallen into the hands of highwaymen.'

The postmistress, alert to every little nuance in the parish, was flabbergasted. How could she have missed it, the build-up, the massive surveillance, liaising with big shots in Dublin and with not a single local guard consulted. She felt cheated of her importance in the community. Some had already begun to take pictures on their mobile phones and Cora reckoned that it was probably to do with his practising as a healer without the necessary qualifications. Fifi knew different. It was more sinister than that. One time, when she found the key to his safe and had opened it, she discovered guns, ammunition, money in different currencies and several passports, each photo of him so radically different, bearded, clean-shaven and once with an implausible red wig. Fidelma ran up far too excited, all her covert passion poured into her words, to vouch for him. Almost condescendingly he motioned her back and as he did, the second policeman snapped the handcuffs over his wrists and shut them tight.

The last image they had was of his tall figure, unbowed but humiliated, starting down the steps of the bus and just as the sun had soaked into the young ash leaves, it now rasped on the bracelets of metal that bound his wrists.

It happened so quickly, so 'low key' as they said, that they were well nigh lost for words. The fact that he had co-operated and hadn't tried to escape was surely a sign that it couldn't be too serious. Yet the mood had changed, everyone felt uneasy and the driver was sweating and cursing his bad luck. A day wasted. Fidelma regretted that she had jumped up and was touched for the first time with a fatalistic terror.

The driver, no longer extolling the beauties of Ben Bulben, threw his hands up and said, 'The longer I live in this insane country, the less I understand it.'

By a show of hands it was agreed that he would drive them back to the stop by the Folk Park where he had collected them.

*

People came out of their shops and out of their houses to repeat to one another what they already knew, talking in grave tones, enumerating the horror, the horrors that might have befallen their children. They came in cars and on scooters, older people with sticks or on walking frames came and even the ducks, disturbed by the hullabaloo, waddled out from the Folk Park into the main street.

A television camera had been set up and a reporter with a handheld microphone approached passers-by to be interviewed, but most were reluctant to speak. Children made faces at the camera.

TJ's was crammed, people craning to have a closer look at their fake healer, who they were told had the sobriquet of 'Beast of Bosnia' and that there were millions on his head. They saw images of him in his wartime swagger, and once with the Russian poet, both men shooting into the town of Sarajevo, as if it were a game, and accompanying it were lines of his poetry:

When the time comes for gun barrels to speak,
For heroic days, valorous nights,
When a foreign army floods your country,
And wreaks havoc and causes damage in it,
That condition must be righted:
Then you roam your homeland on foot,
And your boots fight side by side with you.

On the television one or two spoke of him as the warrior poet, who had always had a mystical conviction of his role in history. He had risen from being an obscure doctor to the global notoriety that he had always craved and was now on his way to the Tribunal in The Hague, to be indicted for crimes that included genocide, ethnic cleansing, massacres, tortures, detaining people in camps and displacing hundreds of thousands. His first request in the detention centre, where he awaited extradition, was for a barber, and so his white locks and his white beard were now, somewhere, on that barber's floor.

What apes they were, taken in by his mesmerism, his tree hugging, his aura, his tripe. A strange youth rushed in and said just after capture he had broken free from detention and shot a guard and another person talked of his having taken his own life with prussic acid. A general delirium prevailed. There was shock, repugnance and disbelief. Plodder Pat sat unusually quiet, thinking what could he have done when not even the sergeant was briefed on the operation. The boys in Dublin wanted all the glory for themselves. Fifi was crying aloud, asking John in God's name why he had not sent her some sign, some guidance from beyond. She would throw the effing gusle into the river, except that the police had taken it, having ransacked the house and in the safe seen the skeleton of a snake, the revolver and the cartridges. They put her through two hours of interrogation. Why had she not gone to them after the very suggestive words scrawled on the pavement in the town – *Where Wolves Fuck*. Why hadn't she? The truth was she was a little soft on him. She remembered once, bringing home a box of young lettuces to plant, when surprisingly he appeared to help, remarking on the clay, saying what good clay it was and little did she guess that in his own country were all these thousands of remains, with worms eating them. He'd fooled everyone. She would never trust a soft-spoken, courteous man again.

They saw the shells of burnt houses, a gutted landscape, marching frightened families, a boy on a pile of rags calling a name and behind the bars of a concentration camp, skeletal young men staring out in gaunt and hopeless despair.

'If it's true, it's sad . . . It's very sad,' Hamish said.

'It's true . . . Very true and very sad,' Fifi replied.

The capture was described in detail, the idyllic country setting, a bus hurtling along, a disingenuous party, mostly of women, heading for Ben Bulben, with its proud association to the great national poet, W. B. Yeats.

He had entered Ireland, so they learnt, by a circuitous route. Having been hidden in monasteries in his own country, he was spirited out, when it became apparent that the authorities were soon to close in on him. By Italy and Malta, through the bay of Biscay to Spain, he had travelled under several names, by boat and then by trawler, before arriving at Clegger Harbour, an unmanned cove, off the coast of Wexford. It was well known to smugglers and paramilitaries, where, because of the rock formation, the tide was always low and small boats or currachs could get in.

'He who walketh on shite,' someone shouted and Father Eamonn, who had never set foot in that bar, came in, leaning on his stick and close to tears, as he was led to the good chair by the fire. He was as baffled as everyone else.

Mona was the most jittery of all, because of her accidental part in the day's happenings. She could barely cope. With Dara not yet returned from the football match in England, she had to call on Dante to draw the pints and the half pints, while she herself did the shorts, her hand shaking uncontrollably, sloshing it. If she were alone she would have turned the blasted thing off. But it was the encounter in the early morning that kept dogging her. When she opened the shop at ten, three men, bruisers, were waiting to come in. They were uncouth, treated the place like a dosshouse, wanting a shower, changing their underpants in front of her and brusquely demanding coffee and toasted sandwiches. One had a crew cut, a second wore a plaid cap that he must have got at the airport and was trying it on in the several bar mirrors, the third wore a hat on the back of his head and had a ginger moustache. The other two referred to him as the Medico. They asked her what time the bus with Dr Vuk would be returning. She said she didn't know, as Dr Vladimir had moved out of the area weeks ago. They knew that and they were the ones to tell her that since he left, he had lived in a caravan on a remote island off the coast of Galway.

They were talking among themselves when a lorry driver rushed in overexcited and said the healer had been taken off the bus in handcuffs and the news was on all the radio stations, how he had been hiding in this remote Irish hamlet. She turned on the radio and the Medico crossed to listen, then conveyed it to the two others, who began to argue and shout, each blaming the other for some wrong she couldn't grasp. They got so obstreperous that she asked the Medico to speak to them and he sent them out, where they shouted and harangued on the street. He crossed to the bar and asked for a coffee with cognac. He sat on a high stool, his head in his hands, grieving that they had not arrived in time to save their friend. They had driven hundreds of kilometres and at great risk to themselves, to do this, because they had heard on the rat line that the authorities, for their own lousy reasons, were about to hand him over to the Tribunal in The Hague. He raged against that coach that they took at Rosslare; were it not for a bloody puncture, they would now be whisking him back on the secret route by which they had come. He was asking her to excuse his tears, but friends were friends. This bloody news had unmanned him. He waxed sentimental, wished to know how popular Vuk was with local people. She sang his praises, citing those he had cured, including Hamish's wife, and that yes he sometimes drank in her bar. She pointed to the leather armchair where he sat, adding that he mostly kept to himself. He enquired about lady friends. A handsome man, without wife or mistress, was bound to feel lonely and in need of some pussy. She corrected him, told him to watch his language. That was when she fell into the trap. She let it slip about Fidelma, the draper's wife, the town beauty. Quick to seize on it, he began to draw her out, asking who the woman was married to and if they were rich and if she was likely to crack under pressure.

'Maybe,' she said and as the word fell out of her she knew that she had said too much. Suddenly he latched onto it, wanting to know where this lady lived, what was her full name, as he would like to pay his condolences. He asked again where she lived and she prevaricated, saying it was miles out the country, but he had heard enough and was on his feet, lifting his hat like a gentleman except he was no gentleman. By the blade-like jut of his shoulder as he went through the half-open door, she felt that he and his cohorts had an agenda, and thought it was probably to do with the vastness of the money on Vlad's head.

*

The pub was so full, the atmosphere so frenetic, that Mujo had to wade his way to the counter. He was carrying cages in one hand and a small dirty white attaché case in the other. He wore a yellow waistcoat that was too big for him and had a grin on his face. He was in a hurry, couldn't stop. Mona tried to sit him down, but he wouldn't.

'Just drink this,' she said and he took the shot of vodka, threw his head back and drank it gallantly in one swallow, like a man, then put the glass back. She knew him well, mothered him, because on his day off, he fetched turf from the bog and wood for both fires, the one in the bar and the one in her bedroom. He was the only one ever to see her clothes strewn around and the purple wallpaper, hanging off in tongues from the damp, in that room.

'I think I speak for all . . .' Mona said sheepishly and looked around for confirmation. 'We should have heeded you Mujo . . . but we didn't . . . we took the part of the wrongdoer because it was easier. We failed you.'

The crowd would have carried him on their shoulders now, but it was all too late. He wanted to be back in his own village, his doves free to fly the skies without hazard.

'I'm going home,' he said.

'But home is gone,' Mona said.

'We build another,' he said and in his child's mind, his mother was already there waiting and they would be in their own orchards, their paradise regained.

Before leaving he handed her a letter that was to be given to his friend Dara. The last they saw of Vlad on the screen was in his long black coat, walking towards the Folk Park on the night of the open-air opera, Fidelma by his side.

'Well, he's caught now . . . the worst is over,' Mona said.

'But the contamination has happened,' Schoolmaster Diarmuid said and there were knowing gasps. Father Eamonn, who had not stirred from the fire, just looked across at her and shook his head, dolefully.

*

Fidelma was not in the bar. She and Jack had been watching in their front room, utterly silent. She was too afraid to look at him in case she betrayed herself. A line of Vlad's poetry then completely unhinged her –

> *Something like a chill is nesting within you.*
> *That spear, that stretched arm glows in your head.*
> *You feel that mortal metal, its presence . . .*

'Turn it off, turn it off,' she said, desperate.

'Go in the kitchen if it disgusts you,' Jack said sharply and she ran in there, where everything was judging her, the heave from the refrigerator, the idiotic magnets, china elves in a bowl and the unwashed egg beater at the side of the sink. She picked up the egg beater that she had used for his omelette and whisked it crazily in the air. There was no disentangling now. How could she bear his child? How could she not bear it? It was inside her, her blood sustaining it. Part of her was conspiring to run, to get out before she was caught and simultaneously a small voice of reasoning was saying *Go back in, throw yourself at his mercy, and tell him everything.*

*

The ring of the doorbell startled them both. Fidelma said it was locals collecting for a father who had drowned himself and left a note to say he was ashamed at not being able to provide for his young family. They had called earlier and she had asked them to come back, since she needed to go to the machine to get money. Jack went to answer it and returned, saying quite brusquely that three foreigners were outside, wanting some information from her.

In the light above the porch she saw the three men. They wore leather jackets, one had a baseball cap and the other, a burly fellow, had a new plaid cap, which he wore backwards. The tall one wore a hat on the back of his head and they referred to him as the Medico. He spoke quite good English.

'How are you this evening?' he asked.

'I'm fine,' she said.

They needed a word with her. The younger one, albino-like,

with pink skin and almost no eyelashes, was sniggering as he looked up and down the length of her body, dribble at the corner of his lip.

'We have questions . . .' the Medico said.

'What questions?' she asked, trying to assume an unnatural calm. She knew it was about Vlad.

'You come with us,' he said.

'You can say what you want to say here,' she said, fear creeping up on her.

'Not with your husband at home.'

'We need go . . . have chat,' the burly one said and grabbed her bare arm above her elbow.

'Who are ye?' she asked.

'Blood brothers,' one answered and opened a folded newspaper with Vlad's picture on the front page, handcuffed, as he was being taken off the bus.

'I know very little about him . . . he rented rooms above our shop,' she said all too quickly.

They shook their heads, let out a series of snorting laughs and said the party was in full swing and she was the guest of honour.

She walked back to get her coat and said to Jack that they needed to get belongings of Vlad's in the clinic, as they were cousins of his, but she knew that he knew she was lying, because of the look of disgust that he threw at her.

'Let's go to TJ's,' she said to the men as she closed her front door softly and with a chilling intuition.

'Too many eyes, too many ears . . . all listen,' the Medico said.

'Then we go to the Castle . . . they have lots of drawing rooms,' and as she said it, she thought how genteel it sounded.

The taxi to which she was being herded was more like a station wagon and the step up was very high. Music blared from it.

'Take seat,' one of them said, suddenly and bafflingly courteous. Seeing she had difficulty, the driver jumped out carrying a little plastic yellow step, to assist her. He was black and they had probably hired him in Sligo. The seat covers were torn and there was a smell of drink, cigarettes and the kebabs they had been eating. She was squeezed in between two of them, with the burly fellow opposite. Nobody spoke. When they got to the town, she leaned forward to give the driver the directions, telling him to turn left, but the Medico shouted, 'Go right.'

'We're going the wrong way,' she said, her voice rising.

'You go to church each Sunday?' one asked.

'What's that got to do with anything?' she replied.

'Bambi . . . Bambi,' the albino said, blowing cigarette smoke into her face. Mustering as much calm as she could, she asked what this was all about. They answered for her, they said, 'Luda Kura bar . . . Madhouse.' It was where her boyfriend used to drink back home, before he met her.

'You fuck with him,' the burly fellow said.

'You can't talk to me like this,' she said. So they knew, they knew everything.

'She scared . . . she think something bad going to happen to her,' he said and they all laughed, heartily.

'I'm not scared,' she said to defy them.

'Maybe she no like the music,' the albino said and asked the driver to put it louder.

They were quite a few miles out now and she glimpsed landmarks, a petrol station, and a white elephant building once meant to be a nightclub that had never opened. A wayside church on a hill with an adjoining graveyard. The taxi driver was also nervous, as she could tell from his erratic driving and they barely missed a crash at the major roundabout.

They objected to the air freshener that hung from the dashboard, said it stank.

'You the boss, man,' the driver said and tugged it off. His name was Tyrone. It was written beside his photo, a black man, managing an uncertain smile. They began asking him then if he had a wife and what she looked like and if she had false teeth and if she took them out, when they fucked. Then they asked why he had come to the west of Ireland and he said he loved the beauty of the place and the church spires because it meant that Jesus was watching over the land. They were making fun of him, but he didn't object, because he was too afraid of them.

'Excuse me . . . but I have to concentrate,' he said, staring ahead at the road. They turned to her then, to make fun of her. The albino asked her if she liked the Medico's moustache. He told her to touch it. He said girls in the Luda Kura bar at home liked it very much. She asked again where they were going.

'We show you countryside,' the burly one said.

'I know the countryside . . . I live here.'

'You bad manners,' the albino said and whacked her on her knee so that she jolted and he kept doing it, to unnerve her.

The smells were oppressive and twice she thought she would be sick, but held it down. She kept looking out the window for signs to hold onto – an advertisement for a pony show, and another for kayaking, Wilderness B & B. Several other signs eluded her because the driver had picked up speed, as they were telling him to hurry. They had gone from one county into another and were in a lonesome area with bog on either side and bog cotton shivering on high stalks, brown peppery seeds, scudding about. The Medico got out a piece of paper and began to read directions.

They came to a slip road, with a long low building up on a hill and a sign for a golf club, then on down to where the road got narrower and turned into a track. She saw a thistly field and absurdly, a sign that said 'Trespassers Will Be Prosecuted'. There were wooden posts with barbed wire that had flecks of sheep's wool in it. Then the Medico wound the window down and told the driver to go off that track and up onto the rough ground, and as he did, the car lurched from side to side and they were flung onto one another. She could glimpse the ruin of a castle, its brown crumbling turrets overlooking the sea far below and a lighthouse at a great distance. It was not yet dark, but soon it would be. The driver missed his grip, swerved, then skidded, as the car sank into a hollow, where a sheep had gone to rest and was summarily pulped. They could hear the cries of the remainder of the flock who ran away in terror. The car bounced and rushed on, then stalled on the prow of the next hill, as if running away with itself. Then they came right up to a house, a deserted ruin, where obviously animals sheltered. There were cows in the fields, black-and-white cows, first staring at the headlights, then rearing into a gallop.

They jumped out and the burly fellow, taking the driver's keys and car phone, ordered him to open the boot. The albino relieved himself against a tree, the one thorn tree that clung to the crevice of a rock. There was no one about, nothing, only sheep and cattle and a metal feeder with hay sprouting from it. She saw everything with a terrible clarity, as if seeing last things.

Alone with the driver, she clutched his collar. Who were these men and what were they going to do to her. Oh man were they soused. They had been drinking vodka since they hired him at ten o'clock that morning, his first job, and he now asked the good Lord to spare him.

'I have four kids and one on the way . . . I want no trouble with police . . . police send me home,' he says as he takes from the glove box an old Bible held together with Sellotape. He starts to read from Psalm 91, reads it slowly and tells her to repeat the words after him, which she does –

You will not fear the terror of night
Nor the arrow that flies by day,
Nor the pestilence that stalks in the darkness.

Music is pouring from the house, it is like a disco in there. She is getting more terrified, asking crazy, unrealisable things. Suddenly Tyrone has a brainwave. It has come from God. It has come from her holding the Bible. She has the woman's means to save herself, to save them both.

'Life reside on the tongue,' he says and then, 'Be sweet . . . Be gentle . . . Do not argue . . . God love woman and he save you . . . God made woman for Adam to be happy. Eve have emotional mind . . . Adam have logical mind . . . Bring them to emotional mind . . . talk to them . . . you have soft voice, remind them that women follow the body of Christ to the tomb . . . all the Apostles they say they are men . . . how come they do not follow the body of Christ to the tomb . . . Ask them to have pity . . . Be wise with them and their craziness pass.'

The albino has come out.

'Gold lounge,' he says as he pulls her out of the car. A song, loud and brazen, is one she vaguely knows, having heard it in TJ's – 'When I'm with you, baby, I go out of my head, I just can't get enough . . .'

She stands on the threshold, thinking that at this very last minute, fate will intervene.

*

Mona was edgy and unable to sleep. She had this awful presentiment, just as she'd had twenty years previous, when her husband didn't arrive back from the Galway races and she knew before Plodder Pat even knocked on her door that Tim was already dead at the wheel. She tried prayer and she tried pacing and eventually, she had to go down to the pub and make herself a hot port. No use blocking it out any longer, she would have to act on her intuition. It was not curiosity, more a general anxiousness that made her open the letter Mujo had left for Dara, his friend. The heading was that of an asylum centre in Dusseldorf and the handwriting was laboured.

> *This is my story*, it began. *One New Year's Eve, I learnt of what happened to my family. A lady told me. She thought I knew, but I didn't. The day soldiers came to our farm, I hid in one of the beehives that was empty. There was shouting and crying and then the lorry drove away and my uncle and my mother were taken. Many days later, I am found in the beehive, but my memory gone. Someone from Red Cross they bring me away. I know that my uncle is dead, but I believe that my mother is still alive, that she is waiting for me and that we will find one another.*

Then pasted onto a separate sheet of paper was evidence, copied from a court document.

A hot day. Guards all stand with machine guns. Hundreds of men in one room beaten and afraid. A father is told to send his son into the next room, where men were taken for more severe beatings and didn't always come back. Unless father send his son in, no one in camp will be left alive. A second name is called and the two young men are pushed into beatings room. My uncle is sitting on a metal table all bloody. Guards already slash him with knives, and guard is pouring water over him in order to keep him alive, so as to kill him again. The young men recognise my uncle, they were friends from the same village, they play basketball together and belong to same pigeon club. One was ordered to hold him down and the second ordered to crouch and bite his balls off and unless it was done no one in whole camp would be left alive. They smear oil all over the lips of the one who is ordered to bite. He did what he had to do. Guards shouting, 'Bite harder bite harder.' My uncle nearly unconscious did not die just yet. Guard bring pigeon and my uncle put his hand out to stroke it, he think it a pet. Then the guard stuff it into his mouth, feathers and all. 'Bite harder,' he shout until my uncle truly dead. The two men ordered to deal with the body.

Mona was stone cold. She read it several times. God or no God she must do what she had to do. *Fidelma must not have this beast's child*. How clearly it all came back, a fresh morning when, after another sleepless night, she had taken a walk over to the river. Fidelma was getting out of her little Citroën, holding a big bunch of lilies, having probably driven to Sligo to get them, white lilies with sienna-coloured stamens, ecstatically happy. A woman in love bearing a gift. Knowing that for years Fidelma had wanted a child, Mona guessed, 'I think it has happened for you.'

'It has,' Fidelma said, and embraced her and swore her to secrecy. The child's father was not Jack, but a different man altogether and she was under oath not to say. She ran, hugging the big bunch of flowers as if it was already an infant she held to herself. Mona guessed correctly when she saw her let herself in the side door of what was once her shop, as Vlad always arrived very early to meditate. Seeing Fidelma so ruefully happy she felt she could not betray her, as a childless woman herself she could not do that, because she like everyone else knew nothing of the man's history. Now she had to do something worse. She would go to their house as soon as it got light and call Fidelma out on some pretext or other and tell her what they had to do. They must go to England, God or no God, that child could not be allowed into the world.

*

It is a large room with a clay floor that smells of animals and dried dung. The light from the big torches gives a merciless glare. They are in their shirt sleeves and dancing a sort of conga, swinging and head butting as the albino pushes her in.

'How are you feeling right now?' he asks.

'She's feeling randy . . . She's a Hot Mama and a Rich Bitch,' another answers. They then begin a sort of excuse-me dance in which she is thrown from one to the other, like a rag doll. They are chatting her up, sometimes insultingly, sometimes not.

'You miss your boyfriend?' the Medico asks.

'I don't know what you're talking about.'

He drinks then from the vodka bottle and passes it to his friends and she asks for some because she needs to be drunk, to get through this. What she believed was that they would rape her, but she was wrong. It is Vlad they want, it is him they have come to revenge themselves upon.

'I thought you were blood brothers,' she says.

'We were . . . We the "Preventiva", we guard him, protect him, move him safe . . . We lose everything, our fathers, our comrades, our lands . . . then peace, lousy peace, and he take the spoils. He do business . . . black market, cigarettes, gasoline, booze . . . He have cement and wood to build houses, many houses . . . We have nothing. He big boss . . . he cover his own arse and not ours.'

'That's not my fault,' she says.

'You had fun, yes.'

'Stop this game,' she says.

'We've only begun, bitch.'

'Harming me won't get you anywhere.'

'We kill anything of his . . . we kill his cat,' and he slides an imaginary blade across her throat.

'Don't kill it,' she says, her hand instinctively going to her belly and in that moment she knows that she has admitted to being pregnant and instantly tries to backtrack. They are feeling her now, pawing her, asking if she has a Bambi tattoo on her belly, swivelling her round for a side view. Suddenly remembering Tyrone's advice about being sweet with them, she says how she has seen the scan and how the skull has not yet formed, it is a little tadpole, it would not harm anyone.

'Blahblahblahblahblah.'

'Abort,' she hears the word twice and it hangs in the air like it might have been spoken by an oracle, lurking in one of the unlit corners.

Then the sound of his cell phone, which is a mimicry of a yapping dog and the Medico picks it up, listens and puts it down abruptly. From a plastic bag he takes out an iron crowbar and dons a plastic bib across his front. She backs away. Her hour has come. She runs into a corner where they follow and hold her, arms and legs flailing, and the Medico shouts to keep her there. That room is pandemonium now, their shouting, her screaming, pounding music, all of it driving out to where Tyrone, though she cannot know this, is reciting from memory, Psalm 91.

'I'll give you money, I'll give you my house, I'll give you anything,' she calls, but in vain.

'Ask him not to do it,' she says to the albino, thinking that because he is the youngest, he will break. He looks at her blank-eyed, as if looking at nothing at all.

'You have a mother,' she says.

'I love my mother.' He is affronted and says his mother's name is Vyjella, which means Violet in English. He is told to undress her. He pulls down her skirt and then more slowly her tights and her knickers, then gazes at the white of her flesh and the thick nest of black hair, with the gaze of a bridegroom.

'I do . . . I do it,' he says all excited and then he grabs the crowbar and straddles her. She can see his legs in his blue jeans and she can smell him.

'You will be sorry if you do it . . . I will haunt you forever,' she says, not screaming now but with a conviction, so that he draws back, shaken by her words, and says to the others, 'She witch . . . she mad.'

The Medico, furious at the time wasted, swaps places with him, takes the bar, holds it between her parted thighs and then rams it into her, slewing and tilting, then raking, as if raking earth. The pain is so violent that she cannot scream, only bleats of terror escape her and her screams are no more. The moaning of a dying animal, except she is not dying fast enough. Bound and held to that spot, she is calling on Jesus, on Christ, her hands pitifully outstretched, wantonly asking her killer to be her saviour. Half-lucid, half-crazed thoughts flit through her mind with each worsening thrust, and she remembers reading that at the very end, a dying person finds the courage to be brave, but no such courage befriends her. He is shouting for the torch to be held higher and for an instant, her sight is blanketed out by the glare and then it begins to happen, a slippage, as if all of her insides are being dislodged and from the two hooligans a shout of victory, as the blood comes churning out in fitful gushes. He withdraws the bar with the same savagery as he inserted it and flings it in disgust so that it hits then capsizes the second torch as both fall with a clang.

They are getting ready to go, the music suddenly turned off, shouting orders to each other as they pack their things. They leave her in utter darkness.

She hears the car drive away and all is quiet for a short time and then the scurries, rats, come to sup and she can hear their tongues lapping up the pools of warm blood.

*

The London flight has landed at the small airport and people have begun to trickle out. Tyrone lurks in a corner by the

Mavourneen coffee shop, trying to be invisible, unable to ring his wife, because they took his phone and all his money. He is waiting for Dara, knows that Dara and others went for the friendly game between Ireland and England.

Dara emerges with his mates, all in green, green jerseys and green scarves, and they scatter, some having mothers or girlfriends to collect them. He sees Dara come towards him bleary-eyed, all smiles now that he is sure of a lift home.

'Ireland scored first . . . the place went wild . . . jumpin' up and down . . . "Fields of Athenry" . . . a great game altogether . . . it was a draw but it felt like we won . . . ten of us in a hostel in Greek Street . . . Bed at four up at five . . . Great day altogether.'

'Something bad happen . . . I think she dead,' Tyrone says as they go out and Dara guesses it is to do with Vlad, as the news has been on every channel.

That drive is frantic, with Tyrone having to talk all the time, because unless he talk he will go crazy:

'They hire me for whole day . . . evening we pick up the woman, she scared like a little sparrow. I see trouble but I must drive. Go go go they say. Road narrow. I slow down. One he grab me from behind, I say mercy man. Before that he okay, he ask me what meat I like, I tell him deer and antelope that live in the bush and eat the sweet things, eat the mango. Now he is maniac. I see big sheet of water and road ending in hollow. I ask God help me. They say stop, and I stop and they jump out. They take keys. Soon music come same as nightclub. Later they take woman, I hear screaming, many many screaming. I think she dead. I have problem to go to police, for fear I lose my licence, go to prison or are sent home. On way to airport they throw bags in lake and wash their faces, laughing laughing laughing.'

It was pitch dark as they entered the house and they could hear scurries.

'I'm kinda afraid of rats,' Dara says and they hold onto one another as they pick their steps to where the body is slumped in a corner. They can't see, they can't tell whether she is breathing or not. Tyrone flicks on his lighter, but the flame keeps sputtering as there is hardly any fuel left.

'Quench it,' Dara shouts and runs, returning with sops of hay that they set light to. It catches fire instantly, sparks flying up, a great phosphorous glare, to reveal a figure that is bleeding and as good as dead.

Dara kneels, listens, then eases her onto her coat and what he would remember ever afterwards of that grim night was the warmth of the coat in which he cradled her, and carried her out and into the back of the car. Neither he nor Tyrone exchanged a single word on that long drive. Tyrone had to drive so slow because with every jolt, she seemed to dismember.

*

Coming back. Broken but not dead. The days, or was it weeks, in the hospital are a blur, being hefted on and off trolleys, hearing voices of doctors and nurses talking to one another, in muffled tones. What had they seen. What had they to do to her, to piece her back together. She would never know. She only knew what happened on the mountain and she pushed it away each time, like pushing a heavy door.

A nurse is singing while combing her hair, in preparation for the important visitors, the VIPs as she calls them.

Now Eileen O'Grady,
A real Irish lady,
I'm longing to call you my own.
I'll not be contented
'Til she has consented
To be Mrs Barney Malone.

It is a small ward with the vases of flowers squeezed onto the ledge that fronts the television.

The nurse is reeling off the next stage of her recovery, the rehabilitation process, learn to cope again and regain control of herself and her body. Staff are there for her, to give care and counselling. Words. Words. There is a place inside her that no care and no counsellor can reach. But she still smiles the grateful smile of the obligated.

'Who's coming?' she asks, nervous.

'The guards, the doctor, the pathologist, the house surgeon who examined you on admission, the gang.'

A baby is not mentioned. It never would be, not by them and not by her either, a sinful clot that had been disposed of. On the windowsill there are some 'Get Well' cards. The Book Club have sent cut-outs of hearts in gold and silver cardboard and Peggy has knitted her a woollen doll. The head was a tangle of mad wool sprouts and the body ended just below the navel, a stump really that she held for courage.

Dante and the boys had sent a message – *Don't let the bastards grind you down.*

'What will they want?' she asked the nurse.

'The oral evidence . . . what happened to you out on the mountain.'

'I can't tell them that.'

'You must tell them . . . you must . . . for the law to do its duty.'

'I don't have the . . . vocabulary.'

'Then you'll have to find the vocabulary.'

'They butchered me . . .' she said and gave a little insane laugh.

'Fidelma,' and now the voice is stern, 'are you or aren't you going to co-operate?'

'Will my husband be with them?'

'Poor man . . . What he's been through . . . Walking around in a daze . . . His pyjamas on under his trousers, not knowing whether it's day or night . . .'

'Do you hate me nurse?'

'I pray for you,' the nurse replied.

They were coming in, a phalanx of men in suits or white coats, the inquisitors, Jack among them. He had a teeny plaster on his chin, where he had cut himself shaving. They surrounded the bed, saying how good it was to see her sitting up and the house doctor read her thermometer off the hanging chart.

'Might I have a few moments alone with my husband?' she asked tentatively and they filed out like recruits.

Once alone, he half fell in over her, his face inches above hers, the hammer of his heart thudding on hers as a slew of obscenities came from him. Words so ugly that she could not believe it was him speaking and she cowered under the covers. It would have been better if he had struck her, it would have been better still if she had died, because he now would be weeping and gnashing on a grave, mourning her.

'I won't come home,' she said.

'Oh yes, you will come home,' he said, the mad blue glitter in his eyes, nailing her.

'I'll go away . . .'

'On what . . . On what . . .' he was shouting now and those who had retreated in deference hurried in. The nurse, in a display of false cheer, asked was it not time for their morning coffee.

'Morning coffee my arse,' Jack said and the house doctor grabbed him by his lapels, took him to one side and spoke to him and then led him outside where he still ranted.

The others stood around the bed in judgement.

She knew what they were thinking, a decent man, a pillar of the community, a faithful husband, dragged down into the mire.

*

'Now missus, nothing is a problem and you know that.' Dara has come, to take her over to Sligo on an errand. He leads her warily down the corridor, into the lift and out to the car park, which is packed. Her whole body feels as if it will fall apart. At first she is silent in the car, listening or pretending to listen to Enya, which he has put in the CD player, thinking she will find it soothing. All of a sudden she is remembering something she had forgotten to remember – one of the rats at her earlobe. He stops the car and lights a cigarette, then makes sure that all the doors are locked. He says if she wants to talk, talk. She says that talking only makes it worse. This is the same journey as she made in the bus, not that long ago and yet every bit of the landscape is altered. The trees are still the same trees, but she senses menace in them. At the sight of the sheep grazing she suddenly recalls the sheep that got mashed when Tyrone's car lurched down into a hollow and the bleating of the flock, as they ran away.

He drops her on the bridge in Sligo. She will be waiting in

that same spot in half an hour. She walks as if something is going to drop out of her. She dreads the very presence of other people. All of a sudden she comes to a stop, then looks around. Yes, it was just there by the museum that she and he met once, by chance and went inside to see the exhibition. *Mingling hands and mingling glances.* In glass cabinets, on display, there were some of Yeats's poems, in his own hand, the brown ink rusted with time and the paper curled at the edges. The room was empty, just them and a dozy girl who took the tickets. He asked her to read one of the poems, to do it, especially for him.

Come away, O human child
To the waters and the wild,
With a faery, hand in hand,
For the world's more full of weeping than you can
understand.

Further up the street, she tripped, but caught herself on a pole that held up part of the awning of a shop. She was in two minds to go back to the bridge, but Dara would not be there, he would be driving around, until it was time to collect her. People sat at an outside cafe in the corner, tables all squeezed together, gales of laughter, a group peeling off their T-shirts, thrills, rowdiness, the froth yellowing on the tumblers of Guinness and waitresses managing three plates on one arm. There was a smell of fries and cakes and drink.

The sales were on. The shop she wanted was in an arcade and a beautiful young boy stood near the entrance, playing the bohrain, the sound sweet and tremulous: *She is far from the land where her young hero sleeps.* He played beautifully and she stood to listen. He wore a white beret at an angle and had a shy, winning smile. She threw coins into his mug and he stopped playing for an instant and held his breath, in courtly gratitude.

From a rack of coats, she chose a heavy black one with a wide box collar and a double row of black buttons down the front. It cost everything she had. She put it on straight away, having come from the hospital just in a cardigan. In the long mirror she was talking to herself and the shop assistant, recognising the strangeness, made no mention of the peculiarity of putting on a heavy coat on such a scorching day.

On the way back she asked Dara if they could go to Cloonoila for a quick visit, as there was something private she needed to do.

She walked up one street, past the feed factory, the baker's, the first pub and the post office, then past her own empty shop with leaflets and circulars scattered on the bare floor. Crossing the road, she passed the row of houses with lace curtains on the downstairs windows and walked slowly along the second street, where there was a butcher's, the second pub and the crèche. Through the open window, she could hear the sounds of children, singing in the classroom, filling her with a lost longing. She moved like a somnambulist, her hands out in front of her, like a blind person feeling the way. No one cast a stone and there was no peeping from behind curtains, but she knew that news of her appearance would quickly circulate. Were anyone to speak to her, she had an answer at her fingertips – *I have been unwell but I am on the mend now . . . And thank you.*

Why was she walking there. It was something to do with the new coat, that had replaced the other, the bloodied coat.

It was a kind of atonement and a kind of defiance. It was also a farewell. She would not be walking those streets again.

PART TWO

South London

First a tube and then an overground train and after that a walk of about twenty minutes along a busy road, to Jasmeen's flat, somewhere in south London.

The tall flats were on three sides, with a rectangle of grass in front and beyond a little gate that opened onto a busy road. The higher floors of the flats had white balconies that stood starkly in the oncoming night. Jasmeen, her future landlady, went first and Fidelma followed, not knowing what she would find. There were a few grey squirrels on the grass, nibbling on the husks of the chestnuts that had fallen from the one massive tree.

'I want to be near trees, or even one tree,' were the words she blurted out during her interview. It was with a charity organisation in a small complex of single-storey houses, not far from Victoria Station. There were many people waiting, all silent except for one man with a black patch over his eye, talking ceaselessly – 'Me Sierra Leone, war war war, *guerre guerre guerre*, we want to believe it don't happen, that is how we get by, we try to escape, we come here, we shout at persons that jump the queue before us, and live rough. My cousin he move back, he hate it here, he say come for a holiday and I go for one month and after one week I am edgy. I paint a wall, dig up weeds, play ball with kids in the street and make small vegetable garden for my auntie. I come back to this city, where I know no one and do my hating alone.'

Intermittently, her name was called. Different people had interviewed her, asking the same questions again and again – Why was she homeless. Where had she slept the previous seven nights. Why did she leave Ireland. What was her relationship with her estranged husband. Had she been in trouble with the police. Had she slept on the street. How long did she intend to stay. How much money had she in her possession? Eventually, she was taken to see Jasmeen in a room next to the refectory and there was a smell of fried bacon and eggs, as homeless people were given their breakfast. Jasmeen's role, as she explained, was to find accommodation for homeless families with children and then to visit them regularly, to make sure that they adapted and to find schools for the children. Unfortunately, as Fidelma was single, she did not fit into that remit, so sadly she was unable to help her.

She came out of there totally dejected and walked aimlessly around. It was restaurants and shops and more restaurants and more shops, with scantily clad mannequins, sickly looking in that neon light. Eventually, she came on a side path that led to a cathedral, where she sat near the back and tried to pray. The soft light through the stained glass gave the nave a warmth and in the side aisles, rows of candles flickered in wayward joyousness. Above, in the gallery, someone practised on an organ and the same notes were struck again and again, corresponding to the same thoughts in her head, where to go next, where to sleep that night. By chance, three or four hours later, still wandering, still walking without any destination in mind, she bumped into Jasmeen, who was leaving work at four thirty and seeing her so lost, invited her home.

The flat was on the ground floor and the hallway poorly lit. There was a puddle at the bottom of the stairs, dog pee or water spilt. From the elevator, a woman's taped voice that seemed to belong to a different, more exclusive milieu kept saying, 'Going up. Going up.' There was an exercise bike just outside the door, laden with clothes and boxes and behind it, a tall plant that looked as if it had withered.

Inside they went first to the sitting room, where there was a huge television set and framed photographs of Jasmeen and of her daughters in different outfits and one of her older daughter in cap and gown, the day she had got her degree. Then she was shown the bedroom. It was the younger daughter's room and there were clothes everywhere, clothes in boxes, clothes on hangers, CDs on the radiator and on the dressing table, glittery bracelets, make up in jars, a teddy bear and birthday cards with the sign of Scorpio. The bed had a buttoned pale green velvet headboard and she lay face down, shutting her mind to everything, telling herself to be grateful for this small respite. Under the pillow was a weeny teddy bear and for some reason, the sight of it moved her to tears. Everything would be better once she knew the routine, when the bathroom was free to be used, where to store her things, likewise the routine of the kitchen and when she might be allowed to cook. Suddenly there was a tap on the door as, since it was her first evening, she was invited to share a meal. Jasmeen said it was the custom in her country to offer hospitality when a visitor came.

It was a fish dish, but it was not like any fish she had ever tasted. Jasmeen told how she had prepared it, marinated it for forty-eight hours, then cooked it with bananas that were not the bananas usually seen in a supermarket, but green bananas, which could only be got in a market on Saturdays, quite a distance away. She then said that the daughter in the photograph wearing cap and gown had graduated in biology and gone home to Africa to teach. She held up a phone, saying it was her special phone to ring Africa, which she did twice a week and lived for those conversations. Her other daughter, Jade, who had moved out some time ago, shared a flat with friends in the East End. It was more trendy and also closer to where her boyfriend, Ronnie, lived. Both daughters in the photograph were beautiful, tall, dark-haired, with polished skin, their eyes moist in wondrous anticipation. Jade, her mother warned, might at any moment reappear, as she often had big bust-ups with Ronnie. Being the younger daughter, she was indulged about everything, including her dreams of becoming an actress.

All of a sudden, Jasmeen jumped out and pulled out a bottle, still in its Christmas wrapping, from the cupboard on which the television rested. It was cava and she poured big glugs into tumblers. She was happy to have someone to talk to. She just nodded to neighbours without ever talking, because it was like that, in flats, in every city in the world. She knew her neighbours only slightly. The young woman they met on the way in, with the little girl eating an apple, had rid herself of a husband who was drunk and violent and the young man with a hood over him was obviously a new boyfriend, so the child had a newcomer in their small kitchen and in her mother's bed. The man in the flat next to hers was from Zimbabwe and couldn't walk very well because of a war injury and he too had a child, a little girl of about ten, but no sign of a mother.

'You're wondering why I brought you home,' she asked and said it was because she never once forgot her own predicament when she first came to London and how lonely and famished she had been. She then went on to tell the story of her life, and those who helped her when she first came. Her husband was an army man, quite high up and with a good income and she was used to privilege, a maid, a chauffeur and a dressmaker, but when the marriage was no longer working, what with a younger bride on the horizon, she set out for England with two daughters, one eight and one three and a half years old. She had a bank draft for two hundred dollars in her purse. Through the council, they found accommodation, one room, about three miles from where she now lived. In the one room there was a big bed with a flowered quilt and it was into that bed they crept every day around three o'clock in the afternoon, because they were so afraid of the dark. They had never known such darkness or such coldness, no more than they knew what troubles that darkness held. They had only bread to eat. It was given out in one of the charity places, where she walked, holding one child by the hand and the younger she carried on her back. It was another African woman that she met on the street who, seeing her and her children in such light clothes, stopped them and brought them to the Salvation Army shop. There they were given warm coats and knitted gloves and caps. That was the night, or rather the evening, that they didn't go to bed at three o'clock, because now that they had coats, they could go out. They went to a restaurant over on the high street and the girls had fish and chips and she ordered one portion of chicken between them all. They didn't say another word, feeling too intimidated, and when the time came to pay and she offered the cheque for the two hundred dollars, the waitress could not change it, so the manager was called. She asked where the bank was, only to be told that banks closed at night time and after a difficult pause, she wrote her name, her address and an IOU, promising to come back on the morrow. She could read his mind, read that he was thinking to himself, 'These people straight out of the bush haven't got a clue.' The elder daughter cried, as this was her first glimpse of the many humiliations that were to befall them.

Next day, in the place where they were given bread, a woman brought her to the bank and after much explaining, entreating and paperwork, the cheque was cashed. She paid the restaurant and on the way home, from a street vendor, bought sweet black grapes for her daughters, which they ate sitting on the bed, and put the seeds into an envelope to plant in the patch of green outside. In time, Sabrina, the elder girl, went to school, where she excelled herself in sport and athletics, growing taller and more beautiful by the day, and Jade was placed in a crèche, where she made friends that she wanted to live with. Meanwhile, she herself went from one place to another to find work and eventually, was hired as a chambermaid in a hotel in Edgware Road. Maureen was the first Irish woman she had met, the one who had helped them and ever after, Jasmeen had a soft spot for the Irish. Maureen, who lived in the flat opposite, agreed to be child minder, collecting the children from the school and the crèche until their mother got home at seven in the evening. It was Maureen who helped them the night a big stone was put through the bedroom window. Jasmeen was in the kitchen, with Jade, preparing a supper, when suddenly Sabrina came screaming. She had been sitting on her bed doing her homework when the stone came hurtling into the room. They went to look at it, the huge stone and broken glass all over the floor. They ran into the hallway to get help, but, as she said, it was not easy to get help because they were black; they were in fact the only black family in that large block. Maureen happened to come in, asking if a letter for her had been delivered there by mistake and instantly brought them across to her place, to ring the police. She was quite firm on the phone, explaining the ugly situation, saying how lucky that the girl had not been badly injured and insisting that they be moved from there.

Next morning, both women went to the station, where she gave a statement and after four weeks they were given another flat, where black people were more acceptable. This assault was an eye-opener for her. She vowed that she would not be a chambermaid for life and started studies, in order to get on the ladder and make a better future for her children. Four nights a week she went to class, where, with thirty others in the same boat, she learned English, phrasing and parsing words over and over again and eventually, after three years, she got a degree, which enabled her to look for proper work.

It may have been the cava that made her nostalgic, but she jumped up, saying there was something she must show Fidelma. She returned carrying a ceremonial dress on its hanger. It was a silk dress, gaily coloured, with a hat to match, a hat that could be dented into different shapes and which she donned proudly. Then she walked around holding the dress in front of her, a sway to her body, the panels softly undulating, the various silks bestrewn with big apricoty blossom.

'When I am wearing this dress . . . I am reaching out,' she said, and she curtsied and smiled, harking back to that other time, her maid, her chauffeur, her dressmaker, her luncheons, her green and salad years.

Fidelma

I dread my dreams. I dream of one or other of them nightly, along with all the other muddle, journeys, crowded carriages, in the Underground unfamiliar, blank, hostile faces. I dream of Jack and our daily routine, putting porridge in the oven overnight to cook and sometimes I dream of him in different circumstances altogether, walking Auburn the red setter that died and that he had cremated in Belfast, keeping the ashes in a silver pot on the mantelpiece. Another time he is walking her on a crocodile leash, somewhere in the warm Mediterranean, reciting a poem by Walter de la Mare, stressing his favourite lines, poor Jack, that were in fact his life's motto –

> *Tell them I came and no one answered,*
> *That I kept my word.*

His tirades in the town were shocking, walking around with a loaded revolver, asking everyone if his wife had done the decent thing by drowning herself, so that he could take his own life with honour. Sister Bonaventure relayed it to me. She was one of the people he accosted, his cheeks hollow, the eyes with that mad blue glitter, talking manically to himself. The nuns took me in. '*The swallow hath her perch.*' Sister Bonaventure led me up the stairs that smelt of wax polish and along a corridor, to their one spare bedroom. I was given my meals on a tray in a private room that was without a window. To all extents and purposes, I had left Cloonoila and nobody knew my whereabouts. There were a few practicalities to be attended to. Sister Bonaventure managed to sell my little car, along with the few antiques from the shop and my jewellery. I kept my locket with my mother's hair in it and I can say it was my first acknowledgement of her importance in my life, the thing called motherhood. In all, I accrued a few hundred pounds so as to set off. They spirited me out of there by night, with my new passport and the photograph of me taken for it, in which I might have been dead, so sepulchral did I look. Father Eamonn came to hear my confession and I knelt on a little kneeler in the room without the window. He kept his eyes lowered throughout and gave me absolution, without my having to enumerate my sin.

I stayed the first three nights in a B & B in Ebury Street, not far from Victoria Station. It was noisy, what with people coming and going at all hours, lugging their suitcases on wheels down the flights of narrow stairs, wheels, more wheels, as if the whole world was on the march. Pigeons cooed in the small back garden in the very early morning and I got up as soon as I had access to the bathroom and was off out, down the street and into another, quieter street, to an outside table and ordered coffee and brioche with strawberry jam. I liked sitting in the cold. I could have been any tourist, except that I wasn't, I had to find work. Father Eamonn had given me a wholesome reference and there was an old write-up about the boutique, in which I was congratulated for being so fashion-conscious. I went to various places on the off chance, but without success, leaving my name and the number of my mobile phone. One shop sold cushions and hangings and I thought how I would fit in there and hide in all that sumptuousness. In a shop on the high street in Kensington the assistants were all young, expertly made up and with false eyelashes and there were racks upon racks of clothes and belting music, but no vacancy. Lastly, I tried a wine shop. When the man who interviewed me asked me if I could cope being alone four nights a week, saying there was an emergency bell under the counter in case of trouble, I faltered.

It was after that that I went to the charity organisation, where I met Jasmeen. First it was a matter of waiting in a cramped room, the many faces all around with the same nervous expression and the one argumentative man with the eye patch.

I dream of Vlad too, his shadow disappearing up the street, his eyes so searching, kissing his ring once as if he were a bishop and the moment in Strandhill where he first made his feelings known to me. Except in that dream, along with the surfers, there are spectators, local men all waiting to kill him. They are goring him with pitchforks, but he is refusing to die.

In all my dreams there is blood. It gushes from the pump in Cloonoila, where several women stand to fill their buckets. They are blaming me for the terrible curse that I have brought on their village. It oozes from mattresses and spills onto the floor, out into the hall and the pathway that leads from Jasmeen's apartment to the entrance gate. I dream of the little mite that I cannot imagine and will not ever give a name or a feature to.

Tomorrow I have an interview.

Bluey

Fidelma sat on a bench nailed to the pavement, killing time until her interview. The wall was too high to actually have a view of the river, but earlier she had stood and looked at it, the water a toffee colour, not like the silvery rivers of home. White pleasure boats were going up one side and down the other, and sometimes a police boat that was painted differently. Twice she enquired the time of passers-by, who looked at her askance.

Finally she got up and went towards the bank along a walkway, where a few young trees, hooped in metal baskets, had something of the tiredness of the city on them. A cradle hung from one of the very high floors of the bank, where obviously someone had been cleaning windows earlier on, and even to look up there at it, in its sway, gave her vertigo. She felt again in her purse for her passport and the two references from home. In the glass of the revolving door, her reflection, as it met her, was none too confident.

The young man who interviewed her had a friendly smile, short curly hair, thick branching eyebrows, full lips and bockled teeth. His name was Bluey and from the very first moments he sought to put her at her ease, fetching a cup of tea from the cafeteria and a weeny carton of milk on the side. They were on a high floor of the bank in a small room that overlooked a huge office. Traders sat at their desks, all of it so quiet, so hushed, with the solemnity of church. Night, as Bluey said, was no different from day. Boats on the Thames, cruisers, pleasure boats, police boats, cargo ships, a part of the city that did not sleep. The place was all glass, glass walls, glass mirrors, everything spick and span and he was proud to tell her that his team of cleaners had won a certificate for excellence three years in a row. Above him was a manager, an administrator and a housekeeper. Pointing to the glass wall, he asked her how she thought it sparkled so. She wasn't sure. Just water, he said, just plain water, as with chemicals of any kind, dust got ingrained in the glass and couldn't be wiped off. He wore two earrings in the same ear; white gold inlaid with diamonds, a gift from his missus, as he said. He had been married for almost six years to an English woman and already he had booked the restaurant for their anniversary dinner.

'My wife she say to me, you are the army Bluey, I am the lover. She want me to teach my kids behave nice and have respect for others. Of course,' he went on, 'when we first marry we have conflict, she cook fish and chips every evening and I try to persuade her to be more adventurous, I tell her everybody different, different tastes, different food, different politics and oh my God, different God.'

It was with a certain pride he went on to say that now his wife experimented with dishes and used her spices, chillies that he grew under glass, in his little garden in Kent, the three colours, the red, the green and the yellow. He also got chilli flakes in the market they went to on Saturdays. His wife loved trinkets and he showered her with them. Soon he rolled up his cotton sleeve to show his mom's name – *Helena* – inside a reddish heart surrounded by a lucky blue dragon. His Mom was his queen, taught him everything he knew, she said to him, *Bluey, there exist some great consciousness between people, but they do not know it and that is why there is war.* His Mom complains to him that he does not love her anymore, because he does not go home to Mozambique and he tells her when he phones her every Saturday that so long as he can see her in his mind, it means he loves her and the day he stops seeing her, then he will go home on a visit. He was not always such a loving son. One night, aged about twelve, he opened the window in his mom's house and he ran. Not found for two days. Lived in a field near a farm and the farmer's wife gave him a potato and a carrot to eat, raw potato and raw carrot.

Soon after he was found, his grandfather, who had been a boxer, brought him to a place where they did cage fighting. Two people in an octagonal cage, naked, and the only thing not allowed is to take the other person's eyes out. Before you start, you don't know who you will fight. Is he taller? Is he stronger? Is he tougher? When you go in you bring everything mean and bad, you use hands, feet and after forty minutes, win or lose, all the bad stuff gone and in the moment you are free. Free.

Fidelma listened, carried away by his stories, but at the same time fretting, because she did not want to go home to Jasmeen and say she had not got the job. It was Jasmeen who had helped her, looking on the internet night after night, and it was Jasmeen who had guided her to fill in her application form. As if he had read her mind, he opened the form, scanned it, then looked at her and said her name aloud.

'Fidelma, a beautiful name, a goddess perhaps . . . Why do you want to work in Bluey's bank?'

'It's complicated,' she said and clammed up, begging him with her eyes not to ask too much.

'Ireland always green,' he said. 'I take my wife and kids one day and we play golf, like it show on the television . . . green

green green,' and he looked at her and said he knew how quick a person can lose heart, lose hope. He had lived and worked in many countries, having left home at a young age, with his bag on his back and a few quid in his pocket, his mom crying by the gate. One thing he never forgot. It was a restaurant in Barcelona and he was looking in the window at people eating shellfish and laughing at the mess they made, just outside looking in, when a waiter in black tails, followed by more waiters, came out and told him to move on. He was dirt in their eyes.

'In those moments I want to kill . . . have you ever wanted to kill, Fidelma?'

'Yes,' she said, much to his surprise.

Then he read the two references she had brought, the one from Gerry her solicitor and the other from Father Eamonn. Gerry was succinct, simply attesting to her character, while Father Eamonn's was more florid. Bluey read bits of it aloud, her breeding, her family descended from kings and queens, her convent education, her cultural yearnings, her love of literature, her French-themed boutique, which, alas, was lost during the financial crisis. There was no mention of her husband and long before she had put her wedding ring in a little box. The letter ended with a quotation from Byron – *She walks in beauty like the night.*

Bluey looked at her, sizing her up, saying that if she walked like beauty in the night, could she clean like beauty in the night?

'So I'm hired,' she said with excitement.

'Not yet.' He needed guidance. He needed to sit alone, meditate and ask his Mom. She would sit downstairs and remember the things Bluey had told her and that he gave everyone the same opportunity, had Latinos, Africans, Eastern Europeans, Angolans, West Indians, Chinese, all under his watch.

She sat in the big hall, with almost nobody around, staring at a ceramic sculpture of an elephant, painted blue and white. A money pot perhaps. Bluey had said that of the thousands of flowers displayed in that bank every day, the money flower was the most popular with the traders. They believed it brought them luck. Money money money. Green green green.

He came on her unawares and as he stepped off the escalator, he was smiling.

'Congratulations,' he said and they moved to a quiet corner, where they sat and he was suddenly formal as her new employer. Her job would commence in one week, she would clock in at eight in the evening and out at six in the morning. She would write her name in a ledger when she arrived and on departure, although very soon the system was due to be digitised. She would be given a tunic and trousers to wear. Light blue tunic and navy trousers. She could bring her own shoes if she wished. She would start on the fourth floor and move up as she progressed. The person immediately above her would be her trainer, for the first six weeks, and would evaluate the work that she did. That person would report to the supervisor and above him was the manager, Lukas. Her trainer was a nice lady, but strict. She wore plaits on the top of her head and they called her Medusa when she was angry. The plaits turned into snakes, but Medusa did not know that. However, there was no need to worry, as each Friday all went to the pub for one hour and drank beers.

'A little bit of your story and a little bit of my story Fidelma . . . and everybody good friend.'

Then he took out a photograph of himself as a very young boy setting off for the world and many adventures. He wore poor clothes and poor shoes, but it was the smile that would carry him. What did she make of the person in the photograph? She hesitated. He said if she had one word to describe him, what would that word be?

'Plucky,' she said. He liked the word. He was certain that they were going to get on well. He must run now – *She walks in beauty like the night.*

He waved to her from beyond the revolving doors.

Dust

Brown dust. White dust. Black dust. The black dust was the most ingrained of all and Fidelma was told that it must be rooted out of the corners. Glass was washed with lukewarm water and wiped down with endless balls of newspaper. In her blue tunic and her hair drawn back severely, Dara would hardly recognise her now. Not that she looked in mirrors, but occasionally, she caught sight of herself in one of the big windows that looked onto the Thames, the water a sheet of dark at night. Sometimes from the pleasure boats, music and the sound of the revellers could be heard through the double-glazed windows.

She watched others as they dusted, trying to learn their techniques, some so brisk, some flicking the cloth, skidding and skiddering over the surfaces, except for Maria, who went about her tasks with great zeal, because everything mattered, even the most menial thing. That was her philosophy, that and the rapture of the tango. Maria believed that one night and enigmatically, a tall man, a big boss in the bank, would appear and with a kindred intention, they would glide down the corridor and break into tango. It was not a dream as she said, it was a fairy tale and in their predicament, fairy tales were crucial.

They were night people, one step away from ghosts, and strangers to each other. Some had husbands, as she guessed by their wedding rings, and many had children, who, contrary to the rules, telephoned in the night to report some crisis. The mothers, knowing that phone calls were forbidden, lurked in corners, to listen. Many had fled horror, countries they could never go back to, while still others yearned for home. They all carried memories and the essence of their first place, known only to them. For Fidelma, it was such a small memory, young grass with the morning sun on it and the night's dew, so that light and water interplayed as in a prism and the top leaves of an ash tree had a halo of diamond from the rain, the surrounding green so safe, so ample, so all-encompassing.

It was her last morning in the convent grounds and Mass had been offered up for her private intention.

'Off your arses . . . off your arses.' It was Medusa's battle cry, as she flitted from floor to floor in her important role as assistant supervisor, the woman with the snakes, eyes darting towards this and that and screaming at the slightest provocation. She was a tiny woman, dark-skinned, all bone, her hair neatly plaited with the plaits arranged on the crown of her head and the brown scalp showing through, somehow saddish-looking.

'Stop looking at me' were her first abrasive words to Fidelma, who had been merely admiring the perfect symmetry of the plaits.

'Sorry,' she said.

'Do I hear a Paddy . . . do I smell a Paddy?' Medusa said, two fingers to her nose, for others to relish the joke.

'I suppose you like snow,' she said then.

'Yes, I like . . . snow,' Fidelma answered.

'Ho ho ho, Honky likes snow because snow is white and I am not white, I am black,' and at that she went off, cackling, saying Mrs Paddy had six weeks' probation to prove herself.

'Don't pay any heed . . . don't let her get to you,' Maria whispered and at the tea break, she gave her a leaflet with a 'Miracle' prayer, which was in Spanish.

*

In the mornings, after they had clocked out, they ran, recklessly, they ran as if they were fleeing catastrophes. The fear that governed their whole lives was now compressed into this urgency to catch a bus or a train to allow a husband or a mother or a cousin to go to work.

Fidelma walked, so as not to arrive until Jasmeen had left for work. Jasmeen was not a morning person and needed her *space*, as she said more than once. The streets were empty, except for the few enthusiastic joggers, who ran and sometimes stopped by a railing to flex their muscles. There was the sad debris of the night, plastic bottles, condoms, cigarette butts, damp wads of newspaper and vacated sleeping bags, on steps and in doorways. The street sweepers, with their saffron stripes, were easy to pick out, meeting each morning at the same place, all foreign, exchanging a few words, even laughing, as they steered the barrows, their wide brooms upright, jutting out.

Along the way, she stopped by a wooden hut, where taxi drivers queued for their breakfast. In the first week they were resentful of her, but as time went on she was admitted, in fact given precedence in the queue and for some reason, they called her Shelagh. *Let Shelagh go . . . good on ya Shelagh.* The man behind the tiny counter remembered her order – a decaffeinated coffee with a little milk, *caldo*.

'*Caldo*,' he repeated and she would nod.

Then she walked by the Embankment, where the floating

restaurants were moored, all white with the splendour of temples, and some of the houseboats with gardens on their decks, or in tubs, flowers and tall rhubarby plants, with the water plashing against them.

*

A little girl always stood behind the long narrow window in the flat that adjoined Jasmeen's. She fitted exactly into it, stock still and quite pensive. Fidelma reckoned she would be five or six and wondered why she waited, so steadfastly, there. Then one morning she waved. It was a very wan wave of the wrist, as if she was answering a command to wave at some dignitary.

Not too long after that, she smiled.

Finally, they met in the communal back garden, where Fidelma had carried out her mug of tea, wanting, as in Cloonoila, to be near nature, even if nature was one square of hummocky grass, with a horse chestnut tree at one end, lesser trees, bushes and forty-eight sets of windows spying on what went on.

The little girl came onto the balcony, smartly dressed in a lilac dress that was padded at the hemline so that it ballooned out and she wore pink leggings and black patent leather shoes. Her skin was golden, like the colour of a walnut shell. There was a perfection to her, the eyes, the pert eyelashes, tiny teeth, nails polished turquoise and the cuticles so perfectly defined.

'Hello,' Fidelma called.

'Sshhh,' and she moved nearer as she spoke. 'It is strictly forbidden to come into the garden . . . I can come on the balcony, but not the garden,' she said. She had had her big bowl of cereal and this was her time for fresh air, but twenty seconds before half past, she must go in again.

'Who forbids it?'

'My daddy . . . It is also strictly forbidden to come into another house.'

'So your daddy is very strict.'

'Sometimes, but when he takes his pills and falls asleep . . . he can't remember the password for the TV and I have to remember it for him,' and she laughed, proud of her mastery over him. Her daddy took naps. Old people took a lot of naps.

'What's your name?'

'It is forbidden to tell,' and at that a stopwatch, hidden somewhere in the vastness of her pockets, gives a muffled alarm and she runs up steps and into her own flat, slamming the door decisively.

Not too long after came the first of many communications. They were top secret. Letters left on a little bird table on Jasmeen's balcony. The writing, sometimes zany, was in different coloured crayon, but with a decided penchant for purple:

I like butterflies. I also like pandas. They are very nice creatures, they are vegetarian. They only eat bamboo. They have no claws.

I can name the three parts of the Trinity – Father, Son and Holy Spirit.

A long time ago, in a land far away, the most terrible beast that ever lived roameyed the countryside. In the morning it would gobble up men as they went to work in the fields. In the afternoon it would break into lonely farmhouses and eat up mothers and children as they sat down to their lunch.

If I lived in Oxford I would go bonkers.

On Monday our eggs arrived. On Tuesday they started to chip. On Wednesday the eggs were cracking. On Thursday eleven chicks hatched. On Friday we had young chicks.

To improve my English, my auntie has told me to write a story. It concerns a princess in a cellar. The cellar is small and grey and there are rats and mice. The poor princess has to stand on a stool all day. It is very scary.

*

It was Friday, the evening when they all went to the pub, but it also happened to be Maria's birthday. Everyone had dressed up for it, different scarves, bright lipsticks, evening purses and whatever bits of jewellery they had. Maria, in her black dress, with the scalloped neckline and sprays of embroidered roses, was Queen. How young she looked and how ravishing, her hair loose, falling over her shoulders and with a beautiful sheen to it. At first they were quite constrained, not really knowing each other and it was left to Bluey, the only man among them, to put them at their ease.

Fidelma had scarcely seen him, because almost as soon as she began work he was promoted and had to look after staff in sister branches all over. He was wearing a paisley waistcoat that he had got at the market and, as he said, must have belonged to some admiral. He knew all their names, the countries they had come from and remembered the names of children and one who was about to make her Holy Communion.

Amaretto was served in coloured liqueur glasses, along with tapas and almond-flavoured biscuits in thin tissue paper. The idea was that the paper, when twirled into a particular shape, could be lit, where it soared up of its own accord, then became invisible and one with the stratosphere. They enjoyed this, making wishes, competing with each other as to whose paper rose highest and they had grown talkative, emboldened from the liqueur, which they gulped, pronouncing it far nicer than the beers or the shandies they were accustomed to.

Maria had done the seating and they were already told that after the first fifteen minutes, the person on one's right had to move up two places and so eventually, Fidelma found herself next to Medusa. Maria had planned it that way, so as to get the snakes out of Medusa's hair. Medusa was so affable, stroked Fidelma's arm, said she had wanted to socialise and now it was happening. At once she explained the reason for her plaits, saying her hair was very strong, like horsehair, and wishing she had soft hair, the same as Fidelma. Then, on her phone, she showed the photographs of her children, a boy and a girl, at a barbecue, along with several other children. The barbecue had been held on her patio, that her boyfriend Kcool had laid. Kcool owned several nightclubs and they were building a place in Majorca, way up in the mountains, a finca. Her kids came first in their classes at everything and had medals in singing and piano playing. She had many questions. Was Fidelma missing her own country. Did she have grown-up kids. Had her husband passed away. Did she go regularly to church. Then a visit was planned. One Sunday in the summer, Fidelma would come, she would take the three changes of train, arriving at Hounslow Station, where they would meet her and take a short cut across an estate to her house.

They would eat on the patio. It would be Cajun chicken with various salads and afterwards, while she and Fidelma lolled and got to know each other better, the children would be riding their ponies in the large paddock that led off their garden.

'Time, ladies, please . . . time, ladies.' It was Bluey with his harsh whistle that had to remind them the little celebration had come to an end and two bottles of Amaretto had been consumed.

Maria and Fidelma stayed on, for a nightcap.

'I suppose you heard about the boyfriend and the clubs.'

'I did . . .'

'And the finca in Majorca . . .'

'I did . . .'

'But thank God and the Virgin that you are friends . . . no more wrangling, no more Mrs Paddy.'

*

The little girl was lugging a branch that was far too heavy for her. The council had lopped the trees and there were a lot of stray branches strewn around, many of which she was attempting to carry across. Several times she stopped and was winded, as the burden was too much. But she persevered and eventually there were enough branches to make a secret hidey-hole under the tree. That done, she lay down on the grass and threw her arms out in abandon.

'I like your haircut,' Fidelma said.

'A friend of my auntie's cut it, he came to her house . . . told me not to blink, but I blinked like mad,' and now she scrunched her eyes and laughed sillily and gaily at the surprise of their being out of doors, breaking rules and about to set up home, where nobody could spy on them.

Over the weeks, they met each morning, unless it was raining, or her auntie had come to do the laundry. Lots and lots of laundry. One day her auntie had brought the wrong washing powder and her father had got a rash and was furious. The other time he was furious was when their letterbox was crammed with circulars. She wore a different dress each time, she had a range of them, all with identical pintucking on the chest, matching leggings. Some days she wore a long wooden necklace, painted with white flowers. Her hair always smelt so clean. Each time she would bring something from the house, a sieve, a broken wooden spoon, a bit of an old mat, cups from a doll's house, from which they would drink imaginary tea, plastic iced buns and serviettes with the name of the Indian takeaway from where her daddy bought their suppers most evenings.

'Are you by yourself in there all day, every day?' Fidelma asked.

'No . . . we are a tribe. A girl tribe. We fight the dinosaurs . . . then we have our lunch and a rest and we fight more . . . Punch punch punch until we are very tired and they leave and go to their own quarters over by Battersea. Then I lie down with Greenie . . . he's my dinosaur . . . he came over to our side when he was injured . . . he plays with Mr Clown.'

'So you spend your day punching.'

'And romping . . . I also have a bronze from my judo class . . . We're graded on knowledge and on courage,' and at that she crawls out from their enclave to demonstrate: one hand raised and the other lowered, as she tackles the imaginary opponent, the blood rushing to her cheeks, gripping him by the lapels, pulling and pushing in order to trap him and get him down. She does it a few times with impassioned effort, finally succeeding in holding him down for the count of ten, by which time he has lost that round. Her judo class is the big adventure in her life, going on the bus with her auntie every Thursday, writing her initial many times on the window when it is steamy. Then in the changing room a big scramble to get into her uniform, white as white and called a *judogi*. Then into the ring for the big fight. She went down the week before, but was up fast, up under the ten-second deadline and fought for a long time and finally won and the teacher praised her stamina. The boy she fought was very thin and was from Sweden. She was very happy to have won. Afterwards, as was the rule, she shook hands with her opponent and both bowed and went back to their seats and her auntie had a fruity drink for her as a reward. It was raspberry-flavoured, because she would go bonkers if she had any more orange juice.

'You have to be very tough to win,' she said, explaining that her belt was red with two yellow stripes, but that she was working up to get a yellow belt, then an orange and one day, a black belt, the highest grade of all.

She took a folded sheet of paper from her copybook and slowly, ceremoniously, opened it, spread it on both their laps, for the revelation. It was a drawing of herself and Fidelma, their arms outstretched, their ears sticking out like a donkey's, gawky legs in high-heeled red shoes and underneath, in bold capitals, the letters of her name, each letter separate from the neighbouring one, with thick purple shading in between –

My name – M I S T L E T O E.

'Mistletoe . . . that's a lovely name . . .'

'I had a different name when I was born. I was called Mary. I was in the hospital in Fulham. I didn't know anything. I didn't know who all the people were, but I knew that I was with my mummy, she was in a bed near me and I was in a cot. Then they brought me home, here, and we all sat on the sofa together, all of us, me in my cot and my mummy and daddy on either side. My mummy is wearing a big floppy jumper and I'm pulling it and she lifts me up and swaddles me, swaddles me tight, because that calms a baby down. My mummy is in America now, so my auntie swaddles me instead.'

'So you miss your mummy . . . ?'

'I am forbidden to say.'

These encounters, often in the freezing cold, were what Fidelma lived for. It softened the stone in her heart. In there, squeezed together, Mistletoe feeling her hair, twirling it, making ringlets, then running her finger over face and neck, supposedly for imperfections, but really in fondness. This now was the fulcrum of her life, gave purpose to it and cancelled out the grinding monotony of the job, Medusa's tempers and the oceans of dust that rose to meet her each evening when she clocked in.

*

She received constant reprimands, some by letter and some spoken. The superintendent, who was English and whom Fidelma had not seen before, told her that there had been complaints from members of the staff. She talked too much at the breaks. She did not do her work properly, there was limescale on a lavatory bowl and the glass door of the chairman's private shower had the pink smear of Windolene. Worst of all, there was a puddle next to his desk. Then things began to go missing, J-cloths, sponges, her rubber gloves. She knew it was foul play, but she endured everything, so as to cling onto this job. She forgot to eat, she forgot to pray, she forgot the seasons, although once, snowdrops appeared in her mind and she reckoned that she must have sighted clumps of them, under trees in the park, milk-white, with their mantles of drooping green.

In her sleep, she ran dusters around lintels, door jambs, mouldings, she knelt by the legs of chairs to make sure there were no foul-smelling puddles and she wakened choking from dust.

Each morning before leaving work, she would shake the dusters into the belly of the vacuum and then wash them and hang them to dry in her corner of the store room, hoping they would not go missing, except that they did. First one. Then more. The same with the products in her basket. Her Mr Muscle, her Toilet Duck, her bleach, her Vim. She knew it was Medusa.

It was Maria's idea to write a candid letter to the supervisor and request an appointment. His name was Herman and he was from Ivory Coast. He sat very erect, behind a large desk in his tiny office, his lips open to show a good set of teeth and his tongue the bright pink of trifle. His desk was strewn with motorcycle manuals and newsletters and there were two photographs of him astride two different motorcycles, one in a street in London and the other in a street in Paris.

At once, she detected the bristle. He did not like what she had to say. Why hadn't she sorted these thefts out with Medusa?

'But she is the one –' she said.

'Are you implying . . .' he cut in sharply.

'I saw my yellow rubber gloves in her locker.'

'So you broke into her locker.'

'No . . . she opened it to fetch something out.'

'This is a very serious accusation. Have you proof? Please answer yes or no.'

'No . . . I just sense it . . .'

'You just sense it . . . in here shooting your mouth off . . . Let me tell you, Medusa is a good person, a churchgoing person and we value her contribution on the team . . . Why would she want your dusters, since she has plenty of her own?'

'Human nature . . . malice,' she said and no sooner had she said the word than she realised her mistake.

'You have made the whole thing up,' he said with scorn.

'Why would I make the whole thing up?'

'Perhaps you are a racist.' And at that he ran his forefinger down the letter Maria had helped her to write, muttering the odd word, *Mr Muscle, Duck, Vim* and when he had read to his satisfaction, he tore it lengthwise, the sound so shearing, and dropped the pieces into the waste basket.

The Waiting Room

You will have to wait, Fidelma is told. The waiting area is in the reception room, along to the left.

'I would rather wait here,' she says, but to no avail. The young woman behind the desk is testy and three phones are ringing at the same moment. She picks up one for either ear and with a cursory nod, points Fidelma to the reception area.

She had worked for five and a half weeks, but when she arrived at the staff entrance, her pass card did not allow her through. She tried several times and then asked one of the security guards, who also tried and failed. She knew he could let her through, but he said he would rather not and it was better that she speak to someone at the reception desk. She asked the receptionist to ring Bluey, which she did, but it was obvious by her frustration that he could not be reached. He must be floating about from floor to floor. The message was being passed on.

The reception room was large, with several armchairs and on a table English and international newspapers neatly laid out. Everything so clean and so hushed. The deep armchairs faced one another, but she chose one opposite the television, on which there was a programme entitled *Money Markers – On the Move*. The screen was the largest she had ever seen. Several images of the American flag hung over the White House and suddenly the steps leading up to it were no longer actual steps, but stairways submerged in pools of water. It was both real and unreal.

Limousines were moving at a dizzying speed, helicopters flew overhead, joints of rare meat were being carved, as businessmen in identical suits, white shirts and ties arrived for a conference. Then the image shifted to different countries, and always alongside the native flag, the American flag hung in solidarity.

Quite soon it was issues of equity and yield, the level of fundraising in capital cities, the mortgage credit score and the action being taken for world rates to remain the same. Apple would soon open a store in Brazil and in Puerto Rico, life was on the brink. Then a long queue of people at an airport, which she assumed to be Puerto Rico, waiting like lost pilgrims, their fates foreknown.

All of a sudden she jumped, finding that she was not alone in that room. A man, unnaturally still, sat at one of the computers that were on a raised platform and it occurred to her that he might be dead. The plants in a long container looked dead, they were green and needly, but with no life in them. Only then for the first time did she look around, walls marbled and one wall dominated by a huge abstract painting in deep red, with red foetuses moving within it. Any minute, Bluey would come, tapping her on the shoulder, saying *What's the story, what's the story?*

She hears footsteps, gets up, but it turns out to be a young woman in stiletto heels, who looks around anxiously, then drags a chair to face the entrance, and consults her phone, which she lays on her lap.

On the screen, for the commercial break, African women in huge headdresses and ceremonial dresses, not unlike Jasmeen's, are walking onto podiums, where they are greeted effusively. The programme that follows is entitled *Women to Watch in African Business*. The whole world is in that room and yet there is no one in it, it is lifeless, it is lonely, it is empty, save for the fidgety woman, the seemingly dead man and the machines. She wants to go to the desk and ask if Bluey has been located, but is afraid to annoy the receptionist, who has already shown her displeasure. Instead, she goes to the hospitality niche to get water and it is then she flips. Everything in that cooler is a vapourish blue, the bottles, the bottle caps, the vapour itself, the water, and as she reaches her hand becomes soft and pliable as putty.

Luckily there is a different woman at the desk. She is matronly with grey hair tied in a bun and listens attentively, then tries one extension after another, until she is actually speaking to someone. She listens, frowns, listens further, puts the phone down carefully and says, 'I am sorry love . . . but Bluey is gone for the day.'

'But I was waiting in there . . . for nearly an hour,' Fidelma says and sensing her anguish, the woman asks her name, looks at her ID and decides that they will try Lukas. She comes off the phone, crestfallen, because Lukas has said he cannot do anything, suggesting that they try Bluey on his cell phone. It is turned off. Callers are told to please try later and not to leave a message.

It had been raining when she arrived, but now, as she re-emerges, it is deluge. London is like black night and the figures moving through it drenched and scowling, herded into one another. It happens to be the day of a tube strike, but crowds have gathered outside the tube station, because it was rumoured that some drivers had refused to strike. She stands with others before the locked gates and then, like them, reconciles herself to walking.

On the Embankment it is a tussle just to get through, figures drenched and half-blinded, bumping into one another. Cars, buses and cyclists all on a collision course, fighting for their footing and the tour buses, coming in twos and threes, send lashings of water in all directions, so that pedestrians are even more wrathful, their patience spent, in their urgency to get to where they belong or half belong. Belligerence peaks by a pedestrian crossing, as the lights do not allow enough time to wade through and people vent their rage by wielding their umbrellas and thumping on the windscreens of the halted taxis.

In the foggy wet, the lit signs of red and blue above offices on the opposite side are not nearly so imposing, nor are the white pleasure boats and the gangplanks leading up to them, water slurping against them, in and out it comes, in hopeless, hungry gurglings. In the various kiosks that she passes, the garish souvenirs look sodden and tawdry and a canvas chair left outside sags with water. In the distance, the hanging cradles from the London Eye do not sway by even a fraction.

The whole moneyed might of the city is at a standstill.

The chapel was set alongside a school, in a street of otherwise unassuming houses, somewhere in Chelsea. It was not palatial, like the one near Westminster, where she had once prayed. The holy water was in a little glass dish, laid into a large circular stone font and the smell that greeted her was of warm wax, that familiar smell from Cloonoila, in chapel, after Mass or benediction. A little woman with one wellington boot and the other foot bare whispered that the chapel was just closing, but then took one look at her and said, 'Come in . . . you craytur.' This was Grainne and her job was to lock up for the night. She was caretaker, did the altars, the candles and also had the thankless job of scraping the wax from the sconces. The priests were very nice to her, gave her things. To prove it, she took out a holy picture with the prone figure of the Lord and a caption that read, 'O Croix – Hail Cross.' '*O Croix*,' she whispers, proud of her French pronunciation. Yes, it was a very nice area and low on crime and guess what – in a bookshop not far from there, hangin' on a wall, was Dirk Bogarde's kitchen clock. *Cross my heart, Dirk Bogarde's clock*. Dirk was a friend of the owners and a good customer. *Put that in your pipe and smoke it*. She could see that Fidelma, apart from being drenched, was in a state, so there was nothing for it but to storm heaven. They knelt in one of the pews halfway up, the church almost in darkness, except for the pale gleam of two sacristy lamps that hung on long chains, a red light for the Sacred Heart and a blue light for Our Lady. Grainne did the praying. It was loud and it was generalised, asking that they be kept safe from assault and would never go hungry and beseeching God, up there in his golden parlour, to reserve a place for them.

'There's a lot of Irish, knocking around London . . . so you're not on your ownio,' she said then, as she drew on the second wellington and embraced Fidelma fiercely, before parting.

*

Jasmeen called out, the moment she heard Fidelma's key in the door and then she appeared, wearing a kaftan over her working clothes. The table was already laid in the kitchen, a red cloth and place settings for three with mitre-shaped napkins in glasses. There was music playing and it seemed to Fidelma that it came from her room.

'Hi there,' a voice said. It was a young girl that she guessed must be Jade, who had moved out some time ago and shared a flat with friends in east London. She was like a moonlight creature, all black and silver, her eyelashes thickly crusted with black and an array of silver bracelets up along her forearm. When they shook hands, she said Mum had been telling her about the heart-to-hearts that they had on the Saturday nights and those wicked glasses of cava.

'I can bring a duvet into the hall,' Fidelma said, but Jade would not hear of it, the bed was plenty big for two and they would be like babes in the wood. She needed sleep, having just got back from Ibiza, where she had spent four amazing days with her boyfriend and friends, raving on the beach until sunrise and then chill-out swims. As a surprise, she had brought a takeaway, yummy things, spicy cashew chilli stir fry, sesame prawn toast, butterfly tigers, sweet-and-sour chicken, crispy duck, egg fried rice and Jude's Very Vanilla ice cream. The wine was already open and she poured liberally into the glasses.

At dinner, she did most of the talking and there was something frantic about her, wildly gesturing, barely touching her food, on edge, waiting for that phone to ring. She had been up for a modelling job, a singing job, an acting job and one of them had to come through.

'But she's famous in Africa,' her mother said proudly, describing how Jade's face was in more than one African country, advertising a cream.

'A skin product Mummy,' Jade corrected her and then made kiss-kiss noises. Jasmeen asked her then to tell Fidelma about the nightclub where she worked as a hostess and Jade drew pictures of a club in the East End that looked grotty from the outside, cool inside, carpets for the celebs, bouncers with crew cuts, the security men who came early to suss out the joint and then the celebs themselves and their hangers-on, all in dark glasses, like a fleet of funeral undertakers. Then there were the beautiful girls, especially the beautiful Russian girls, who always came with the richest men and sometimes the catfights if their men so much as looked at another woman. Now and then she was sent over champagne, but as it was not allowed, Huey, an old man who took coats, hid the glasses in a cupboard and in the mornings, before she cycled home to her pad, herself and Huey had a few swigs. Huey was her best friend there. He had come down in the world. He had been married several times, including once to a lady-in-waiting to the Queen and he could enter the palace by one of the side doors in the yard. That wife was gentle, never raised her voice and was always embroidering. Three other wives were vultures, only in it for the lolly. He saw his son occasionally, during school holidays, but he was never able to bring him to his lodgings for a night, as she felt it was beneath them. Bizarre things happened in that club – all night men and women trooping to the lavatories for their lines of cocaine and coming out giggling.

'You promised,' Jasmeen said, suddenly distraught.

'I promise,' Jade said and jumped up and hugged her mother, quoting from the psalm they both knew – 'Rebuke me not in thine anger, neither chasten me in thy hot displeasure.'

In the bedroom Jade was opening drawers that Fidelma had not dared touch, pulling things out, jeans, scarves, her lucky spider scarab, her Pout Box, her lipstick palette, lip liners, glosses, strewing them about and then, without even thinking, she began to make up a face that was already painted. She put on an ermine bolero that she found, ran it down her cheeks, caressing it. Suddenly she is talking, arguing, expostulating, a whirling dervish of contradictions. Her dream was to be an actress. She had played Portia, wife of Brutus, in a school play and audiences were blown away. Night after night, her emotions brimming – 'Is my place only on the outskirts of your happiness?' – and then she broke down.

She sat on the bed, like a little girl, hugging herself in the ermine bolero. 'Shit . . . Rat . . .' and it all came out in a tumble and how she couldn't tell Mum, but something awful had happened and she would never see Ronnie again.

'Get this,' she said and described only a few hours previous, walking up to a theatre, where she was to meet him, to go to a show with friends and his coming down the street towards her. What's wrong? He wouldn't say. He couldn't say. Eventually he did and it was horrid. When he got to the ticket desk, there had been a mistake and there were only five tickets on the booking sheet, with not a chance of a sixth, as there was a big queue, people waiting for returns. He couldn't do it to his friends, couldn't let them down, especially as they were going back to Cornwall and the Isle of Wight the next morning and poor Muggins would understand. Understand! Fidelma heard then how she called him every name under the sun, and he just turned around and walked off, and she went the other way, towards Seven Dials and sat on the steps howling, people looking at her, phoning him twice, except his phone was turned off, and eventually calling in sick at the club, and doing her face in a pub loo, so as to come home to Mummy, all sparkly, not cry on her shoulder, just to be home. It was over. No it wasn't. They were soulmates. She wouldn't see him again, ever. There was a gig in Hackney at the weekend and she would go with friends and sit at a table and completely snub him.

They sat side by side on the bed then and Fidelma tried to

calm her, telling her, without actually believing it, that it would all be all right.

'I know he loves me,' Jade kept saying.

'Of course he loves you,' Fidelma said and then Jade did something sudden and profound. She pulled off her wig and was barely recognisable, her hair straight and lank, her prowess summarily gone. She cried from the depths of her heart – 'I am a child of Africa . . . A child of Africa . . . that is who I am.'

Mistletoe's Father

It was almost quiet, but of course never a total silence in that apartment block, with over thirty families, small children and always a dog yapping, including dogs from neighbourhoods way beyond answering at a different pitch.

Fidelma was in her room. In the adjoining room, Jasmeen would be praying, as she did each night before the altar she had fitted up and decorated with candles, incense sticks and eucalyptus leaves. Each week the leaves were changed.

The knocking on their door was thunderous.

It was Mistletoe's father, a stocky man with shaven head, in overalls and short-sleeved vest, Mistletoe standing behind him.

'It is not right . . . it is forbidden' are his first words, which he repeats, in a more admonitory tone.

'What is not right . . . what is forbidden?' Jasmeen asks. Fidelma guesses that it is to do with their little ceremonies in the garden.

'My child is being brainwashed,' and to prove it, he snaps open a pink suitcase that he has been carrying.

'You see, you see,' he says and shows a cardigan, two pairs of tights, dresses, pyjamas, Greenie, a small bar of soap and an apple, all the necessities for a journey.

The two of them are drawn in purple crayon, voyagers setting out for distant places. Underneath she has written:

Mistletoe and Fidelma on a rickshaw

Mistletoe and Fidelma join a circus

Mistletoe and Fidelma help with the harvest

There is also a drawing of a roaring lion, a gaily dressed harlequin on a tightrope, and a clown with tears running down his cheeks. This episode concludes with Mistletoe and Fidelma on their way to China and the scenery replete with pagodas and palm trees.

'It's a game . . . that's all,' Fidelma says.

'A game!' He exploded at the word. Either they were conspiring to go away, which was a criminal offence, or they were not and so the child's expectations were shredded. Shredded. He liked the authority of that word.

'She is trying to kidnap my child,' he said pointing to Fidelma, and the word was too much, too extreme altogether for Mistletoe, who throughout had been inching her way from behind his back. She stands before them now, her eyes feverish with excitement. Soon she is making faces, orchestrating her annoyance with her forefinger, and prodding his back with short, perfunctory stabs.

'She's alone all day . . . not at school . . . so she invents things,' and as she says it, Fidelma sees the utter and naked panic in the man's frame. So this is the nub of it. His whole life with his child is one of fear, hiding from authority, hiding from the law, hiding from the police, on the very brink of disaster. He thinks that she is plotting with Mistletoe's mother. It is useless to tell him that she doesn't know Mistletoe's mother. It is useless to say that she meant no harm, because for all his shouting, he is the one on trial.

'This will have consequences,' he says and stops suddenly, as if he cannot remember what these consequences are.

'It won't happen again,' Fidelma says. She would like to say more, she would like to invite them in, but she can't. The tension that this intrusion has caused is incalculable.

'I think it's time we all got some sleep,' Jasmeen says tartly and the father looks for Mistletoe's hand, but she wriggles out of it.

The sight of them going the short bit of corridor, the father limping, the child maintaining her distance, was strangely pathetic.

At the very last moment, Mistletoe turned and waved. It was a wan wave, identical to when they first met, a wave bringing the curtain down on their world of make-believe.

'He moved in here three and a half years ago and we never exchanged a word . . . now this . . . this,' Jasmeen says and though barefoot, she kicks as she walks, kicking anything that will get in her way.

The Centre

It was a cul de sac, under the flyover, with the constant thump-thump of traffic overhead. It was poorly lit, with dilapidated buildings on one side and on the other, a wall cutting off a main road. That wall was a symbol of protest, inch upon inch covered with graffiti, in red, blue, white, yellow, purple, indigo, magenta, terracotta, a tableau of screaming indignations. A few idlers stood by or crouched, not asking, not seeking, not threatening, not begging, just standing there, as if by some sovereign edict they would be picked up and absorbed into the throbbing heart of the city.

Fidelma worried that Maria might have already gone in. It was called the Centre and people from all over came in search of advice, then once a fortnight they gathered to share the stories of their fractured lives.

When Maria did arrive with her friend Lupa, there was no time for chat, so they hurried in up the stone stairs, to the little room. It is almost full. They are there because they have nowhere else to go. Nobodies, mere numbers on paper or computer, the hunted, the haunted, the raped, the defeated, the mutilated, the banished, the flotsam of the world, unable to go home, wherever home is. They sit wherever they can, on milk stools or kitchen chairs, or saddish cushions, that have been donated. Many have to stand. Fidelma is by a small table, with an image of a mandala made from fresh coffee beans and the smell is pleasing.

Varya, who runs the office, welcomes them, calling some by their names. She is a tall, well-built woman, her short hair streaked with different, vibrant colours, her eyes a soft, dark honeyed hue and her arms always open to the world. She runs a charity centre in the adjoining offices and like everyone else in that room, she is a refugee, but as she keeps reminding them, she is a survivor and it is the duty of survivors to help others. She lived through the siege of Sarajevo, as did her elderly mother, with all the fear, hunger and privation that it entailed, yet as she says with a certain irony, there was a time when Sarajevo was thought to be the biggest issue in the world, but that time was no more. She has provided this refuge, to give them a haven, where they can come at any hour of the day and sit and brood and admit to their homesickness. Thursdays she encourages stories, so that they all know at least something of one another, such as who has children and who has had to leave children behind in a far land, who is legal and who is not. She well knows that in telling their story, some say the exact opposite to what they feel, some lie, some clam up, but by just being there, she believes that gradually some small shift may happen inside, that they may feel that little bit less alone.

Last week it was Maria's turn and this week Lupa is invited to speak. As was true for Maria, she admits to the especial music of the tango, in her head and in her soul. She is from Argentina and though still in her thirties she is a grandmother, which is the story she tells, how it came about and the responsibilities that it brought. She has to hold down two jobs, one in a municipal garden and some nights in a mortuary. Her daughter Isabella, as she tells it, not yet fifteen, was brought to a party by some friends she had just met. 'There, she dance with a young man who tell her he loves her and she goes with him that night. She returns to school as usual, and after three months she know she miss her period, but think it normal, until it go five months and then she know for sure. Her friends no want to help her. I go to the headmistress and she say, "Keep it secret, do not give bad example." I go to the house where the party was and they say there were lots of people, including many strangers, at that party and they close the door in my face. They do not believe she was raped. They say she is a liar. They say I am a liar for her. I kneel down and talk through the letterbox, I plead, I say my daughter was raped and I ask them to have a little compassion, but the woman inside repeat that we are liars and that if I go to police it will bring trouble for everyone, because so many are illegal. My daughter, she stop school after seven months. She do not want her friends to jeer at her. At times she hit her head again and again on the wall and scream and say *Why, why me?* and then she say she want to die. She also say if it a boy she will kill it. She will smother it with a pillow. Her time come and I am with her in the hospital and I am allowed to watch and I look and I hold my breath as I see it come out. It is a little girl and I say she cannot kill it now and we bring it home, our second Isabella. My daughter she sometime love it, sometime not, spending too much time in depression, living too much alone, won't go to park or museum, won't get out of bed. But because there is a baby, judge give me extension for one year on my visa and please Gods my daughter will come to love her child once it starts to walk and to talk and engage with her.'

After Lupa had finished and as always with each story, there was a silence, out of respect of what had been said.

Then it was Nahir's turn, but he was reluctant. He began by

laughing. He was shortish, his hair in a crew cut and his eyes hooded behind heavy, sallow lids. There was something unnerving about his hesitancy, as if he might just break out of this abnormal calm and erupt. Varya introduced him, said that like her he was from Bosnia, though from a different part, and how he had been taken to what in official language was a reception centre, but was in fact a killing factory. The several killing factories had innocuous names – the Red Room, the White Room, the Hangar and so on, the very names belying the butchery that went on. Upon hearing mention of Bosnia, Fidelma froze and wanted to leave, but something, perhaps her own timidity, kept her there.

Quietly, he began – 'I say war is a lottery . . . count your lucky stars that you are here . . . I used to be very serious, now I read old cowboy books. A lot of laughing for no reason. If people throw stones at me, I don't throw stones back, I laugh. I follow the football of my own country, even though I no longer live there. I live in Dagenham and my girlfriend she live in Oxford and we meet once a month.'

'Tell what happened,' Varya says gently and at her bidding he stands, unsure, as if asking either to be pitied or pilloried.

'One morning at dawn the soldiers come and break down all the doors in the street one by one. My brother and I are both called. Our mother run from the bedroom and walk with us as far as the little gate. You will come back, you will come back. *Da* I said for both of us, meaning yes, yes. She give my brother the key of the house, because she know that she too will be taken, the whole village will be cleansed. The last thing I see before they put on the blindfold is the grey mist in the forest, shrouding the trees and I wonder if I will ever see that mist and those trees again. But I did. I am one of the lucky ones, though maybe death is luckier. From the bus we are put on boxcars on a train, we know it is a train because of the sound of the whistle and we are brought to camp, my brother in one house and me in another. Many bodies packed in there on top of each other, one toilet for hundreds and all the time shouting, guards shouting and people being beaten, begging until they had no breath. Our interrogators are people I know before war began. The torturers are people I know before the war began. A sad thought occurred to me one day. Had that urge to torture and to kill been there all along, even when we were friends. My brother tries to get me to talk about it, but I can't. I tell him I feel nothing, no pain, no hurt, no revenge, deep in a limbo of my own. He is filled with hatred. He sees I have no hatred and he can't forgive me that. He tells me to try and remember it or at least to imagine it, the cries, the boy from our village beaten senseless with "*Pusti me da živim*": "Let me live", played loud over and over again and I tell him that all I can imagine is my head breaking apart inside and there is no room for memory. He says I surely remember the sweeping up, bits of bodies, tufts of hair, bloodied T-shirts and he is about to strike me for not remembering and I say don't strike me, I am not ready to remember and maybe I never will be.

'I got out sooner than he. One night a guard, who was our language teacher in school, pulled me out and brought me to a boiler room. He had a knife. I think he going to kill me. Instead, he give me the knife and he say go go go. He maybe do it because that day we saw him kill someone, like a pig. We watched it and lived through it and maybe he had pang of conscience or else he was drunk, but anyhow, he let me go. A woman who lived nearby and who delivered their grog took me in. She hated the soldiers. The daughters all around were repeatedly raped, but would not talk about it, because guards threatened them that if they told worse things would happen, their homes would be torched. Their parents would be slaughtered. From there I eventually got to a camp run by the Red Cross and after seventeen months I was released on condition that I would not return to Bosnia. I think I have breakdown in some centre in Holland. I laugh a lot and talk to trees. My brother did not get out till much later and was eventually swapped in an exchange of prisoners. He went back to where we once lived, because he had the key, he never lost it. There is nothing of our house, only a burnt shell and the stumps of the fruit trees, in a blackened landscape. He say his heart is blackened also, but purified by going back. He say it is essential to remember and that nothing must be forgotten. I say the opposite. Slowly, painfully, he start to build a new house where our house stood. It is for me to return. He also have hives and honey bees. I go home because he want me to. The honey is thick and tastes of blossom. He say we walk in the forest to reconnect. He ask what I remember night after night in that room of madness. I say I remember the magic of the rivers, especially in the spring, in the thaw, when the torrent come down the mountain and he go mad with me and say I have no feeling, I am behaving as if I had nothing to do with it and I say to him he is tracing spectres. We cannot connect. He takes the key that he wears around his neck and keeps saying "The key, the key," as if that should unite us. I tell him that I want to be a good person, I want not to hate. Forgive me, but as you see I am a man of few words.' Suddenly he ceased talking and Varya thanked him. Nobody spoke.

Then to lessen the awkwardness and the strained silence, she asked him if he were to get a gift what would it be and he said a saucepan, a cast-iron saucepan that he could clean properly and not a Teflon one. There was laughter at the idea of a saucepan! Suni, who was next to him, put her hand up and said a turkey baster, yes, definitely a turkey baster, as Christmas was not that far away and she and Mildred were an item now and yet again, she told how it happened, like lightning, on a tennis court, Mildred kissed her, said, 'Get real Suni,' and that was it, even though before that she'd had boyfriends. Yes, definitely a turkey baster. Allissos wished for a gift token for a nail parlour and her nails to be painted a metallic violet. Also that she could see the lights in Trafalgar Square on New Year's Eve.

Varya then announced that the theme for the latter part of the evening was 'Mother', because Allissos's mother had died the week previous. They knew already a little of Allissos's life, in a house in Acton, with seventeen others, all waiting for a letter from the Home Office, all standing in the hallway each day waiting for that letter from the Home Office. Then one day a lady accused her of stealing her letter that had the permission in it and she said no, but no matter how she said no, the woman harangued and followed her up the stairs still accusing her. They knew that she rarely ate in the kitchen, bringing her rice to her bedroom three times a day, either with or without sauce, and that she listened to the phone-in on LBC and talked back to it, asking when she would hear from the Home Office and be allowed to stay. Allissos crouched down, all abashed, but Varya pleaded with her to stand up, saying her story would be a gift to all the others. She was a slender girl, with long black glossy hair, which she stroked all the time as if it were a friend and she grew in confidence as her story went on.

'I was about thirteen and I hated my hair, so a friend recommended a chemical to relax it. I went into the bathroom and locked the door. Very soon my hair went green and came off in my hand in tufts. I ran and told my mother that I had lost all my hair. "Serves you right," and she slapped me hard on both cheeks. She was in a bad mood. I always felt she did not want me. It's the culture. They only want sons who will grow up to be big and strong and bring food. I was not glad in my own house and it was worse when my mother and father broke up. I had arguments with my mother every day. My father went to another woman in a different village and I would run away from my mother and go to him, but his new wife did not want me. He would send me home and tell me to accept my mother as she was, as I would never succeed in changing her. At sixteen, an aunt made an offer to take me to France and I lived in the countryside where there are vineyards and I learnt to press grapes. I am there for four years. Then a cousin invites me to England, she says it is better if I come to England, as there are more opportunities and English is the first language all around the world. My cousin lives outside London. She meets me off the train. She has a room that is also a bedroom and she makes me very welcome. She opens a bottle of wine and I never drink wine before. She starts to tell me that she and her boyfriend are not happy. She has met an Italian and is moving to Rimini to be with him, but I am to stay. I say I do not want to be in the same room as her boyfriend. She swear he will leave me alone, he has lots of girlfriends, oodles. That first evening he is polite and gives me fish fingers for dinner. My cousin has already left. When it is time for bed I say I will sleep on the floor, he scoffs. I take a pillow and a big towel from the bathroom and lie down. He walks around naked and he cannot understand why I won't get into bed with him. He says it is thanks to him I have a roof over my head and that I owe him everything. As the week goes by he gets nastier. There is only one key to that house that he takes with him to work, so I cannot go out for a walk. I go to church one Sunday when he is sleeping and I come back and he is all dressed up like a peacock in a blue shirt and red shoes. Very late that night he comes home drunk and he falls onto the bed, shoes and all. Next evening, I ask can I go for a walk, as it is summer and very hot in that room. I go down one long street and then a side street and pass an allotment where girls are picking berries from bushes. I stay looking at them for a while. They ask me if I want to join them. When I come back he will not answer the bell. He calls out through the window and says my clothes are in the wheelie bin by the gate. I go back to the church where I had been on Sundays and a woman takes me home and next day she rings various agencies and in time I am given a room in the house in Acton. It is three years now since I start to claim asylum. The asylum has been refused, but I appeal and with a solicitor we go to the immigration office every six months to re-claim. All those years I think of my mama and how I would like to make up with her, but when I ring she is screaming at me and telling me I have no nature and to stay away from her. I send her a small gift of a powder compact. I get a part-time job in a hotel when they have functions and need extra staff. The functions are in a ballroom, with ladies all dressed up, wearing masses of jewellery and in low-cut dresses. Talking loudly. I know it is illegal to work there, but I need money to phone Senegal. Each day, like the others, I wait for the decision. Then four nights ago very late I am asleep and my phone rings and I grab it. It is my father and he is distressed. Since my mother got sick he is a lot at her house, feels sorry for her. Except I didn't know she was sick. When he told me she had trouble breathing the line went dead. My phone had run out of credit. I had to wait until morning to go to the shop to get a new card. I call my dad and he is crying now. It is very noisy in the background, as there are a lot of people in the house and my mother has died and is in the bed, where they have put flowers around her hair. I can picture it, her thin face, her eyes shut, the fresh flowers falling onto the pillow. It is awful to be told this on the phone. I want to be there to say goodbye to my mama and at that moment I realise that the thing I want most in this world is for her not to be dead and for her to forgive me. I want that even more than asylum. My father says a few more words and then I am alone in the room and I know I will never stop wanting my mother to forgive me.'

Suni is indignant. She makes it known with sudden and abrupt movements of arms, wrists and fingers. She goes ballistic, asking why they have to listen to this crap when they are there to talk politics and not somebody's mother. Varya interrupts and very gently points out that everything in this world is political. The bread you eat, the water you drink, the mattress you lie down on, war or peace, everything at root is political. She said it was insensitive to upbraid Allissos, and to remember the primal connection between mother and child, no matter who you are. Many in the group applauded, including Nahir.

Oghowen is already standing and eager to tell her story, which she has rehearsed on the bus. She is a largish woman in a short-sleeved blue calico dress, even though winter had come and the clocks changed the previous Sunday. She begins by praising God, *God is in control*, then starts her story.

'My name is Oghowen, it means Only One. I bring trouble

into my mother's life. She did not want to be pregnant and so she went to the native doctor and was given medicines. The baby is born premature and dies after a few days. Then one week later, my mother is on the road and she starts to feel pain and contractions and she bleed. She was pregnant with twins, but the native doctor did not see that. She go into the bush where I am born. She wish I were a boy. Girls are disposable. I am the person she persecute from the very start. She take me to the witch doctor who heat a clay pot with different stuffs to rub all over my body. Then with the razor she make slits for the devil to get out and they all cheer and say, "You won't be one of the bad ones anymore." But my mother she still pick on me, all the time. She and two aunts bring me one night to a hut in the bush. They tell me, "You are going to be circumcised," and I ask why. An aunt say it is tradition and another say it is to stop me flirting or allow boys to play with me. My mother she say it is for me to be clean and not have dirty feelings for boys. There is another girl waiting there and she is holding a knitted doll and she is squeezing it, squeezing it. She is called in before me. I hear her screaming, maybe thirty, maybe forty minutes, maybe more. I am brought in and told to lie on the floor. It is a clay floor. I dig my fingers into the clay because I have nothing to hold onto. The room smell of Dettol and I see razors and a small scissors on the table and I know. One ask if I want a rag over my head but I say no, I want to see. Even then I know God's plan for me is to live my life with my eyes open. God is in control. Then she hold my legs apart, a second woman lift my arms and I begin to shake uncontrollably. They tell me not to shake, otherwise there will be a mistake and everything will be worse. The nurse, she begin to cut the clitoris and I scream and roar like an animal. My mother, she tell them how stubborn I am. I roar until there no more roaring and afterwards they stand me up and I am bleeding. I am told to wash with warm water and salt for seven days and then I am to come back to take the threads out.

'At sixteen or so a cousin invite me to England and I live with them and I am much happier. They are all church members. At home we read the psalms and the holy books that do inspire. On Sundays we go to church and sing God's praises and afterwards we have coffee or tea in the church grounds and we mingle with other people. After two years I meet a young man from my own country. He relocated from Holland and had temporary visa because he worked there. He court me, walking and sitting in parks and we make plans. We have beautiful wedding and the pastor allow us to have the celebration on the church lawn. He say we are the best churchgoers of all and we are tireless helping others. When I conceived I knew it would be a girl and it was. She looked at me with tender eyes from the very start. She exceptional. She helps. She tidies. At school she tell bold girls to be polite to teacher and not answer back. We make sponge cake for teacher at the weekend. She knows everything. If I cry she knows why I am crying. It is so we won't be sent back, because if we are, they will do the same things to my daughter that they did to me. I don't know where in the world my mother is, but if we go back she will find us. I am afraid for what will happen. God knows my pain and God is in control. He tells me to be there for other people and I am and it helps me a lot. Very much thanks,' she said when she had concluded, her bare brown arms outstretched in clemency.

Then it was Fidelma's turn. She was bewildered. She thought she would recount some dream or nightmare that might hint obliquely at her history, but no dream or nightmare came to her.

Hearing the word 'Sarajevo' had brought it all back. He had materialised before her, the very same as when he had walked up their main street, his voice so quiet and weighty and that last bitter rebuking, the morning he saw the graffiti, the obscenity that was a prelude to all that came after.

She searched for the words and began, her voice strained and unnatural –

'It rains quite a lot in Ireland, hence the cliché the Emerald Isle, green fields and moss on walls and tombstones. Many things have changed for the better, more so in the cities; in the countryside there is still a lot of prejudice and they crave scandal as if it were nectar. I ruined things for my husband and for our reputation, by being faithless. It turned out that a new man came amongst us in the guise of a prophet, but he had done appalling things, had ordered and orchestrated thousands of deaths, in his own blighted land. I feel that by having been with him I am an accomplice to those appalling things. I feel a guilt that is, if you like, counterfeit guilt and so I stand accused. On my last morning, I stood on a hillock outside the convent, where I had been given shelter after my downfall, and spoke to the landscape itself, saying I wanted to cleanse my house, my soul, myself. There is a poem, a beautiful poem by Emily Dickinson that says "When it comes, the landscape listens – Shadows – hold their breath – When it goes, 'tis like the distance on the look of death."

Suddenly she stopped, knowing that it was not truthful, that it was too inconclusive, too lofty, and as they shuffled out, Maria waved to her in dismay. Varya had signalled to her to stay behind.

*

How long have they been there? A leaden silence had settled over the place and the person whose turn it was to do the cleaning had left and they had heard a door shut as she went out. Fidelma has come back to the room, herself again, the self that she wears for the world. She has been sitting and talking for some time. It is Varya's private office, with Varya in her swivel chair and Fidelma also in a comfortable chair and she is holding a glass, but she does not remember it being handed to her. She sees the coloured drawing of the South African flower and the various newspaper clippings about refugees, human rights and asylum seekers. Every iota of her being is poured into her telling. She knew the man Varya spoke of, the man who had derided the deaths of those queuing for bread in the market place, saying that it was a stunt and the dead and wounded were those of mannequins and corpses from wars long past. That man was her lover. How ugly the word sounds now, how incongruous their coupling. She tells it in fits and starts. How he came on a winter night and the word spread like wildfire, that a healer had come among them. She fell for him, a little at first, more like a schoolgirl crush, then deeper, then the full fall. After that, she contrived to meet him, left notes, a runic stone and often cheese straws that she made herself. Later they went away together and in time she got pregnant as she had wanted to and he diagnosed it by waving the glass pendulum that he wore on a long cord around his neck and that he used for psychic predictions, placing his hand down the length of her naked body and saying, 'Yes, a nice little Serb boy or girl is planted there.' It was in his consulting room during lunch hour, when there were no patients around. Then rumours, the graffiti, his disappearance, his fleeting return, the capture on the bus and the full screed of his history, unfolding on television. Then the three brutes. Their smells, their sunglasses, one mended with Sellotape, the hut with the clay floor and nothing to hold onto, when it happened. When it happened. Belting music and her screams. Each thrust of the crowbar like it could get no worse, except it got worse and worse and the screams went out of her, fighting for her life with the last funnels of breath, while also wanting to be dead. Then the three men going and the silence soon broken by the scurry of the rats.

'It is as though they have never taken the crowbar out,' she said and looked for the first time into the eyes of the woman, soft, befriending and with immeasurable hurt.

'I hate him, I want to inflict every punishment on him, including taking his voice, his voice box out, and strangling it syllable by syllable. I want the three men pulped, I hate myself and my own body, I think only violence will end the violence. This hate fills my heart, my soul and my being. When I menstruate I want to wipe my face in it, to add to the defilement. You see, I have lost all connection between what is natural and what is unnatural. I hear the stories of the other women in that room, fates far harder than mine, excruciating, and I am moved, but I am not moved enough to stamp out the hate that is strangling me.'

She looked at Varya, shook her head and looked away. It was late. A train was still running and in that ghastly light, the carriages were a bleached white, like a convoy of hearses, following one upon another to a doomed destination.

Kennels

Fidelma has met Violet and Elvis and Beth and Toby and Cher and Holly and Pearl and Benjy. She has seen them not in darkness but in the sombre light of the kennels, as the only window is in the outer hall and elsewhere it is gloomy.

Lara, a young girl, is walking her along a corridor, to familiarise her with the place. In her cotton dress and her wellington boots, she looks like a milkmaid, chatting as she goes, saying who is jumpy, who is a pretty boy, who loves company, who is a loner and so forth and with the sound of her voice the hounds come leaping forward, to sniff and have a lick of her hand. She praises them, extols their silken coats like young calves, their soft ears and their hearts beating like a human's.

Outside each kennel, the names of the dogs are chalked in pink on little blackboards and soon the multiple lash of their tails on the wire mesh is like a summons to riot. A couple have remained on their raised beds, half concealed on thrones of shredded paper, staring out with such sad eyes, such sad stories in those pensive eyes.

All of a sudden one starts to growl, thrusts itself forward, frothing and barking in an attempt to break out. This is Bella, who suffers from epilepsy and hence has a kennel to herself. At the mere tread of a stranger, she is sent into a frenzy and soon others have joined in the fray, hurling themselves against their confines, a swell of savage and discordant barking, so that

Lara's soft words of appeasement are of no avail. The place is bedlam.

This consternation is what Fidelma will remember and howl back to, in the night, in whatever lodgings they aim to find for her.

It happened like this.

*

She is in a snack bar in a London side street, near where the hospitals and nursing homes are, with ambulances parked all around and nurses with blue capes over their white uniforms, hurrying from one address to another. The place is crammed with workmen, all standing as they down their coffee, sharing the one free newspaper and discussing favourites for the afternoon race. Written on a board, in a neat, cryptic hand, are the specialities of the house – *Panini, Ciabatta, Bagel, Tuna Melt, Jacket Potato, Mixed Fillings*. The two men behind the counter look like twins, in identical Breton caps, and despite the crush, manage a few friendly words with each customer. There he stands, the same Bluey, the same shiftiness, the same smile, the gold earring and the broken teeth.

'May God strike me dead if I am to blame,' he is saying, hands raised in contrition, insisting he wasn't even there the day her pass was refused. Medusa wanted the job for her niece and sent many negative reports to the person at the very top.

'What kind of negative?' Fidelma asks.

'Oh . . . stuff . . .'

'What kind of stuff?'

'Look, forget it . . . As a night cleaner you are supposed to be invisible. You do not exist as a person. You are there to work and not to blab.'

'But I didn't cry,' she says, the colour rising in her cheeks, a knot in the gut, because she knows full well that at work, she held herself together and it was only on the walk home in the early morning that she sometimes shed a few tears. At that moment she pictures Medusa, diminutive, the skin brown and taut like the canvas of a ship, eyes darting and mistrustful, the whites a wounded yellow gristle, and plaits arranged symmetrically on the crown of her head, avid for confrontation.

Bluey hushes her, says not to dwell on the past, as her ship has come in. He has work for her. Her heart leapt at the news. It was not in the bank, but out in the countryside and he knew that she loved nature, birds, trees, rivers, though how he knew remained a mystery to her. It was a centre for greyhounds, not too far from London. Lovely lovely animals, who, when they had to retire from either age or injury, had a tough time of it. A greyhound who did not come first, second or third in the first five races was scrapped and then it was either a bullet through the head, a brick or a retirement home. His friend Tracy ran a centre and as it happened, needed temporary help, as Cressida was unexpectedly pregnant. He'd been there himself, gobsmacked at how devoted the staff were, walkers from all over coming every day and Tracy praying that some of her hounds would be adopted, as there was a big queue of those wanting to be let in.

'I'm not sure,' Fidelma said.

'Trainers and owners often slaughter them for cash,' he said. The word *cash* sprang at her. She had almost nothing left, and though no harsh words had been uttered, she felt she was becoming a liability to Jasmeen.

'Why don't we go and have a look,' and he paid for the coffee and picked up a clean coffee coaster as a souvenir.

They drove through streets with tall blocks of flats, all an identical mustard colour, then into the financial district, towers of steel and glass, stacked almost against each other, higher and higher in the bid for supremacy. He named them for her. She has her first sight of the Tower of London, a fawn sprawling building that with its turrets and its lesser towers appeared to be a city in itself. He'd taken his kids on a guided tour, and what they loved was hearing the ghoulish bits, little Princes getting the chop.

In the long tunnels, the trapped wind whined and it was a relief at last to come out into the open, by some more buildings and then low-lying land and a great expanse of sky that stretched from end to end, with dawdling clouds piling softly over it. She had not seen such a vast sky since she left home. Pylons, though fixed, seemed to be marching across the landscape and in between there were windmills, thrashing ceaselessly. Bluey was talkative. It was to keep her from brooding. When they entered the Thames estuary, he said what a famous shipping route it had been, tankers and carriers from all over the world and how Francis Drake in 1577, with his guns and his one hundred and sixty-four men, set out for South America, at the behest of the Queen, to do maximum damage to Spanish galleons on which she wished to be avenged. When he returned, three years later, with far fewer men on board, the gold and ducats he had brought for the Queen exceeded the country's national debt. It was from that to nature. The marshes and the wetlands, more than three thousand acres, brimming with wildlife. He reeled off the names of birds, Brent geese, red warblers, skylarks, godwits, flocks of curlews and various species of gulls. Yet when she looked, Fidelma saw neither sky nor wetland.

They were on a dual carriageway, with a glimpse of busy laneways underneath, cars and lorries whizzing by at a terrific speed and the grass within the steel barrier that divided the motorway limp and grimed. It was not countryside as she had known it.

Car factories, small warehouses with signs for coach parts, camper vans, garage doors and free buggies along the way. On a large poster, a warning read *Hands Off Our Sports Club*. At intervals, there were the competing prices of Sunday roasts in different carveries. There was even an enticement to try Twilight Golf. More and more she questioned the common sense of this expedition. He kept going astray. These signs and a clump of hollyhocks returned faithfully, as did a double white gate that was the entrance to an equestrian centre. His sympathies for the unwanted greyhounds magnified, as they went round and round and she hoped that soon he would be impelled to turn back and once again they would be in the tunnels, the financial district, seeing the blue and white girders that supported the might of London Bridge.

The van was borrowed and the satnav, he said, had lost its navigating marbles. A woman with a cultivated accent kept telling them to turn left after fifteen metres, which they did, only to return to the exact same settlement of houses, and the white gate to the equestrian centre. When he rang the kennels to get directions, Fidelma could hear incessant barking and Bluey was told to hurry up, as they were about to start preparing the dinners.

It was in a builder's yard, with various working sheds, some roofless, some not, and to one side, small buildings were marked Units and all numbered. There were workmen everywhere and a pile of rubble was stacked at one end that opened onto a flat field and horizon beyond.

It was down three steps to another ramshackle building, with duvets drying on a railing and window boxes planted with gaily coloured flowers. On a length of wire, between two poles, there was a row of wagtails, eerily silent.

The aluminium door, though drawn, was unlocked and Bluey called out as they went in. Soon she was introduced to Tracy, a hearty woman in wellington boots and a big smile, saying to Bluey that she knew he wouldn't let her down. The smell of urine was nauseating, even though the place had been scrubbed and was now being hosed down. On the wall there were collars and leads and muzzles and brushes and toys and fleeces and coloured photographs of star greyhounds with clean pink tongues, massive white molars and rapturous eyes.

*

Lara suggests they take a pair of dogs, a him and a her, who share a kennel and are yelping happily at the surprise of a second walk. Fidelma has her first lesson in gripping the long mouth for the muzzle to be slipped on, her nervousness imparting itself to the jittery dog. 'Not too loose, not too tight.'

Out in the field and to her surprise, the dog doesn't thrash or strain at the leash, happy to be away from the dark and the enclosure. The short grass is hummocky, with clods of earth thrown up by horses, who stand at the far end, restless.

Other walkers, on their way back, call out to them gaily, dangling their pooh bags, which were of a ruby colour, dangling them with an insouciance, as if they were evening bags. Lara's dog then shat and Lara demonstrated how to pick it up. With a deftness, she turned the bag inside out, then, pinching her fingers, drew in the contents before she tied the two ends of the bag in a knot. Soon it was Fidelma's turn and she was barely able to keep herself from retching. She needed a second bag and even with that, she messed things, and in the end had to dry her hands on the short, trodden grass.

'You'll get used to it,' Lara said as they walked on and she talked of the excitement of a new dog that she and her partner had got a few days previous. It was a collie. They saw it on the Battersea Dogs Home website and immediately knew that that dog needed them. It would mean having eleven dogs in all, including the hounds. She had to go alone to London as her partner was working and when she got there, there was a second collie, as the one she had seen had been taken the day before. The two dogs were obviously from the same family and had been found abandoned outside a vet's clinic. So it had to be this one. The dog was called Prudence, but Lara decided that was not the right name and there and then she named her Rosie. That was the easy part. Getting her back to Essex was not. For a start, she was hysterical at being among people and not answering to her new name and scared on the escalator, even though she was being carried, so much so that when they got into the Underground, she hid under a seat and would not come out and they missed a stop and had to go back again. As the train was not full, she decided to be brave and put her on a seat and opposite was a nice gentleman, who didn't object.

Outside the kennels, Fidelma stood alone for a few moments, to take stock. One big tree and then on the horizon, a line of trees squeezed together and bordering a bit of sky that was a pewter colour. That great brimming of nature that Bluey had predicted was nowhere to be seen. She clutched at her throat so that no sound of dismay might escape from it. It was this or nothing.

A fugue of barking had started up inside, but without the hysteria and venom of earlier; it was dinnertime and the dogs knew it. She watched as Lara prepared their feeds – dried biscuits, tinned meat, brown bread, iron, seaweed and cod liver oil, all mixed with warm water and pounded into a sort of stirabout, the dogs all the while crazed with excitement.

Since it was her first day, Tracy said Fidelma could sit and watch the routine, as the dogs were brought singly or in pairs to the paddock. The paddock, without a blade of grass, was a cement floor, with blue tarpaulin and sheets overhead, to keep off rain or sunshine. As each bowl was laid into a tripod, that dinner was wolfed and then the dogs licked whatever might have got spattered onto the wire meshing. It was all done briskly, as there were forty-four dogs to be fed. Tracy sat with her, discussing the dogs' characters, their personalities, the ones that still carried scars and the ones with carefree dispositions, adding of course that one never gets the back story. When her dog Mr Fitzpatrick had downed his grub, he was brought to be held in her arms, while she recited his history. Ever so nervous when he was brought in, terrified of everyone, but especially men. Full of scars and cuts, one ear bitten, covered in lice, his teeth rotten, too dangerous to be put with any other dogs, a tearaway. Threw his plate around, and his food and the toys she got him. He had been found up in Yorkshire, half wild and hunting rabbits and from his tattoo she was able to trace that he had been an Irish dog and had run races there, but was dumped, when he could race no longer.

'Never puts the teeth in anyone now . . . or hardly ever,' she said and Mr Fitzpatrick replied with little taps on her collarbone, like the tapping of a baton.

'You'll get to love one of them and that'll be it . . . that's how it happens . . . you'll look back on this day as a big stepping stone in your life,' she said, as she encouraged Fidelma to give Mr Fitzpatrick a petting.

It was time to lock up. Night descending, long before night itself. On their raised beds the dogs lay close to one another, except for Bella who slept apart. Did they dream. According to Tracy, yes. They dreamt, they ran races, their legs jigging, running the Grand National all over again. She said then that they had short memories and would sleep and sleep until the sound of the first car the following morning.

As they tiptoed out, up steps and across the yard, Fidelma looked back at the building, so silent, such a forsaken quality to it now.

*

In the room above the pub Fidelma hears murmurs, but not too loud. There is the steady drone from the two large television screens and being poker night, all is quiet and intent. She bought fish and chips from the van that was parked nearby, a selection of cockles, winkles, prawns and mussels, and ate them quickly, but the chips had gone a bit sodden. Then she takes a slug from the bottle of prune syrup, which she'd bought on the way in the Costcutter where Bluey stopped to get a special honey for his wife, who was finicky. The sweet taste of the syrup brought back memories of home. She had a sudden picture of Jack in their kitchen, fending for himself and it was like they were two people in some vast ruin, who, although they could not communicate, still knew of each other's existence and one day would have to meet. *O there above the little grave we kissed again with tears*. She picked up a leaflet from the pile Lara had given her and read about the hounds, pushed to their physical limits, their short careers and injuries from racing on small, tight-cornered tracks and soon, unwanted to face an uncertain future.

She put it down hurriedly and went downstairs.

In the bar, no one bothers her. The poker players are very intense and barely speak, except to acknowledge some annoyance or some coup.

'Okay darlin',' one man called across and his friend told her not to mind him. On the next bench is a woman in an eau de nil dress with short puff sleeves and a frill around the hem. She is a very large woman, sitting so close to her man that she is almost like a jelly, moulded into him. They barely talk, but they are as one. All of it so temperate, so still. Fidelma is drinking a concoction of soda and crème de menthe, which the girl behind the counter recommended to her as a sedative. Behind her, on the windowsill, there are a few flowers in a small vase and when she touches one, she jumps in terror, dismayed by that tenderness, that touch.

A Letter

The letterhead had the name of the convent and the handwriting was scratchy.

> *Well, my dear Fidelma, you must have wondered what happened to your old Bony, for not being in touch. I nearly left earth for the higher kingdom. What happened was this: I was bringing a beautiful vestment over for a young priest in Manor Hamilton and I stopped off here at the chapel to get some bottles of Holy Water, but when I got into my car to set out I felt very strange in my head, I was sort of out of it. So I said to myself, 'Don't drive Bony, just sit and let it pass,' and so I did and apparently was there for an hour or maybe more. It was the grace of God that Father Eustace happened to be passing by, going into the chapel for Evening Mass and saw me slouched at the wheel. The upshot was I ended up in the regional hospital, not knowing where I was or who I was. I'd had a stroke, which affected the whole right side of my body, including my brain. Couldn't speak, couldn't move, couldn't anything. For two weeks I was out of it and then I was moved to another hospital for the slow recovery, which entailed vigorous physiotherapy and psychotherapy. Learning to walk and talk again, like a child, taught me a lesson, of just how fragile we humans are and how grateful we should be. My illness and the seemingly miraculous recovery was written up in the local paper, along*

with a photograph of yours truly at the car boot sale with my pots of jam and marmalade. I received over one thousand messages of sympathy and Mass cards and as soon as I was able to read them I began to feel better, I realised I was wanted. I believe it was those good wishes, in all their sincerity, along with the marvellous nurses and doctors that implored the Lord for the miracle. After many weeks I am slowly walking and my speech is back, though I can suddenly forget a name and it vexes me. Our Lord and Our Lady were watching over me and my faith is my rock. I have thought of you a lot and the one thing I keep praying for and will not cease to pray for is to see Jack shaking your hand in forgiveness. I pray for that. I believe he has got very thin and often refuses food. Peggy says he is starving himself to punish us. How are you in that big lonely city, where I have heard that over one hundred different languages are spoken? I tend not to look at the prison wall of life, but to look up at the sky, as it is more beautiful and more spacious. Try to do that and remember that you are wanted. Your good friend, old Bonaventure.

James

A man called James had returned to collect his dog, Jenny, who had been boarding for a few days. Jenny fretted, did not eat or mix with the other dogs and constantly listened with eyes and ears for her master's return. When she saw him, she scaled the wire mesh, both sets of paws thudding on it, delirious to be reunited, and when she was let out, he almost keeled over in the welcome he received. Then she rolled and rerolled on the floor to proclaim her joy. He was a tall, lean man with sallow skin, his hair silvered, and he wore a leather jerkin over his knitted pullover. His eyes, which were deep-set, were grey and yet with a wonderful alertness. The way he broached it was so subtle, stroking Jenny all the while, saying that there was a spare room in his house, which she was welcome to, should she wish it. Had Tracy been talking to him, giving a hint? The pub was friendly but in truth, a bit shambolic and the prospect of a quiet room in a house, and probably the use of the kitchen, appealed to her. He mentioned then that he went away every six weeks and she would be left to herself, to keep watch.

'His house is ever so lovely,' Tracy, who had overheard him, said and mentioned a visit one summer, cream tea in the garden and hollyhocks as tall as himself.

'I'm sure it's lovely,' Fidelma said, that bit shy, but inside she was euphoric.

The following Saturday, which was her day off, he came to

pick her up. She had just the one small suitcase, the rest of her clobber in an open basket. The staff in the pub made a point of coming out to see her off, even though she was only going five miles away and the manager had presented her with a bottle of port. James rolled the hood down and soon they were on a narrow road that had once been a highway and was the major route between London and the outback. Trunks of trees from the high bank on one side bent forward, as if they might topple onto the road. Green light and leaves in a ceaseless rustle, as he drove from hamlet to hamlet, all with the long-ago names, Pilgrim's Hatch, South Weald, Sandpit Lane, and after a few miles they came to his small village, which was a hamlet really. There was a pub, a post office, a few coloured timber houses and a church with its bell tower, built, as he said, from old Roman bricks and stone. His cottage, which was an old almshouse, was one of four, at the very end, by a lane with a public footpath that led to fields and woodlands beyond. The small porch was smothered with wisteria, light blue fobs in thickets of green, with fat bees buzzing inside it.

The kitchen was stone-floored and dark, because not much light came from the mullioned window, and he indicated a few practical things, including where the matches were kept, in an alcove above the gas stove. Then it was into the little pantry, muslin cloths over cheese and butter, because he believed that refrigerators killed the taste of certain things. A little refrigerator stood on a trestle table, bravely emitting the odd juddery lurch. He said that for the most part they would eat separately, since he kept odd hours, stuck in his habits, a bit of a curmudgeon from living alone. However, the place was hers to feel at home in. It was with something of a flourish that he led her to the next room, which he called his 'snug'. It was cluttered with books and guide books, papers everywhere, on the table and on a long stool under the table, on a desk, the floor and the one windowsill. He confessed that since retiring as a teacher, he was writing something, which he reckoned would never be finished and which he probably never intended to finish. In one corner, on a whatnot, she saw a silver tray with a whisky bottle, a jug for water and a single cut glass. A fire of sorts flickered in the small grate and he said he always had a peat fire going, because he liked the smell and so did Jenny – *Don't you.* Jenny leapt and went ahead of them up the steep stairs to the room that was to be for Fidelma.

A small room, it looked out onto a garden, where there were borders of yellow tulips, the centrepiece being a huge boulder, which he told her was of Scottish granite and which he and his wife had hauled from a garden centre, one Saturday. It had been fitted with a fountain and for a time, that fountain flourished. There was a womanly touch to the room, the cotton coverlet on the single bed bleached white, with traces of roses, and a picture of a young barefoot girl in a haze of gold with a mop of golden hair, which must surely be that absent wife. He left the room suddenly, as there was something he had forgotten. Alone, she stood spellbound in front of a little bureau with a lace runner and thought, I can sit here, I can read my books here, I can write my diary here and I can feel safe. Then she touched the various shells in a bowl that other hands had picked on a seashore and put there. He returned with a wooden rocking chair, which he set down to face the window, Jenny all the while frothing with excitement. When she enquired about the rent he was evasive, he said to pay whatever she could afford, to put it in a jug down in the kitchen window, and if there were times that she wanted to indulge in the haute couture of Brentwood, the rent could be postponed.

*

That summer was scorching. Hotter than the Sahara as people said and the workmen in the kennels were bare-chested, wore shorts, larking and pouring buckets of water over each other. The dogs felt it too. Many sat far back in their beds to escape even a ray of sunlight and some panted and others shivered in the heat. Fidelma had to put wet cloths over them, to keep them cool and strangely, she came to grow a little fonder of them. It was something to do with the cloth between them and her, a shield, as if naked intimacy was once removed and she no longer retched from the pervading smell. She had a soft spot for one called Lola, who was smaller than the others and with affectionate eyes, but the big affiliation, the *You'll fall in love with one and that'll be it* that Tracy had predicted, did not transpire. However, she saw the little things that made them happy and the joy each morning when she and Lara arrived at six thirty, that gratitude at night being over. Then it was the brisk morning routine, making sure there were no illnesses, then taking them to an enclosure that overlooked the field, cleaning their beds, forking the shredded paper or removing it, then the floors, first scrubbed and then rinsed one after the other, and finally the entire place hosed down. Volunteers arrived around eight and the front hall was all agog, chatter, cups of tea or coffee, the radio on low, with music and phone-ins and every hour news bulletins, which she did not listen to, because she did not want to engage with the world outside.

*

It was her day off, but she still wakened at five and hurried out to sit in the garden, the grass covered in dew and a small bed of mauve flowers opening their petals to the world, just like daisies. Despite burning the midnight oil, James also rose early, because Jenny wished it, Jenny it seemed was something of a sun worshipper and had to be up in the woods to salute it. Normally he went by with his mug of tea and gave a mere nod, but on this particular morning he had something to show her.

They walked along a track with fields on either side, corn and rapeseed, gold and yellow in a patchwork of glory, Jenny sniffing the ground and every so often turning to her master, with a friendly chattering of her teeth. It was why he had chosen her, having walked several dogs in the kennels, trying to decide which one to adopt, but Jenny bewitched him with this conversational trick of hers.

The wood they came to was immense, a sacred wood as he said, beech, chestnut, ash and most of all oak, in their full splendour, and the ground underneath a carpet of soft wavy young fern. The walk was winding and they were mainly silent, until they came to what he had promised to show her. She recognised it as they approached. It was an oak tree, riven apart by lightning, the bark black and charred, a tree that had died and yet, as he said, in one part of itself it lived. On the opposite side, young branches in leaf extended in all directions, a freak of nature, dead on one side and living on the other, a reason to hope. Circling it were the badger burrows, their round openings clogged with clay, as a decoy and long deep tunnels stretching far within. The badgers themselves were already on the prowl. Jenny whined and chafed at being tied up, because she could smell prey, but as he said, if she were let loose, she would be gone in ten seconds, her hound's instinct returned, sprinting like a cheetah.

'You may have wondered,' he began, 'seeing that there are still a few of my wife's belongings in cupboards, her raincoat and those lavender sachets that she hung everywhere. We had a child that was stillborn. She blamed herself. It gutted her. Wouldn't let go. She held onto the creature for hours, willing it to breathe, holding a mirror for it to haw on. She would have named it Gabriel. When she came home from the hospital, the trouble began. Life was an endless mourning. She did nothing but sit and stare. I would come home from work after seven – I taught in the college at that time – and she was already in her pyjamas, prepared for bed, and she would merely look up and acknowledge me and I thanked God if she smiled. I knew she would have spent her day, or a great part of it, at the computer, studying foetuses and stillborn babies, all abnormalities relating to the ovaries. "Annie, Annie." I might as well have been calling to the wall. I still loved her, but I wanted the old Annie back, the girl I courted, the girl that made hotpot and apple strudel, the girl that would meet me halfway up the road if we'd had a bit of exciting news, such as planning permission approval for that shed at the end of the garden.

'Eventually, the time came when the doctor said she would benefit from a spell in a nuthouse, not that he used that word. She needed to get away, a change of milieu, sea air, sedation, all that gab. After a big search, a place was found in lovely countryside in Dorset and one Monday we drove there. It was like all those places with gates and an avenue up to it, but the grandeur and the friendliness stopped at the front door, where it had a rather functional appearance. A little maid admitted us, gave a flabbergasted start with "Oh Jesus," genuflected more than once and repeatedly hit a brass bell that was on the table. It could be heard in Timbuktu. Annie squeezed my hand, like a child going back to boarding school.

'I used to go and see her every second weekend. We'd walk in the grounds, never without patients tagging along, because she was so popular. So it was jabber-jabber-jabber, one man, with a fishing rod, casting his line, a hook that would take the eye out of you. He professed to be a confidant of Charles Darwin, before Darwin made his theories known to the world. In my fairly elementary knowledge of loony people, it is always a king, a queen or a potentate they aspire to be, never Joe Bloggs.

'Annie and I rarely talked about her coming home, or rather she kept postponing it. It was something to do with the room, the room you are in now. She couldn't face it. The expense was considerable, but I had a vintage Railton that I sold and for which I got a good sum. There is something I must emphasise here, in case I have painted a bilious picture of my wife. She was one of the most generous and giving creatures alive. She would not have wanted me to sell it. One day I turned up and she was effervescent. It was raining and we were in the garden, rain slopping into the urns and the asters in the flowerbeds and our fisherman in full throw as she whispered her plan. We were to have dinner the following week in a five-star establishment that was not too far away. She had looked it up. It was an old manor dating back to the times of William and Mary, with taffeta-lined niches for the diners to feel exclusive. To make it the special evening it must be, I was to arrive in the Railton and not my old van. I had to lie, say the Railton needed servicing and so I had hired the Rolls-Royce from Jerry in the town, whom she knew, and who uses it for weddings. She came down the steps of that place like a bride-to-be, in a white linen skirt that Maggie, one of the inmates, had made for her, a cream lace blouse and white satin gloves that went up to the elbow. She got the gloves in the local vintage shop. The less loopy ones were allowed out under supervision and had cream teas in some cafe and always a visit to the vintage shop, to fit on hats and muffs and coatees. Her hair was curled at the ends and fell in an unbroken ringlet along the nape of her neck. She looked a picture. The menu was most peculiar. It was a tasting menu. We had marrowbones with jellied anchovies, followed by frogs' legs with parsley and lovage. We had snails and porridge and octopus and it was all delicious. We drank. We made plans relating to the future. She wanted two forked trellises in two vats outside the bedroom window in order to grow sweet peas, because the smell of sweet pea was the sweetest, the airiest and the one she could recapture in her mind at will. My wife was an artist *manqué*. The paintings of flowers that she loved were numerous, especially Van Gogh's last tempestuous orchards. She also loved the gentler ones, Redon's twigs, leaves and budding roses, Chardin, a sedate bunch of red and white squeezed into a blue vase. She had oodles of postcards all along the windowsill and in that chest in the hall. Friends sent some on vacation and she bought several when we went up to London and visited one of the galleries. How she pored over paintings and often we sat and gazed while others were tearing around, so as to fit everything in. Once we saw Edvard Munch's lonely houses and lonely isolated people, that both saddened and appealed to her. She did not have the courage to paint, her reason being a fear of the false. She detested falseness.

Even to the point of saying that some of the loonies exaggerated their conditions. One foreign woman, who had read of a doctor in some European clinic who used masks to prevent screaming, went around trying on the crude cardboard masks that she made incessantly. Annie hid what she was feeling, nothing exaggerated in her behaviour, everything concealed, like she must have lived in a black hole, or maybe it was a grey hole, which is worse. I drove her back to the place and at some point in that night of our celebration, she did it. Quite a painting it was. She had cut the veins on the front and the surround of her belly, but had left the cream blouse on. It was more abattoir than Van Gogh's riotous orchards. I had not realised how far gone she was and how much she dreaded the homecoming, the ghost. We don't know others. They are an enigma. We can't know them, especially those we are most intimate with, because habit blurs us and hope blinds us to the truth. She left me a note – *I feel so very tranquil now* was what it said.'

Here he stopped and turned aside and it was several minutes before he resumed. 'Do I forgive her . . . at times I do and at times I do not. Now and then I see a sunset, a great carnival of colour that trails off into islets and I want her to be there, seeing it with me. Her family blamed me of course and took her remains to their burial place in Northumberland. They were mining people and very clannish. I destroyed all the postcards with their pretty posies, used them for kindling. Not a nice thing to do, but I had to kill something. There is one thing I often ponder. It is the note. When was it written. A week before. A day before. That very evening as she got ready and Maggie had to come and tie the little white buttons up the length of her forearm. Or even after our fond goodnight. You see, I think she wanted not to do it as much as she wanted to do it, and that is the hardest thing to bear. Why am I telling you all this?'

He said it quietly, then answered for her – 'There is something in you that I saw in her, some likeness, an evanescence. The same hands, so small, so timid, and a trust that is only found in the very innocent. But she lacked something. She bent, as the reed bends. You see, she had gone under to the black beneath, but she didn't say and she didn't ask . . . Oh my God, the awful loneliness of it, the finality,' and at that he clammed up. Spent and haggard, he was like a figure suddenly stripped naked. Sitting within inches of one another on that log, she could see him visibly gathering his strength to be the hesitant rooted man he always seemed, the man for whom nature was everything. She thinks *He has done this for me . . . he has done this to give me courage* and she bowed her head in deference.

He was standing then, looking up at a buzzard that hovered in the upper air, the thermal air as he named it, circling and climbing until it would spot its prey far down below and then dive with an exact and murderous swiftness. Crows, blackbirds, jackdaws, pigeons and the wild doves, all lying in wait for the pickings.

It was time to leave the place that had been sacred to him and was now to her.

A world had transpired in there and now they were out in the open, with the sun blazing on the hot fields, as they walked in single file along a worn track. Further on the path forked in all directions, so that they passed through young spruce woods and open clearings, then back to woods again, alternating light and shadow.

Penge

There was a bite in the air and the stars frozen in the heavens. Frost weighed down the dead stalks, and the tiled roof had the sparkle of saltpetre. Branches of the wisteria that climbed up the porch were ashen, like old bones, clawing their way. The lawn there was an unblemished cape of frost.

James had brought out a wee dram to keep warm, as they stood listening for the taxi. Jenny was in the porch, her tartan coat still on, reluctant to venture forth.

> *O thin men of Haddam,*
> *Why do you imagine golden birds?*
> *Do you not see how the blackbird*
> *Walks around the feet*
> *Of the women about you?*

They had both memorised that poem, because in the evenings he sometimes invited her into his snug to read to him. It was there they came to be familiar with John Clare, John Keats, Wallace Stevens, Elizabeth Bishop, Marianne Moore and many another. They used to wonder about these poëts, how haughty, or how amenable they might be. James reckoned that Keats would hide like the little wren in the ivy, from the formidable, bosomy Marianne. Strange as he said, that she, who advocated silence, wrote reams, but still, as he conceded, she was the woman who gave the world 'by darkness a star is perfected'.

He was restless, tapping the minute crystals off the glass of the thermometer, then staking some straggling rose bushes and wandering up to the road for the sound of a car. Her new suitcase on the gravelled path seemed an affront.

There was a total silence, birds hiding in the trees and the chimney pots, except for one little creature, its feathers covered in snow, that appeared as the messenger from the famished bird world. They were listening intently for the taxi, fearing it might not come. But finally a car swung into the lane at a hectic speed, and the young animated driver, believing that both were travelling, opened both back doors. James, fleetingly thrown, said, 'Someone has to stay at home and mind the house.' It was an awful moment.

Then he shook her hand for the first time ever, but the constraint was such that he had to pick up Jenny, who was shivering with cold, and her cries so ostentatious in themselves, served as a goodbye for both of them.

*

As the train pulled into Liverpool Street Station, she felt the zippiness of the city, people rushing in all directions, going through the turnstiles like fiends and from the cafes there was a smell of coffee and warm bread rolls. Christmas already featured, six weeks too soon. There were novelties in the souvenir shops and the necklaces and chains in the jewellers were stranded with tinsel, to give an added glitter. The Christmas tree reached almost to the domed roof and was laden with bells, baubles, wings of white gauze to simulate butterflies and small boxes wrapped in crimson paper. Gifts for a children's hospital were in a big pile and from the street, the sound of 'Jingle Bells' and Santa rattling his collection box. A young man, wearing a baseball cap, handed her a small tin for free and she held it like a trophy. In the Underground, before opening it, she read that it was a very low-volume lager, cut with cloudy lemon. *Keep the planet tidy, recycle this little fella*, it said in small print on the back. It tasted too sweet, but she drank it nevertheless.

Penge had not yet decked herself for Christmas, but preparations had begun. Around each of the lampposts, there was different paraphernalia, bicycle chains, umbrella spokes, broken lamps and the separated strings of a golden harp. A man with white hair, in old coat tails, a sort of Pied Piper, moved up and down the street, extolling the would-be decorations, saying the lights would soon be turned on and that it would be a big occasion, with choirs from neighbouring boroughs coming to sing carols and free mulled wine. *All are welcome, all are welcome*, he said as she passed by.

Jasmeen opened the front lock from the inside and as Fidelma passed the adjoining window, Mistletoe was standing, staring. It was as if she had not left that spot in the intervening months, an effigy with a look of injury.

Jasmeen hugged her like a sister and Jade appeared in the ermine bolero, yawning, saying she would put coffee on. They were all talking at once. She must see the new electric cooker, with its high oven, no more bending down and Jasmeen had also been given a brand new swish Peugeot by the company. Jade had hooked up with a band, where she had a solo spot singing two of her own songs that they had put to music.

'Ah, the letter,' Jasmeen said then and went to fetch it from under an ornament, a letter she had been meaning to forward, but of course forgot.

The envelope had the name of Fidelma's solicitor in Galway. She shook as she opened it.

Dear Fidelma,

Long time no see. I hope London is good to you. I am writing to inform you that as of each month, starting now, I am to deposit the sum of two thousand six hundred pounds to your bank account there. Please let me have details, name of bank, account number, sort code and IBAN. The donor wishes to remain anonymous and when I'm told something, I am a good boy and that is what I do. Give us a shout when you are over. Yours, Gerry.

So Jack had forgiven her, but not entirely. How well she remembered those estrangements, long before the actual ending came. He had begun to suspect her infidelity, saying with sarcasm, what a little traveller she had become. One evening he came down from his snooze, wearing his maroon velvet smoking jacket, as if they might be expecting company, which they weren't. Then he got out his LPs, and put his favourite jazz piece on the wind-up gramophone. At first he listened, his eyes filling up with emotion and then very chivalrously, he asked her to dance. They danced slowly, closer and closer, and she could feel his erection, pressing on her, in it his need, his suspicion, his love, his hatred. She froze, her body detaching itself from him, and even though they remained dancing, until the record had played itself out completely, it was like a dance of death.

*

It was almost a repetition of what happened once before, Mistletoe's father standing in the doorway, in his shirt sleeves, except this time he was not indignant, he was pleading. The child was not well. He said it ominously and more than once. She had refused to eat her supper, refused to speak and was shaking with fever. He came to ask if perhaps the ladies could give an opinion.

He led them out and into his narrow hall, that smelt of creosote, a work bench full of tools taking up most of the space, so that they had to squeeze past, to get to the room. Her clothes were on the floor, along with her slippers, sheaves of paper on which she had done drawings and a mangy Greenie stationed on top of the chipped radiator. The eyes, black and glittering, appeared above the coverlet, like a little animal.

'You see . . . you see,' the father kept saying and it was unclear whether he was referring to the state of the room or Mistletoe's fit. She was indeed quivering and her teeth chattered as she gulped for air. It was clear to Fidelma that she was genuinely overwrought, but with their arrival, her upset had gained fresh momentum. Suddenly she began to cry, loud and piercingly, willing herself to cry more, to punish them, but especially to punish the father, over whom it was evident she now had total mastery, as he looked on, bashfully, asking God what to do with her, what would become of them.

'You see, you see,' he kept repeating.

'What's wrong Mistletoe?' Fidelma asked, only to be snubbed and then there were craven offers of fruit, raisins, hot chocolate or toast with peanut butter.

'Maybe if she slept,' Jasmeen said, but that was not what Mistletoe wanted, she wanted her audience and was beginning to bask in it. Yet the thaw had not happened, she merely pulled at Fidelma's sleeve, pulled and pulled, as if it were elasticated. Then it was her hair, she slapped it, to show her disapproval.

'You remember I had long hair,' she said at last, directly to Fidelma, but the castigation was for her father. The short hair was not becoming and gave her a pinched, wizened look.

'You remember,' she repeated and there followed a slew of wrongs. She had not been allowed out on Bonfire Night, where other children were, her new cardigan was several sizes too big, her judo teacher said she was selfish, and she had caught a cold standing out in the garden in the day with everybody ignoring her. To crown matters, Greenie was not well and she referred to the various battles he had recently been in. As he was returned to her, she remarked on where his amber eyes had once been and said poor Greenie was retiring.

Before long she was propped up on pillows, her hair smoothed back and Fidelma wiping her face with a warm flannel. Then she produced a silk handkerchief to dry the face. The handkerchief had strawberries on it and she began to count them, diligently, one by one, and this was a sign that she would eat.

'In Barcelona . . . I ate a steak every evening,' she told them.

'You didn't,' Fidelma said, but the father answered, saying his employer sent him on a business trip, hoping their garden furniture range might appeal to people in Spain, as it had done in Lithuania. When his meetings were over, Mistletoe and he had a walk along a wide avenue that was known as Las Ramblas and afterwards they ate in some restaurant or other, where Mistletoe had her steak. Then one evening and to their surprise, there was a pageant, white horses trooping up that avenue, riders in scarlet and black fur hats, the onlookers pushed back onto the pavement, some trying to imitate the dancers, in their frilled skirts, clicking the castanets, and behind, sitting high on a machine, a man in uniform was collecting the horse dung. At this, Mistletoe laughed and it was her father's cue to become a horse. Holding imaginary reins, he lifted his right leg, then his left leg and with complete absorption, began to trot around the bed, his face a long grotesquerie, in a semblance of what a horse might look like. Then he danced, prancing about the small space, letting out snorts and whinnies, enthusiastic and foolish and awkward and above all, desperate to please her. In conclusion, he towered above her bed, bowed and called her Princess. This led to waves of hilarity from Mistletoe, her laughing now as hysterical as her crying had been a little while before.

It was time for them to leave. In the doorway, Fidelma saw the finger curling to beckon her back.

'I thought I would never see you again,' Mistletoe said, so earnest, the eyes reproachful, like a little mourner.

Next morning there was a bulletin under Jasmeen's hall door. Two pages in her usual violet crayon with accompanying realistic drawings.

> *Not long after I went to sleep the zombies came without warning. They had new men, small freaks with invisible weapons and they kept stabbing and stabbing at me and Greenie, until I had to SOS for reserves as we could not fight them alone. Luckily T-Rex, the big dinosaur and his men came to the rescue. It was a bloody night with casualties on both sides and it lasted many hours. By daylight most of the zombies were*

dead and some had fled. T-Rex lay down under the tree for a rest and as a reward I gave him a medal, a sticker and the livers of the zombies. The meat was raw and fleshy, the way zombies like it. Afterwards they left for their own place near Battersea.

At the end, in different coloured crayon she had written – *Can we go to the High Street for cappuccino and a mince pie?*

Sarajevo

'They think they know . . . they weren't there.' This is Zelmic, drunk, slurring her words, her eyes with a vacancy to them. Fidelma knows her from the Thursday evenings in the Centre, where she often sat, quiet and withdrawn, but now, in her leather skirt and knee-high boots, she is gushing and talkative.

Sarajevo, her city, as she says, not the same anymore, the heart gone out of it. Once upon a time she and her friends sat in cafes discussing Nietzsche and existentialism and now it's young unemployed men looking at models on TV, evaluating pussy. But everyone still smoked and that was something. Yes, she will be going home for Christmas, has presents for her mother and all the people who help her mother, presents for each one, and also money. Her mother has gone a bit strange and no wonder. To make matters worse, her mother is getting threatening phone calls, which she believes are from some weird sect about to harm her and she has begun collecting money to build a church to be safe in. Her uncle has gone back to the mountain.

'You have lovely skin,' she says, tugging her hair back, so that she can see Fidelma's face clearly. Her thick chestnut hair keeps falling onto her face and repeatedly she throws it back, so that they are close to one another. But this intimacy, this marvelling at their paths crossing again, is unnerving to Fidelma.

They are in one of the little alcoves off the main room, where the party is in full swing. It has been organised by Varya and is a celebration of migrant and refugee women from all corners of the world. A sign painted on a white sheet that hangs over the stage reads *We Help Victims Become Heroines*. Fidelma can hear laughter, the smart snap and fizzle of crackers being pulled, along with random surges of exhilaration. They are at a small table with a white candle, the flame guttering this way and that and at other tables, white candles burn and teeter in random gusts. Zelmic has dragged her in to talk, puts her long necklace around them both and ropes them in. The necklace is labradorite, bought in Portobello Road from a Roma lady, who also does horoscopes.

'Dark eras, dark eras,' she goes on, 'everybody starving, my uncle going crazy, asking *Why did I come away from the mountain*. He'd come to defend us. One evening a girl, she must have been about twelve, was hanging from the tree in the communal garden outside and everyone was too afraid to go to her, just dangling there. Her family lived upstairs and the parents had suddenly left. Mixed family, half Serbian and half Muslim. Maybe they had gone to find somewhere else to live and then send for her, but as it happened, there was no need. Once the siege started, they withdrew into themselves, not a word, not even on the stairs. That's what war does. Over three hundred shells a day smashed into our city. Cowering in our apartments. Window frames with broken glass, no electricity, no heat, no water, no nothing. We got a can of oil and two cans of beans each week from the Red Cross, but as we had no wood, we began to burn household stuff, curtains and bedspreads and then shoes. Shoes stink when burnt, especially rubber shoes. We were a bookish family. We loved our books, but before long they were lined up next to the stove and my mother and my uncle fought over which should go first and which should be saved to the very last. The *Iliad* was a beautiful first edition, the pride of our library, but it too went: Agamemnon king of men, Nestor, flower of Achaean chivalry, the Black Ships, Patroclus' corpse, Helen's bracelets, Cassandra's shrieks, all met the flames, for the sake of two or three suppers. My uncle was loath to let Mark Twain go . . . Huckleberry Finn and his river did not deserve such an ignominious end. My uncle was the one who went out and cut the little girl down, said her lips were rimed with dew, as if she was still breathing.' She is scanning Fidelma's face for a reaction.

'You are not appalled,' she says sharply.

'I am appalled,' Fidelma said.

But it wasn't enough. Somehow she knew it was about to turn ugly.

'I must tell you . . .' Zelmic is saying, even more confidential, 'I had this dream about you. We were all in some kind of hangar that was also a medical centre . . . lots of patients and a nurse was taking blood from each one of us. Afterwards, we became her assistants. We were in a line, waiting, and suddenly you put a knife in my back, right into the centre of my back between my shoulder blades, you who wouldn't hurt a fly – what do you make of it Fidelma?'

'I don't really know what to make of it . . . it's your dream.'

'Was the fucking good?' the question fired at her. Can she mean it. Of course she can mean it. This is the whole reason for the tête-à-tête.

'Beast of Bosnia . . . pumping his evil into you . . . a bayonet up the vagina . . . his words . . . his poetry,' and at that she takes from either pocket a phone, one silver, the other black. She pats the silver phone, as she might a little dog, then takes the black phone and presto, her snap album unfolds, as she scrolls up and down and Fidelma is made to see image after image of Dr Vlad, the man whom day by day in the intervening twenty months she has pushed away, or thought she had pushed away, and now he materialises again with a hovering immediacy and she feels the inverse of love, which is repugnance and shame. Then a recent photo of him in which he is rotund, the smiling, jovial clown, contrasting with the earlier ones, him in his prime, Prometheus with hair flying in the wind and still another, the sombre Commando in a long dark overcoat, surveying his troops in a field in east Bosnia. Interspersed with them are pictures of gravediggers, the slung earth littered with bones and women, old before their time, bent and broken, huddled beneath tombstones.

What follows next is a summary of his thinking and his opinions –

I am an author, a writer, a man of letters, a psychiatrist. Bullshit.

Sarajevo was never under siege. Bullshit.

As a psychiatrist I can say that what goes on in our minds has nothing to do with real events. The whole of psychiatry revolves around irrealities, illusions and deceits. More bullshit.

'I don't want to see it . . . I don't want to,' Fidelma says as she shields her eyes, but the knife is going in, in, as this woman, gnawed with hatred and athirst for revenge, will not let up.

'What was it, apart from the thrills . . . what drew you to him, you must have had a whiff of something wrong . . . something very very wrong . . . his accomplice, his whore, his slut.' She is filled now with glee, exhilaration, all her suffering, her grievances, the little hanged girl, her uncle, all discharged into this orgy of humiliation.

'I did not survive that siege for nothing,' she says bitterly.

'I don't know what to say,' Fidelma replies.

'You don't know your problem,' Zelmic goes on. 'You're in denial. If I am honest I think you have a nerve to be here . . . there are some great women here.'

It has gone too far.

'Yes, I am sure there are some great women here,' Fidelma begins, 'and anyone would be justified in thinking that we are all united . . . sisters . . . All from the bleeding places . . . we bring flowers and wine and gifts . . . but not you . . . Zelmic, you bring poison, the Rottweiler . . . you drag me in here for what . . . for kicks, for your smut, to satisfy your fantasies.' While she speaks she is tugging at the necklace and at last the string gives way and the beads begin to roll and sidle all over the floor.

'Shit,' Zelmic says and bends to retrieve them, then stumbles and has to grab at the nearest table, where she sits, drops her head down and her shoulders begin to heave, as if she is about to cry.

The black phone is on the other table and Fidelma runs her hands over it, as if by some conjury, she could exorcise the contents stored in its heartless crater.

She felt very threatened. She prayed then that someone would come from the other room and sit with her and talk idly about things that did not matter.

All she wanted was that.

PART THREE

The Courtroom

The sun shall be turned into darkness and the moon into blood. Such was Fidelma's nervous state that she envisaged the final hearing as being apocalyptic.

But it was not like that at all. Fidelma arrived early, fearing there would be a great crush for the final hearing and that the place would be swarmed. Instead the doors were not even open and two signs, one reading *VIP*, the other *Press*, added to her confusion.

It was a long, low, unassuming building fronted with cream-coloured tiles, facing a crescent-shaped pond, water from two fountains rising and falling with a faithful predictability. The street nearby was lined with the flags of all the various nations and even at a glance the colour red predominated, red for blood-shed, yet their gaiety and their furling decrying all catastrophe.

A man was dredging the debris from the muddy water and pointing to the sculpture of a stork, he said it was the official symbol of Den Haag, a stork on a gold escutcheon with an eel in its mouth.

'Put that in your pipe and smoke it.' He had an Irish accent and it was a relief that he was a stranger to her. She had come hoping no one she knew would be there. It was Varya who had persuaded her to come, pleaded with her, saying it would be a victory for all of them.

'It's unofficial . . . but this lake is the bane of my life . . . bird shit, especially pigeon shit,' he was saying, as he scraped with the hoe, grousing that it had to be drained and scrubbed several times a year.

'I thought there would be a bigger crowd,' she said.

'Oh Christ, the day he was coming in here it was hectic . . . getting the cell right, new furniture . . . a bigger desk . . . feather pillows . . . I was run off my feet, up and down to the town, to the various suppliers . . .'

'So you're head bottle washer,' she said with a smile.

'What brings you here?' He was friendly now.

'God knows,' and she walked on.

Going through security was simple, and far less frenzied than the airport in London the previous evening. Then she went through the turnstile and down a narrow path and up steps into the great hall that, with its magnificence and its stout marble columns, was made for banqueting, yet there was no mistaking where she was. A vast poster read 'Bringing War Criminals to Justice and Justice to Victims'.

The stairs were also marbled, the steps steep and without a banister. On the first landing there was a bas relief, warriors and their cohorts, some with weapons, some mere hewers of wood and water, all with erect, chiselled, marbled penises. The women, and they were few, stood behind in deference, one bearing a bowl that contained food, the second nursing a newborn infant and the third in mute anticipation.

They climbed, were handed their headsets and so silent, so neutral was the atmosphere, it was impossible to guess who was friend and who was foe.

Her seat was in the first row, next to four women identically dressed, who sat close together and looked at her with suspicion, as if she was a traitor. Beyond the thick plate-glass wall, the barristers and their juniors were moving about briskly, their folders under their arms, their black robes brushing one another as they hurried to confer, leaving nothing to chance.

When Vlad entered the trial chamber, she shook uncontrollably, as if he was someone come back from the dead. Inconceivable that he was still alive, or had not descended into madness or infirmity. But there he was, in a smart suit, a nondescript tie, courteous, disarming, still in possession of those insatiate powers that had made him so feared. His guard stood stock still behind him, girt around his waist a belt with a set of keys and a revolver and he seemed curiously roused as he gazed about. From the corner of her eye, Fidelma saw how the four women seized the moment. It was as if a sudden energy possessed them, an urgency, as they stared unequivocally into that trial chamber, making their abhorrence known. He did not look out at the court and as he sat, one of his team, a young woman, crossed and whispered something to him, to which he gave a slight, affirmative smile.

A clerk called, 'All rise,' and as they did, the four judges, in scarlet, entered, walked towards their thrones and in what seemed to be the best of spirits, friendly flourishes were exchanged, *'Good morning . . . Good morning all . . . Your Honour . . . Your Honours . . . Your Excellencies . . . My apologies . . .'*

The ruling judge spoke first, saying how, pursuant to Rule 86 and after many years, the court had reached this stage of the proceedings. The prosecution and defence would be permitted ten hours each to present their closing arguments and then one and a half hours each for rebuttals and rejoinder argument.

The prosecuting barrister then stood, his hands outstretched and yielding almost to pathos, said, 'Let me give you the sad picture.' Then calmly and sedulously he summarised events beginning in 1992, when Bosnian Muslim and Bosnian Croatian communities were terrorised and destroyed, carnage that the world would come to know of in time. He enumerated the thousands of civilians arrested, brutalised, killed, the tens of thousands uprooted by force, the hundreds of thousands besieged for months, years, killing sprees, cyclones of revenge, detainees held in dreadful places of detention and hundreds executed. Yet, when the accused was confronted with these multiple crimes, he deflected them with claims of victimisation or offered implausible explanations. He was the driving force who bragged about the strategies he had devised and was now pretending that they did not happen, or blaming those who did his dirty work, while he had orchestrated the whole plunder and crafted a defence based on falsehood.

At first, Vlad listened, mumbling to himself, his hands moving to his thought, but soon and with a fierce irascibility, he was making notes, which he passed to his team, then with wild gesture, refuting what has been said or is about to be said. The women still with their basilisk stares.

The court then heard of three particular cases that had been selected from the mass of evidence. A man in Sarajevo was never again to see the wife who had made her way to the market to try and pick up powdered milk for their children. She was killed by a mortar and buried at night, it being the only time mourners dared risk burying their dead, for fear of attack.

Next, it was a seventeen-year-old boy in Srebrenica, who, with his father, was endeavouring to join a column fleeing towards Tuzia, but they became separated. Then the boy joined another column that was made to surrender, all of them loaded onto a bus and driven to the execution site. In broiling heat, beaten and abused, soaking in their own urine, so desperate was the scene that they cried out, 'Give us water and then kill us.' This boy miraculously escaped death and rolling over corpses, he found another survivor and together they crawled for days to safer territory.

On Fidelma's other side, an artist is doing various drawings of Vlad, whose outrage is mounting with each and every revelation. The crayon is orange and the artist draws quickly, jerkily, covering several pages of his sketchbook, the likeness becoming a little bit more authentic with each stroke, capturing the full hair, the abrupt swivels of the neck, the jowls, but not the eyes. In the drawing, the eyes have a yielding compassion that bears no resemblance to the man sitting there.

The third case to be cited was of a doctor who had worked for the UN in Africa, and who became a prisoner in Omarska Camp, where he did everything he could to help others. But one morning, when his name was called and he was told to bring his things, he picked up a few cigarettes in a nylon bag, then his shirt, and his fellow prisoners solemnly thanked him, knowing they were never to see him again.

On and on, camp beatings, killing sprees, women forced to clean the cement floors of the warehouses after executions, bloodied T-shirts, drawn teeth, tufts of hair. At night, mothers helpless at hearing their daughters' screams as they were repeatedly violated, these conquests scored on the wooden slats of the cots, by rabid drunken soldiers.

When, at the end of the second day, the case for the prosecution was closed, the four women stood as Dr Vlad was being led off. Then they walked to the glass panel, silently, defiantly, dispensing their curses.

'You cannot interact with the accused,' a furious clerk told them, and seeing he was ignored, he called in a loud and threatening voice, 'Please leave now at once,' except that they did not leave, they waited until their doomings were complete. In those moments, as by some command, an electric blind began, stealthily, to come down on the other side, its dark blue canvas, lowering inch by inch, covering the plate glass, cutting out all confrontation, cutting him off from them.

Downstairs, one of them handed Fidelma a card and watched as she read it. It said *The Mothers of Srebrenica and Zepa Enclaves* in English and in what she presumed to be Serbian. Never would she forget the expression in their eyes, a cold desolation, a remoteness from life, from hope, from pity, from this whole apparatus of justice, that could not lead them to where their sons lay, never to be permitted the sacred ritual of burial.

On the third morning, when he was to defend himself, he walked into the trial chamber, insouciant, like a man setting out on holiday. His barristers flocked around him, acolytes at his behest, while among journalists and visitors there was suspense, as if something very dangerous might ensue. The four chairs where the mothers had sat were empty.

In his opening address he was conciliatory, confessing to feeling handicapped in his plea and likely to appear more as an amateur, and for this, he begged the chamber to excuse his lack of form. But then, with schematic zeal, he set about reminding the chamber of the world's ignorance of the conflict. He had been a martyr to his people, he had done everything to avoid war, had told his own parliament that it was going down the road to hell. It was only when he realised that his country and his people were about to be torn apart that he became a reluctant player. His corps never once neglected the laws of war, the legitimate customs of war, always comporting themselves with the maximum degree of responsibility. As president, he supervised the delivery of humanitarian aid and performed many works of mercy. Yes, he drew up borders, because he had to. If in a multi-ethnic society, as he argued, peoples could not live together, surely common sense dictated that they live apart. In territories in which he was accused of ethnic cleansing, people had left of their own accord, droves of them, seen at six each morning crossing the bridge. He called on his opponents to take shelter with friends in other parts, he invited Croats and Muslims to establish their own administrative organisations and as commander of his troops, many times he stopped his army when they were close to victory.

But this reasonableness was short-lived and as the hours went on, in vivid strophes and with blazing contempt, he painted the errors of the prosecution. It had based its case about Sarajevo on the theory that there existed a Serbian policy of producing terror and intimidating citizens, which was not so. Lies, falsehoods, bogus evidence squeezed from witnesses and manifestly partial. Military observers sat in their shelters gathering information from Muslim and other sources with a total sloppiness, unable even to discern who had died on the front and who had died natural deaths. Mass graves, bones, amputees, were from old wars and not his war, he told the chamber with a blasé assurance. The enemy conducted manoeuvres, gathering and hauling weapons, including large-calibre ones, with the intention of massacring their own people and then blaming it on Serbs. That self-same enemy constantly assumed victim status, used and abused UN insignia, painted their vehicles white to deceive international observers and used every trick under the sun, to appear harmless.

'Genocide, genocide, genocide,' he thundered, saying yes, hundreds of thousands were killed, but by whom. It was not established beyond any reasonable doubt where snipers' rounds or mortar fire had come from. Fatim is sitting on a tram in Sarajevo, sees a flare and presumes she knows the direction from where the mortar was fired. Her head was turned upside down, the way the map of Sarajevo was turned upside down. The direction on the map was changed by ninety degrees, in order to pretend that a specific projectile had been fired by one of his men. Nonsense. Bunkum. In Sarajevo, because of its elevation and its many hills surrounding the urban core, it was impossible, forensically, to identify from where a mortar had been fired. General Francis Ray, representative of the UN Force, had himself said that the exact position from which a mortar was fired was very imprecise and that different possibilities had to be taken into account. Moreover, it was not on the defence that the onus rested to prove where sniper shells came from, it was something the prosecution must prove. Sarajevo, he said then, the voice lowering to a cadence, Sarajevo was his adopted city, the city he loved and every shell that fell there hurt him personally. As he looked out towards his muted audience, he was like a man on the brink of his own creation.

They sat politely, bludgeoned from the sheer onslaught of rhetoric and evidence, as he cited document after document, raved, ranted, repeated himself and finally, declared that Serbs did not have any intention of taking that city, that there had been no siege and that it was a delusion and invention on the enemy's part.

The place was stifling. Suddenly it occurred to her that a trace of him still lurked in her, minute and spectral, that effluvial stain that would be her stigmata forever. It was then that she resolved to ask for an appointment to see him, as things had to be settled between them.

The interpreters were having a hard time keeping up with him and sometimes words were jumbled and precise meaning was lost for those who listened through their headphones. The presiding judge asked him to go slower and he seethed at that, but after a second resumed his composure, saying he was adducing the facts as best he could and that it was in everyone's interest to learn the truth.

On the next day, which was his last day of evidence, as evening was coming and dusk was creeping around the walls of the building and over the stacks of bicycles and misting the pond, he assumed a messianic calm, appealing to what was best and most reasonable in mankind. Suddenly and with great theatricality he broke into English, his voice booming, pervading every corner of that chamber, fortified with his own bravura – 'If I am crazy then patriotism itself is crazy.' Then, with a sweep of his arm, he told the four judges and those that might send him down of the larger certainty, insisting that he would leave that court a free man.

There was a hush. No one spoke. All was suspended as a judge informed them that the verdict would not be for eight or nine months. She looked around at the faces, but there was not a single gasp or cry, or tear; no swearing, no catcalls, a numbness, a negation, as if they had all been sucked into some vortex, some mass hallucination, or turned to stone, just a huddle of people endeavouring to get out and down that stairs, as they fled towards forgetfulness.

His barrister came towards her in the hall, all smiles. He was an enthusiastic man, marvelling at how well things had gone, his client's élan, that sureness of knowledge, the non-fatalism and the certainty of his own innocence. Then, with even greater zeal, he was proud to tell her that her request for a visit had been granted and she quaked at having ever asked for it.

'I think you will like him too much,' he said.

The inference made her blush. She could almost smell it, the clay of that garden, mixed in with smells of flowers and an over-sweet flowering shrub, her soul intoxicated, as she was carried aloft to her unbidden destiny.

The Prison Visit

The prison was a few kilometres outside the centre, in a seaside suburb. The taxi driver chose the scenic route, so that Fidelma had a passing view of the North Sea, with one ship ploughing the grey bleak waters, big waves rising around it, a cold lonely sea that was a continuum of all loneliness. On the promenade, a few stoics were walking their dogs, there were lights in the shops in the town, several signs for museums and a bolder one in red that flashed *Casino Casino*.

The prison was flanked by two tall towers, and though it was only four o'clock, darkness was descending and the brick facade was the colour of dried blood.

Security was far more strict than at the court and she was passed from one guard to the next, their faces under the fluorescent lighting pallid and identical, sour and sullen, eyeing her with suspicion. The detention rooms, where he and half a dozen others were being held, were at the end of a long corridor and as she followed the broad back of a guard, her decisiveness was faltering.

He greeted her warmly, arm outstretched: 'Let me look at you . . . still beautiful . . . a little too thin perhaps.' He seemed, with his excessive compliments, to be oblivious to the guard, who was also standing there as he continued with many other tributes. She had come in his hour of need.

'How are you Vlad?' He smiled at the recollection of the old name and the old days. They were at a little metal table that was stacked with a batch of papers which he began to lay out.

'I brought this,' she said and she took out the black chiffon scarf with the smell of verbena, with which he had blindfolded her. He seemed to ignore it.

'Don't you remember . . .' she said and she held it up for him to see and maybe even to smell. He acted as if he did not understand her, or as if perhaps she was some simpleton he had met long before.

'You were in that court Fidelma,' his voice booming now, 'you saw . . . you heard . . . they paint me a monster, when all the time I was seeking to create a homogeneous peace. You know me . . . you knew me . . . in our personal association did you find me a monster?'

'It's the only good memory I have of us,' she said, crushing the scarf in her hand.

'I am a poet, I am an artist, I am a humanist for Christ's sake, caged in this stinking universe for crimes I have not committed.'

'I wanted to write to you, but I did not know how to put it,' she said, leaning towards him and more anxious now.

'Oh Kafka, come back and help me overcome those shitty ladies and gentlemen enrobed, on their high thrones, because truthfulness is dead and I am the one who must prove it.'

'The morning you were taken off the bus, the news travelled like wildfire . . . TJ's was packed. People drove from all over to watch on the big screen . . . there you were, the you they did not know . . . the you I did not know, but then witnesses told their stories and shoes were pelted at your face on the screen . . . Fifi fainted . . .'

Nothing of emotion or even surprise registered on his face, as he held up a sheaf of papers to show her.

'Not a single piece of evidence ordering atrocities was ever signed by me.'

The pages were scrawled in different inks, with question marks and annotations all over.

'I was watching in my house with my husband . . . he knew nothing of our . . . our love,' she went on.

'For example,' and he reeled them off, page and paragraph, 'D1329, D2335, D2986, D2168, D2170, D3575, D3302, D2172, D2336, D2512, D2513, D2605–606 . . .'

It was not only a matter of will now, but of alacrity, of who could outdo whom – 'I was ten weeks pregnant . . . there was no one I could tell . . . not even you . . . its father.'

He looked at her, then shook his head slowly and sternly from side to side. How dare she compromise him in the presence of a menial.

'I am not a nationalist,' he said addressing the guard now, 'but I think races should not mix . . . when I meet a real Frenchman or a real German or a real Irishman . . . they have something that flowers have . . . a distinct scent of their own.'

It was being said to deflect her, but she was more determined now, her anger mounting.

'Three men knocked on our door . . . my husband answered it . . . they had business with me, or rather with you, whom they had come for . . .'

'Yes,' he went on, 'I have received many prominent awards . . . Books in several languages, also a comedy and a novel – *The Wondrous Chronicles of the Night* . . .'

'They brought me way up the mountain, to a hut,' refusing to be thwarted, '... the one they called Medico took out a crowbar ...'

'One does not talk about a rope Fidelma, in the house of a hanged man,' he says.

'You have to hear me out,' she answers.

'You mustn't dramatise Fidelma.'

'My world in bits ... and the child ...'

'People who converse with God know that I am innocent.' He is bellowing it in her ear.

'You know everything you have done ... in a way I wish you were mad, but you are not mad ... you are one of Lucifer's lying liars ... a monster.'

There is the instantaneous eruption as he stands, papers flying in all directions, '*Uit, uit*: Out, out,' he orders the guard in Dutch and English.

She is gripped by the elbows from behind, the blades of both shoulders lifted in a clinch and then marched outside, to where the burly one is seated and together they proceed up the corridor, towards the doorman at the end. The two who held her talked to him in their own language and she wondered what they were saying – that she assaulted the prisoner, that she was a nutcase, that she should be placed under arrest.

'I've done nothing wrong,' she says but is ignored. She knows they could understand, but the intention was to intimidate her. She has to wait on their pleasure, their whim, their tyranny. With a sudden alarming grab, the doorman takes her handbag and empties the contents onto a table. The usual things – a wallet, a comb, a compact, loose coins and ground biscuits, because each day she had brought biscuits to the court for her lunch and most were uneaten. He sees the ticket of admission to Court Number 02. It interested him greatly, this small white card with lettering in black and in red, *Closing Arguments*.

The companion with the thick eyebrows also studies it carefully, as for some clue. Then the doorman takes an official sheet of paper and slowly, laboriously, writes down each item that was in the bag. She thinks, these brutes have absolute power over me now. When he finishes, he signs and stamps it, goes halfway down the corridor and disappears through a doorway, while his fellow guard stood over her. Never once did he meet her eye and was deaf to her repeated question as to what was going to happen to her. The only person she could phone, that is if she was allowed to phone, was the young girl at the Tribunal, who acted as interpreter, but she had not brought that number.

'I am staying at Hotel Corona,' she said, as if that would exonerate her. A sneering look came on his face and stayed there, while they waited alone.

Finally, she heard voices and two men, one already known to her and a stranger, came towards them. She ran to them, tears in her eyes, and foolishly said, 'All I want is to go home.'

With a dogged indifference, they pretended not to have heard and went on talking in low voices, when suddenly the one who had emptied the contents of the handbag, as if exasperated, or realising it was his suppertime, gestured to the third one to put the stuff back in the bag and get done with it. She was made to sign the letter he had written and then slowly he took a key and still more slowly moved it into the lock. That squeal of metal would live forever in her memory.

Outside was deserted, the searchlight showing mist on the plot of grass over which she ran, wildly, not once daring to look back, passing a little row of dwellings with plants and china dogs in the window, up onto the road, in search of a taxi, except there was none.

Boarding the first bus that came along, there was a hiatus, as she could not remember the name of the street where the hotel was.

'Den Haag Holland Spoor,' the driver said, and she shook her head.

'Salonboot Rondvaart Den Haag,' he said and she was even more bewildered.

'Holland Spoor . . . Rhijnspoor . . . Staatsspoor,' he continued and used the moment's baulk to pick at one of his teeth.

People in the bus were becoming impatient, muttering to one another.

'To where do you wish to go?' a woman near the front called.

'The centre,' she said.

'Centraal,' the woman said and the driver repeated it and now Centraal, like Sunday morning bells, rang jubilantly as they set off.

In the glass of the window, going through leafy suburbs, she saw her startled self and then his face, appearing, floating out there, the vengeful eyes, the lip snarled to one side, *Uit uit* and she huddled into her coat for protection.

The Conjugal Room

The conjugal room is functional, a bed, a zinc washbasin, a shower room divided off by a folding door and some fawn towels. It is larger than the previous cell and there is no guard on duty.

How well she looks, *très chic*, in her fur, not unlike Anna Karenina. She is wearing it in her assumed role as huntress, saw it in a boutique in a side street, near the hotel, when she stood to look, but because it was Sunday the shop was closed. However, a woman next door alerted the owner and before long, she was tucking the fur collar around Fidelma's neck and steering her towards the swivel mirrors, which allowed for a front and back view. She had been upstairs making dumplings to put in the chicken broth for her husband, who was very ill, in fact dying. The fur collar was the last of the winter collection and money did not matter now, all that mattered was that her husband, her good husband, be tended to in the last six weeks of his life.

'Quite the little traveller you are,' Dr Vlad says, coming towards her, soft and prowling, the way he once was and when his body is flush with hers, she can feel the heat of his balls and that waddle under the casual navy trousers. He is about to kiss her when she staves him off with a flick of her wrist. May she comb his hair?

'You may.' He is happy at the courtesan approach and with the feigned dutifulness of a little boy, he sits in a chair facing the barred window.

The comb she chooses is large and white, a country comb, what her grandmother would call a rack, with wide gaps between the teeth, to collect the dirt. His mop of hair, which was recently washed, is easy to go through and his curiosity is boundless as to what female tricks she is up to.

Suddenly, without any undue pressure, the comb breaks and she holds the two halves in her hands, stunned with disbelief. So it was true what that cracked old man used to say, how in his long years as a ship's barber he had combed many heads, famous and infamous, and unfailingly, where there was evil within, the comb broke to tell the tale, to confirm it.

'Evil,' she says.

'Evil you say.' He has turned sharply to look.

'Evil I said,' and she repeats the story of the ship's barber and his certainty that character could be deciphered through a comb.

For a moment he is silent, then he kicks himself free of all caution, stands so quickly that the chair falls backwards and staring at her with hatred, he takes the broken comb and snaps it in pieces.

'I have more combs,' she says, tumbling the contents of a shopping bag onto the floor, where they fall and lie in an assorted mass of black, brown, white and tortoiseshell. Perhaps it is this uncustomary audacity that unnerves him, because she sees that he is shaking. She has gained a small victory over him. He is ranting. What is this bunkum, this electromagnetic bunkum, this gypsy scaremongering. He swears and blames himself for this most private of visits, then mimics her, the little draper's wife in her cheap fur, on a quest for truth, justice, atonement.

'Who says you have any claim on me, who – who,' he asks.

'I have no claim on you . . . except that we knew each other once.'

He is silent for a moment, then surprises her, treating the whole thing as a jest and from the floor he picks up the numerous combs, makes little tunes on them, runs them through his hair, through her hair, to no terrible consequence, and recalls her blushing, how wonderfully appealing her blushes were, an artwork in the making.

'Shall we dance?' he says, but he has already taken her in his arms and leads her into steps that she is unaccustomed to. It is to gain power over her. Soon they are coiling wordlessly around one another, but she knows this is only a ruse, as there are scores to be settled and he is a vengeful man.

'Evil is a strange word for you to have spoken,' he tells her.

'Not so strange . . . when you think of the atrocities you have inflicted on mankind.'

He looks at her as if he might strike her and would have struck her were they elsewhere, with no one on guard beyond the door. His face is within inches of hers, the whites of his eyes becoming bloodshot.

'Who sent you . . . what organisation is behind this . . . this dirty work?'

'No one . . . I came alone . . . I had to.'

Her answer throws him, as he takes a few steps back and turns to regain his composure.

'When we made love, what was on your mind?' she asks quietly.

'Pleasure,' he answers.

'When you were carving your pure homeland, with your guns opening fire even on ambulances, what was on your mind, or did the sheer numbers, the hundreds of thousands, deaden the truth of it all?'

For a second he freezes at the audaciousness of the question and she freezes too.

'What has happened to you?' he asks, looking her up and down.

'A lot,' she says unflinching, determined to stand her ground.

'But you are well now,' he says, suddenly, falsely solicitous. He lets go of her arm, walks towards the window and looks out, like a man conscious of his confinement.

'I had looked forward to this visit . . . made myself personable,' he says without turning.

'I had looked forward to it, also.'

'Then why destroy it . . . why bring evil into this room?'

'Because it's here, here . . . in every pore of your being.'

'Take it back . . . Take it back,' he says wildly, jabbing at the air, where it hangs like a viper, a nest of vipers, Macbeth's unseen daggers.

'I can't take it back Vlad,' and he starts at hearing the old name, the fond name, then tears at his hair, his skull, with an infantile mania.

'That smorgasbord of crime of which I am accused is false,' he says going towards her, 'untrue, shibboleths . . . with breakdown happening in my country, in my people, in my psyche, what ought I have done, lain down like a lamb for the wolves to arrive . . .'

'Do you not have bad dreams, nightmares?' she says.

'No . . . I sleep well . . . I dream well . . . I dream of women . . . I dream of my mountains . . . and I will, like Virgil, return home to die.'

'You will be an old man if ever that happens . . .'

'I am in breach of not a single crime of which I am accused,' he says, his arm fending her off.

'Was your essential nature always evil . . . were you ever innocent?' she asks and he answers with a baffled look.

'You remember in Cloonoila,' she begins. 'One day, in the classroom, you read the children a speech from Shakespeare about the Seven Ages of Man – *They have their exits and their entrances, and one man in his time plays many parts*. You must have known it then that you had chosen the wrong part, the worst part, the way you know it now . . . that it could all have been different, you might be the poet you boasted of being and not one of the damned . . . it will find you yet . . . in all that solitude . . . it always does . . .'

'Don't go,' he says and in that moment he is almost repentant, the mendicant, the broken Faustus, finally at a loss.

Something falls. There is a thud as she wakens from her dream to find that she is not in that conjugal room, but in the hotel, where the maid with the little muslin bonnet has come in and tripped over something.

'Sorry madam, I come back later,' the maid says and she sits up, startled, looking at the bedside clock.

When she comes to her senses, she rings down to ask if there is any message or fax for her and yet again, the answer is no.

Bar Den Haag

Each evening, Fidelma went down to the cellar bar. She decided it was where the strays went. Dimly lit, or rather just enough light to see the barman and an array of spirit and liquor bottles on shelves, the amber liquids and the labels reflected in the back mirrors. A toper's dream.

The blind man was led in faithfully, by one of the hotel staff, seated in the same corner and had the same tipple – a warm port wine in a glass beaker with a curved handle, that he could feel for. Sometimes, a pair of lovers, ordering one drink for two and gorging on the nuts. There was a student bent over his iPad and swaddled in sheepskin. Nobody spoke, but the atmosphere was friendly.

On this particular evening, she was alone. She had gone in the day, as was usual, to the gallery, the same route each morning, under the lime trees, where, according to a brochure: *The sunlight filters through onto The Hague's most distinguished boulevard, Lange Voorhout, lined with gracious mansions and neo-classical palaces, in the heart of Europe's most picturesque destination and steps from the sun-drenched shores of the North Sea.* Steps also from the un-sun-drenched walls of the detention centre. It was a suspended time, torn between going home and seeing him one last time.

As always, at the busy intersection where three lanes met, she waited to cross, when others were crossing, so as to make sure that she looked in the right direction. By the tram stop there were the noisy students, eating apples and spitting out the apple butts, and from a tour bus each morning older people emerged, heading as she was, for the museum.

She stood with the group, listening to one or other of the guides, in front of a massive painting of a young bull that dominated the entrance room. The brown velvet coat bore one rippled streak of white, like a gash, and inevitably the guide pointed to that and also to the incidental figures, a kid, a lamb, a ewe and a hatted farmer, but with no mention of the copulation that was about to happen.

In the next room there were flowers, panels of them, lily and iris and rose in such a wondrous crush, brimming out of their vases, so alive, as if they might leave their rust-coloured stalks and fly about. The view of Delft, in the adjoining room, was mesmerising to sit before, signature of morning and setting out, the sheet of blue water looking as if it too had been washed clean and the loop of sky girding it, also a ravishing blue.

In the evenings, when she returned and enquired at the desk, the same receptionist, or one equally brusque, said that if there were a message it would be sent to her room, except that there wasn't.

He was a big man, his face a bit puffy and eyes bleary from drink. She recognised him from the court, always sat in the aisle opposite to hers, where Vlad's cohorts sat and at the breaks, he tore down the stairs, never stopping at the water font, hurrying out to have a smoke. He too remembered her, dimly, had not come to seek her out, just wandered in off the street, beguiled maybe by the swank of the outside and doormen in full livery.

'May I?' he said, but he was already seated, his frame far too big, too clumsy, for the dainty velvet chair. Then he slapped his thighs to show he was settling in. His voice was sometimes slurry – 'How am I. No bad. How are you. No bad. Switzerland very nice place, very cold. I drive all over. Belgium no payee, lousy roads, two kilometres into France and you're away. Not as big a turnout in the court as one would expect. Played his part well, big player in his time. Put on weight. He cooks for the gang, six of them in the detention wing, the VIPs, erstwhile enemies, all buddies now, united in their hatred for the International Tribunal in Den Haag. Table football, pottery classes, classroom languages and at night they swap jokes. What's the difference between a Muslim, a Croat and a Serb? Muslim will smile to your face and stab you in the back, Croat won't smile but maybe won't stab you in the back, Serb will look at you proudly and deal with you like a man. They sing the old songs, the songs of the fatherland. Maybe you heard, we had border issues in my part of the world. Give the VIPs the opportunity, let them free and they will do the same thing all over again, take the lands and murder one another. You think I am Italian,' and he laughed and shouted to the barman, who was not to be seen, to bring a refill.

'If I drink, I drink all night,' he said, looking to make sure she did not escape. 'We live side by side, different religions, Catholic, Orthodox and Muslim, we celebrate the feasts, Christmas, January 6, St Bartholomew, Easter. We never talk religion, we drink, we sing, but old wounds suppurating away. Bloody hell, sixty years of peace too much for warring men. Negativity. Unrest. The ideology caught on. Mobs enlisting. Our front. Their front. The shit happen. Our dogs know it before we do. Bang bang. Expansion, consolidation, elimination. He become president, supreme commander of the armed forces. Tongue of an angel – *war is alchemy*. He play the tyrant when he has to. Wolf-weaned, like Romulus, wolf-weaned in the mountains of Montenegro, that is also my country. *Clean the bloody place of the scum*. Friends become foes, a necessity of history. Dogs going crazy to get to dead bodies clogging up the culverts in the dams. Drivers of buses also ordered to shoot prisoners, so that everyone is implicated. I get the letter with the army heading – *You must report to Army Base.* I am assigned to Kosovo to be a tank driver. I tell my mother I fetch food from UN Headquarters to deliver to the needy and she believe me. Big tank. Forty-eight tonnes of metal. Tank the size of this establishment. Six of us, two drivers, one mechanic, one loader, two gunners and commander up on top giving orders – *Fire, fire, twenty degrees to the left, twenty degrees to the right*, out in the countryside and in the villages. Different crew each week, so that we never meet, never have time to be friendly. I like to be friendly, it's why I'm talking to you,' and he peers at her for a reaction.

'I came down here to have a quiet drink,' she says, to brush him off.

'Sorry, most sorry. Tell me go away . . . you see, I have to let off steam, today big occasion, landmark. I am you understand a small fish in the larger story, a little unhinged, but nothing to worry about. I am a driver now by profession. I carry electrical goods from one country to another. It happen. Flashback. Nice road, flat country, nice fat cows in the fields chewing and there they are, boys and men on the road, praying, calling out to those they loved. Faces I know from school. *Saber, the one on whom happiness falls*. I have to stop the truck and pull in. Fright goes on for many minutes. If it was a dream it would be okay, but it not.'

Everything that came out of his mouth was so wild and splintered and she wished that the barman would not keep disappearing, as there was an urgency waiting to be let loose.

'We come through a mountain pass onto a road, nearly dark,' he went on, 'trouble break out in a village eight kilometres away and on the road, bodies just lying there . . . either to be shot or brought to execution site. No time to lose. *Drive over them, drive over them*, the commander he shout. I am a soldier, I take orders. The wheels buckle, the tank go bumpety bump and we lurch for a few hundred yards . . . I see nothing, I feel nothing, I think there will be mess, pieces stuck to the wheels when we get to the town, where trouble has started up. I know some of those boys from school, their names now on record, written on a stone slab. My shrink, she tell me I must make friends with them, they are dead, they will not hurt me, Saber, the one on whom happiness falls, Sayed, the one who is grateful for everything, grateful to be pulped. Jesus. My shrink she say they forgive. She talk of channelling. Conversations between them and me. The minutiae, the minutiae. I tell her unplug me, unplug me. My friend in Brussels, if he here now he would think I am a nutcase, sometimes I am a nutcase. That is what war does. All that killing and nobody any better off. I go in pub with him in Brussels, we drink grappa and we talk of the night we deserted, five of us, in the dark . . . handguns and grenades under our uniforms, stuffed to our chests. Whole place mined. One of our comrades, Agon, he step on a mine, only seven minutes away from freedom, of Albanian border. *Finito*. Wiped out. My friend in Brussels say how lucky we are, everything rosy. We have food, we have job. He has kids. He say kids bring him through, they listen and they cuddle, what do you say, do you say kids bring one through . . .'

'I don't know . . .'

'I never liked vodka,' was his reply, calling for a large grappa and some wine for the lady.

'I have plenty,' she said.

'I saw you in the court, next to the mothers . . . a lot of bitterness in that room. Mixed bunch, journalists, diplomats, friends, enemies et cetera. Friends very loyal, especially ladies. His portrait next to their skin, him playing gusle. They know killing not in his heart, they know he sad for the places of his childhood. You are an acquaintance, or maybe a psych, a nice English lady come to help with the trauma, to delineate the dark, bullshit. Psychs they mess me up, too much headache. My psych she make me talk it over and over again. I cancel appointment, I say I am wanted in Antwerp and Lower Saxony. Psychs no much help, too much talk. Intersubjectivity crap. You get my drift. But you are not going to tell me why you have come to Den Haag. Something of a quasi-romantic nature perhaps. Ladies they always fell for him. Should have seen his hair in those days, killer hair, better than Charles Bronson, the child of Lithuania. *The meanest man in the west, Charles Bronson*. Flew twenty-five missions, awarded a Purple Heart for wounds received in World War Two. You think he will get twenty years, thirty years, more. Something between you both, you go back a bit as the saying goes, you knew him, he opened up to you, things he never told anyone else, the sweetheart moment . . . so you visit every six weeks or so and in between you write letters, tendresse – *Darling, I'm afraid I'm getting awfully fond of you* . . . Bullshit.'

'Yes, bullshit . . . you talk too much.'

'No hard feelings lady . . . let's have one for the road, as they say in England . . . Churchill he split our lands . . . drew up our borders . . . I've been as far as Dover . . . many many Albanians in High Wycombe . . . maybe you have met some, maybe you have drink with them . . .'

'I am not a girlfriend and I am not a psych and I have not drunk with Albanians in High Wycombe.'

'You're thinking he will get life . . . the mothers are hoping for that, locked up somewhere very cold, where the sun it never riseth.'

'I have no idea what his sentence will be.'

'You must have some fucking idea . . . some fucking opinion, either pro or con . . . you come all this way in your nice coat with your nice handbag to hear a twisted version of the truth,' and he half stood, the roused sentry, bearing down on her.

'I'm sick of your fucking talk and your fucking tank and your minutiae, as you call it.'

'I could smash this place up,' he was saying.

'I know you could, but you won't . . .'

'How are you so sure?'

'Two reasons – one, you would be seized in seconds and two, it wouldn't help . . . the boys, the men, the Sabers and the Sayeds are waiting for you . . . they're on the road . . . they'll never be not on the road, they're inside you . . .'

'Jesus Christ,' and he looked now in terror, at her, the messenger, then down at his hands, the instruments of slaughter, as he stared about with a mounting helplessness.

'I shouldn't have come . . . it bring the whole thing back . . . the proximity,' and then the mumbling began, mumbling to himself, the sweat pouring from his face, his wiping it with the thick wool scarf that he wore, trying to stave it off, but couldn't. He began to shake. It was terrible to see such a big man become incontinent in a matter of moments, not just the hands, but the torso, the feet, all jabber jabber jabber. So lonely to witness, like watching someone slip over into death, except for one fraction of his mind that followed the awfulness of it.

'I am with you,' she said leaning over, speaking very quietly, but not touching him. It went on for many more minutes and sometimes he almost thought he had returned, but was then pulled back into it.

Afterwards he sat, grateful, abashed, unable to look up.

'I want to give you something,' he said. He began to search in various pockets and eventually pulled out a small, folded business card that was torn off at the end. It had the name of his sister's hair salon in Zagreb. Josefina. Should she ever be in Zagreb, his sister would do her hair and give her very good price.

'Where do you live . . . do you live local?' she said, looking from him to the card and back again.

'I tell myself that I would like a wife, I would put my arms around her and she would make me feel okay, at least for some of the time, she and me saying things, she saying that it's over, over, no use lingering on the past. And we walk towards our little house on the edge of a wood and the smoke already coming out of the chimney, because one of our friendly neighbours would have lit a fire for us, no border issues, the peace that passeth understanding.'

'I knew your president,' she said and although he had risen to go, he hesitated.

'I had a part in his life, a walk-on part . . . but still significant . . . he came to our village as a healer – *The stranger who dwells among us shall be as home born* – people were bewitched, especially women. He gave me a child at my own bewitched entreaties . . . it ended badly . . . I came here.'

'You came for him . . .'

'Yes . . .'

'Big mistake.'

'I wanted to believe he would show some grain of remorse . . . a single word . . . what goes on inside him . . . the inner footage. What is it, that need to kill, that desire to kill, what was it. Tell me. Tell me.'

He looked offended, then asked aloud where was the gents, and turning as he went, called back, 'You want answers . . . Explain himself . . . you won't get it . . . he can't . . . feelings not the same, from where you are to where he is . . . carnage . . . Go home.'

She waited, but he did not come back. His scarf was still there, a whorl of red on the table.

The overhead light was quenched and then the lights behind the bar, leaving her in relative darkness, except for little beads of light around the edges of the glass table.

'It's on the house,' the barman said as he put a glass of wine in front of her and went out.

Jack

Fidelma could swear it was the same robin, same little terracotta chest, puffed out, same tilt to the head, the little flirt, with her tricks, landing, then darting off back into the thickets. A winter evening, the air so tender and the boughs of the trees wet and mossy. She had come back for a few days to see Sister Bonaventure, her room in the wing of the convent, exactly as it was. The window slightly ajar and a metal crucifix on the pillow. The only change was in poor Boney, her speech much slower as she searched for the words that tumbled about, in her brain, rudderless.

There was a permanence here, a familiarity, the wood so quiet, the thin brown branches scrolling the air, a stillness, that hyphen between evening and night. She sat, both to remember and to forget, and the robin with that tantalising promise of nearness kept hovering about. The phone in her pocket began to judder, and she reckoned that it was the telephone company welcoming her to Ireland and giving the rates for local and international calls. She stayed, watching the water come up to the tide line, then recede again and so on and so on and soon it would be dark, it would be dark in about twenty minutes and the water would be dark too.

Then the phone vibrated again and again and finally she took it out and in the dusk she read the text that was from her estranged husband – *Go down to the water Fidelma and baptise yourself as you once did long ago.*

How did he know that. How had he divined that. Who had given him her number?

She read it a few times and then, like a somnambulist, she went down the muddy slope to the river, stooped and put her hands in and then her face, as she had done once before. The water was freezing cold, but fresh, and it freshened her and gave her courage.

The house was in darkness and as she went up the front path she could see rimed bunches of rose hips above the porch. The steps were slippery, as the frost had come on hard. She touched the door before she opened it, in some kind of propitiation. Her key was on her key ring, along with the three keys from her London life.

Jack shuffled down the hall in slippers, holding something that rattled. It was the globe in the oil lamp that had never fitted securely. There had been a power cut. He went into the front room and she followed. He had to strike match after match after match, because the sooted wick had not been lit or trimmed in ages. Eventually it took and a small, unsettled flame tapered upwards. There was dust on everything. Dust, her old nemesis, had sealed and settled on objects she once treasured, on the silver salver, the fender, the china shepherdesses, a thick veneer of it. It was like a room in an auction house, with all these things about to be put up for sale. Rust streaked down the cream wallpaper from all the rain and the jamb of the wooden door had gone soft in the damp. There was the old soda syphon on the trolley and his set of golf clubs in a corner, the shuddery lamplight giving to everything the added aura of neglect.

Jack sat on the arm of the sofa and she sat on a straight wicker chair, facing him. He paused to gather his strength, then took her hand and began to speak in a very confidential voice – 'We loved one another . . . we were sweethearts, like Darby and Joan, walking along the shore linked, people laughing behind our backs . . . but then . . . evil came, more evil than we could ever comprehend, and it fell to you child, to be susceptible to it . . . the Prince of Darkness . . . you were the one for whom the bell tolled . . . and now you are home.'

He was breathing fast, too fast, and then he let out a strange unyielding cry, its echo reverberating throughout the entire house, as he sank back into the well of the chair, his fawn slipper falling off, thudless. She was witnessing something strange and terrifying that was both of this world and the next and she was powerless to stop it. He had waited to die until she returned. The knowledge that made him summon her from the river was something she never could or would explain.

'Oh Jack,' she said, as if he might heed or hear her. She was still holding his hand, which went limp in hers. His eyes were wide open, gnawed and staring, and she looked away, petrified.

Beyond the window, a land white and sheathed with frost, that frost biting into everything, even the cattle trough in the neighbour's field, a night crystal clear, cold and implacable, like death herself.

Home

I am not a stranger here anymore. They all know me in the Centre and have given me the nickname of Delphi. There is a postcard of Delphi on the wall, a vacated temple, with stone pillars where, from somewhere within, the Oracle spoke her riddles. There are many newspaper cuttings, all of people in predicaments, migrants with babes in arms fleeing atrocities and heading for nowhere. Each day more clippings and still more, so that the wall now is a heaving tableau of history. There is also a blown-up picture of the South African daisy, called Jerawala.

The world comes in here every day. They trudge up that stairs from the moment the door is opened. We never know what to expect. Father. Mother. Brother. Sister. Shattered worlds. Lost embryos.

A family of five came yesterday, a young father, a very young mother, a baby and two children with nowhere to put their heads down. The children's footwear was bits of duvet wrapped around them and tied with string. They sat in the hall for hours, quiet and mannerly, like figures in a frieze. I rang centre after centre and it was only with imploring that one woman relented, said they could sleep in the passage of her already crowded hostel for one night. That one night to them, on that floor, was home. Then on the morrow, up and off, and before night footsore and weary, craving the valleys and small instances of mercy.

It is all very brisk and very busy here and for the most part, good-humoured. It is quite frugal, but visitors always get something, usually biscuits, as there is a big box of biscuits to dive into. Varya saw to that. She is the one who brought me here, or I should say encouraged me to come. We were in a pub when she put the question – *Why could I not go home, big house, four bedrooms, walled kitchen garden, a veranda, the lot.* I told her I could not go home until I could come home to myself.

'I know,' she said, and I knew she knew.

What brings peace. What brings certainty.

I asked the interpreter in The Hague to ask the Mothers of Srebrenica and they listened attentively and then one spoke – *A bone*, she said. To find the smallest piece of bone of one of her children, or better still to find the bones of each of her three children. Her eyes were brimming with hope and grievance.

Little Allissos has been turned down again by the Home Office. More waiting. She had to leave the house in Acton and Varya found her a place, temporarily, in a big commune out in the country, where a philanthropist keeps the unwanted, in return for working the farm. She eats potatoes now instead of rice. They enter their potatoes at various horticultural shows and it seems the method of judging is that six men look ponderously at the potatoes, on a platter, and then, like stevedores, cut them open, to get to the inside.

I see Mistletoe every fortnight. Her father or auntie drops her at Ladbroke Grove Station and she runs up the steep flight of steps, as if a wind is propelling her. We have tea in a cafe where they make assorted crepes to order. She touches my face as she used to, runs her hand along my neck, ignoring the imperfections. We are to make a journey in the spring. *Stonehenge.* Why Stonehenge, I asked. *Gods*, she said. *Gods*.

At Christmas, we put on a play. It was a very free interpretation of *A Midsummer Night's Dream*. Actors strolled on in motley attire, togas, crowns, scraggy beards, gauds, ribbons and ill-fitting pumps. Lions roared, asses brayed, infatuations abounded, as the fairy world mingled with the rustics and Robin Goodfellow the Puck, with his goblins, squeezed a love juice into the eyes of the unsuspecting.

Jade spoke the first lines, to set the theme of love:

One turf shall serve as pillow for us both,
One heart, one bed, two bosoms and one troth.

Cupid, blindfolded and on his bicycle, was thus to deliver love pizzas to wrong addresses, presaging the mayhem that was to follow.

Poor Snout the baker, who became a wall, through which Pyramus and Thisbe 'did whisper', had an avalanche of loam thrown in his face. Nathaniel, the son of the coaching teacher, had brought along his child's bucket and spade, and kept tossing indiscriminately, 'Mud in your eye, mud in your eye.'

The forest was represented by little clumps of pine cone and some fading castor oil plants. From a swinging cage a foul-mouthed parrot kept saying 'Silly sluts, silly sluts,' but the cage was whisked away for fear of greater obscenities.

Lips were kissing cherries, dewdrops were pearls, a nigh-nigh, lullaby-lullaby accompanying the sweet moments. True love melted like snow, dotage was contagious, betrothals broken and paramours, with seething brains, roamed the forest, seeking revenge.

Helena, the spurned maiden, was heard to say, 'I am your spaniel; and, Demetrius, the more you beat me, I will fawn on you.' Demetrius, for his part, warned her not to tempt too much the hatred of his spirit.

Kings and queens lost their usual froideur. Theseus the King, who had won Hippolyta's love by the injuries he caused her in war, lifted her gown with his spear, in order for her to flaunt her bruises. Oghowen, as his wife, began to undo each hook and eye of her black lace corset, proud of these stigmata, and consequently held up the action of the play.

Titania, who was played by Maria and who was supposed to remain asleep until much further on in the drama, sat up from her drugged sleep, and seeing the weaver, Nick Bottom, with an ass's head upon him, loudly exclaimed, 'What angel wakes me from my flowery bed?' Even she, finding it all so beautifully ludicrous, yielded to laughter, while Bluey as Oberon, her abjuring husband, breaking from strict pentameter, called loudly, 'Get your ass over here Titania,' much to the delights of the audience.

Nahir also broke from strict tradition, having acquitted himself well as a meddling monkey, now metamorphosed to a clown – 'Nay, I can gleek upon occasion.' With a small magnifying glass, he went to sniff out the secrets of other lovers, except that he had forgotten his wooing lines, and plucking the air with a pitiousness, cried out, 'The thing is gone from me,' which clearly it was.

'Thou runaway,' some of the actors called, and followed him into the audience, where he had fled, and there en route, and again stepping out of character, stopped to ask friends or family if they were enjoying the evening. Although it was due to a technical hitch backstage, and not an artistic consideration, the house went dark, yells and shouts rose out and actors down there continued with a rousing repetition of 'O grim-looked night! O night with hue so dark!'

On stage, it was left to Allissos and her Maenads in their rainbow chiffons, to advance the beguilements, with ringlet and roundel dance, encouraging the audience to participate.

The entertainment came to a conclusion, with Robin Goodfellow recalling the zanies and all the actors made to join hands, as wrongs were righted, true love and its virtuous properties restored. Nuptials were celebrated, twine rings exchanged, and packets of rice wantonly thrown on the heads of the eternally betrothed.

Give me your hands if we be friends,
And Robin shall restore amends.

For the finale, the word *Home* was to be sung and chanted in the thirty-five different languages of the performers.

At first, even after many rehearsals, it was awry, the voices grated, the very harmony they had aspired to was missing, and then one woman stepped forward and took command, her voice rich and supple, a wine-dark sea filled with the drowned memories of love and belonging. Soon others followed, until at last thirty-five tongues, as one, joined in a soaring, transcendent Magnificat. *Home. Home. Home*. It rose and swelled, it reached to the rafters and through the walls, out onto the lit street, to countryside with its marsh and meadow, by graveyard and sheep fold, through dumbstruck forests, to the lonely savannahs and reeking slums, over seas and beyond, to endless, longed-for destinations.

You would not believe how many words there are for *home* and what savage music there can be wrung from it.

Acknowledgements

I received immeasurable help writing this book from people in Galway, Roscommon, London, New York, Bosnia and the ICTT in The Hague. Words fail me to express my enormous and abiding gratitude and the list could go on and on. I do want to give a robust thanks to my inspired and painstaking editors, Lee Brackstone and Judy Clain, to Ed Victor, most staunch agent and ally and lastly, but by no means least, to Nadia Proudian, who typed draft after draft with all the expertise and readiness at her disposal.

Permission to print from *Gilgamesh*, the book by Robert Temple.

I was made welcome at Pilgrims Hatch Dog Kennels many times.